feels therefore that she has a foot in both cultures. She has four children and five grandchildren. For many years she taught in schools to the north of Birmingham. An accident put paid to her teaching career and, after moving to North Wales, Anne turned to the other great love of her life and began to write seriously. Despite many challenges, including many years in a wheelchair – from which she miraculously recovered – a serious stroke, and losing her beloved husband Dennis, she has never lost her love of storytelling.

Visit www.annebennett.co.uk to find out more about Anne and her books.

By the same author

A Little Learning
Pack Up Your Troubles
Walking Back to Happiness
Till the Sun Shines Through
Danny Boy
Daughter of Mine
Mother's Only Child
To Have and to Hold
A Sister's Promise
A Daughter's Secret
A Mother's Spirit
The Child Left Behind
Keep the Home Fires Burning
Far From Home
If You Were the Only Girl
A Girl Can Dream
A Strong Hand to Hold
Love Me Tender
Another Man's Child
Forget-Me-Not Child
The Child on the Doorstep

ANNE BENNETT

AS TIME GOES BY

HarperCollins*Publishers*

HarperCollins*Publishers* Ltd
The News Building,
1 London Bridge Street,
London SE1 9GF

www.harpercollins.co.uk

HarperCollins*Publishers*
1st Floor, Watermarque Building, Ringsend Road
Dublin 4, Ireland

A Paperback Original 2021
1

A catalogue record for this book
is available from the British Library

ISBN: 978-0-00-816235-1

Typeset in Sabon LT Std by
Palimpsest Book Production Ltd, Falkirk, Stirlingshire

Printed and Bound in the UK using
100% Renewable Electricity at CPI Group (UK) Ltd

The only people I can dedicate this book to are the tremendous medical staff in Morfa Ward, Llandudno General Hospital, where the staff looked after me so well for the many months after my stroke in 2017. Without them I might not be here today, and I will *definitely* not forget the staff in the gym who worked very hard with me to recover physically and who helped to keep my sanity intact. Thank you all so much.

ONE

After the harsh winter of 1931/1932 everyone was looking forward to the spring. *And it's a long time coming,* Angela McClusky reflected to herself, for it was late March – and nearly time for the schools to break up for the Easter holidays – and there was still a nip in the morning. *Maybe it's like the children's rhyme, 'March comes in like a lion and goes out like a lamb',* she thought with a smile as she picked up the letter from the mat and put it in her apron pocket to read later.

She knew the letter was from Harry, George Maitland's nephew who had travelled from America to run the shop left to his father by his uncle under the terms of his will. Albert had been surprised by his brother's actions, feeling sure everything would have been left to his wife, Matilda.

Harry didn't know if George regretted his marriage or not, for it was never mentioned in his letters home, but he had told them of the new assistant, Angela McClusky, who had taken the place of the lad he'd had previously.

In fact, he'd made so many references about Angela McClusky that his father had said, 'You don't think there's anything funny going on, do you? You know . . .?'

Harry was shocked. 'What are you saying, Dad? Angela is just a young girl.'

'Well, you know what they say – no fool like an old fool.'

Anyway, whatever the state of George Maitland's marriage, he'd stuck with it until the day he died, and who was to inherit the shop wasn't apparent immediately. Harry was surprised when his father said, 'You know, our George thought the world of that shop. He was always in it, trailing around after our dad. It used to bore me rigid, but to hear George talk, it was like our dad owned some great emporium. I got a letter from his assistant, Angela McClusky. I wrote to her, you know, because I wasn't sure the will was right, and she said that George was certainly of sound mind when he drew it up. Matilda never served in the shop, never even entered it if she could help it, and was only interested in the proceeds. Angela thinks George would have known the first thing she would do was sell it.'

'I'd say that was the best option.'

'It might be the best option, but not the best moral one.'

'How d'you mean?'

'I think that's why George left it to me. I don't think he expected me to just sell it.'

'Dad, this is crazy! We live in New York in the USA, and the shop is in Birmingham, England.'

'All right, but I don't want to sell it without at least

seeing it once more,' Albert said. 'Point is, the doc says my ticker might not stand the journey.'

'You mean you asked him?'

'Of course – I'm serious about this.'

'But if the doc says you're not fit to go, then you can't go.'

'I know that.'

'Well, then . . .?'

'How would you feel about going in my stead?' asked Albert.

'Why would I want to do that?'

'Because it means a lot to me.'

Harry looked completely flabbergasted. 'But I already have a job.'

'Harry, *I* employ you,' Albert sad. 'I'd obviously give you leave of absence. All I want is for you to take a look, and give me your honest opinion.'

'Even if my honest opinion is to sell it?'

'Even then. If you have seen it with your own eyes, I will be guided by you.'

And so Harry had sailed to England and met the famous Angela McClusky, and could quite understand his uncle's preoccupation with her, for he was quite smitten himself. She was so very beautiful, as well as kind and considerate. No longer a young girl, her husband had died in the war and she had a young daughter to bring up.

What his father hadn't been aware of was that Angela seemed to be in a relationship with someone called Stan Bishop, whom she introduced as an old friend. He seemed a decent enough fellow, but Harry soon guessed he was much more to Angela than an old friend, or a friend of any description, so he didn't say or give any indication to Angela of how he really felt about her. He thought she liked him but he liked Stan too and risked losing that friendship by muscling in where he wasn't really wanted. He had worked in the shop alongside Stan and when he had to leave – just a few years after he'd arrived, due to his father's illness – he asked Stan to take it on. And Stan, who liked working in the shop, agreed readily.

Angela was delighted that Harry had soon grown as fond of the shop as George had been and was also a polite and personable man. Angela liked him a great deal and was sorry when he had to return to America earlier than he thought he would have to.

She wasn't prepared for him appearing at the pub one night and asking her to go back to America with him as his wife. He confessed he'd loved her for years, but had said nothing because he'd thought there might be something between her and Stan, but Stan had convinced him the coast was clear. Angela had been astonished and embarrassed at Harry's words, for she had to refuse him because she didn't feel for him that way, and she had her daughter, Connie, to consider.

Harry was upset, but knew he had slightly shocked Angela with his surprise announcement, but he couldn't delay his departure as his family were depending on him. He was travelling in November, which wasn't a great time to cross the Atlantic Ocean, but he wanted to be home for Thanksgiving.

'Will you write to me, Angela?' he asked.

'I surely will, Harry,' Angela said, 'but you must write first and tell me you are safe in America, for crossing the Atlantic so late in the year could be hazardous, and I will worry until I get that letter.'

Harry did as Angela asked and she replied, and so a regular correspondence began between them. Harry was hoping to get to know Angela better through the letters exchanged so that he might eventually convince her to travel to America for a holiday. Once there, after meeting his parents and seeing the set-up for herself, she might look more favourably on his proposal. He knew it might take some time, but he was a patient man.

Angela knew nothing of Harry's hopes and enjoyed reading his letters, for he wrote as he spoke, so it was like having him in the room. She took out the letter that had arrived that morning from her apron and began to read. As usual, it was full of family news, as well as what was happening in that brave new world. She was awed by tales of the America she'd read so much about in the newspapers – the wide, straight roads full of petrol-driven automobiles, tall skyscrapers, elegant shops, the neon lights of Times Square, and trains running underground beneath those roads and the pavements they called sidewalks. At the end of the letter Harry wrote: 'When you write back, can you tell me how the shop is faring with Stan in charge? I write to his son Daniel, but he just says everything is fine, but you know shop work, and I would be glad of your opinion.'

Angela folded up the letter, suffused with guilt, because she hadn't been near the shop, though she had promised

Harry she would. Surely it wouldn't have hurt her to pop in now and then, but she'd not seen Stan since that last awful encounter when he had expressed his feelings for her for the first time and she had rejected him. She had been unable to see how she could possibly give herself totally to a man with such a secret on her soul – a secret she could never share with him, for she valued his opinion too much to risk telling him. She knew she had hurt him, but it had been a good while ago now. There'd been plenty of water under the bridge since then, and she fervently hoped they could put it behind them and at the very least, regain the deep friendship they'd once both enjoyed.

She decided she would go the very next day, early, before the shop became busy. If anything, she owed it to Harry. She remembered she had fully intended to visit the shop before, and had actually set out twice, until nerves had got the better of her, and both times she had returned home.

Angela got up even earlier than usual the next morning. She wasn't surprised she had the place to herself, but knew if her daughter Connie heard her moving about, she'd probably assume she'd gone to the local pub, The Swan, as she did the cleaning there. She'd been very grateful to the then landlord, Paddy Larkin, for offering her a job after the war, but a little surprised, for she couldn't in all honesty say either her father-in-law Matt or her husband Barry had been regular visitors. She hadn't been there long when Breda Larkin caught sight of her one morning. Breda told Paddy she was wasted on the cleaning – she was needed behind the bar to bring the punters in. So Angela agreed to work behind the bar at the weekend as well. She was more than happy to have a job though, especially when so many didn't. And with Connie at school and her mother-in-law Mary to see to her in the holidays, evenings and weekends, it was perfect for them all.

Back to that cold spring day. Angela had asked for that morning off – she didn't go into details, just said she wanted the time off for personal reasons, and because she was such a hard worker and had never asked for time off before. The Larkins had retired, and handed over the pub to Muriel and Noel Lampeter, who readily agreed to Angela's request.

Connie had heard Angela get up, wondering at the time because it was a full hour before she usually got up to clean at the pub, but she didn't think too much about it. When she heard the front door slam, she padded across the room to watch her mother going down the street, and in one glance, Connie knew she wasn't going to do any cleaning, for she was wearing the coat and hat she wore for Mass, with stockings and her best black court shoes. Well, that was a mystery, all right. She wondered where her mother was going at this early hour, dressed to the nines. She sighed. Probably there was some perfectly logical explanation. She would have to wait till her mother came home to hear all about it.

As Angela made her way to Maitland's grocery shop, which was right over the other side of Edgbaston, she reflected anew about all the changes brought about because so many men had not returned from the Great War. She remembered what George Maitland, her old employer, had said on a similar subject.

He had no children and this was a great regret for him, but when the war began and the casualty figures began appearing in the paper, he said to Angela one day, 'You know, I've never had chick nor child belonging to me, and at times that has been a cross to bear, for I would have loved a family. But now I look at my customers and see the ones who have lost sons, and wonder if it is worse for them, who have given birth to a boy and reared him with such a powerful love that they would willingly give their own life to save him. But they are unable to save him from war, and when he dies for King and Country, the loss must be an overwhelming one. I have had women in the shop crying broken-heartedly about their beloved sons who will never return, and at times I am almost thankful I have had no sons of my own to suffer the same fate.'

Angela knew what he meant. She remembered the morning in the late spring of 1919 when she had come upon Eric Moorcroft (who then owned the grocery shop on Bell Barn Road) up a ladder outside his shop. He came down as he saw Angela approach and folded the ladder up. 'Did you want something from the shop?' he'd asked.

Angela shook her head. 'Not yet,' she said. 'I'm on my way to work, but I'll likely call on the way back.'

Eric nodded and lifted the ladder and turned to go into the back yard with it, looking suddenly so woebegone that Angela, although knowing she hadn't the time to stand

and talk, found herself saying, 'You have a fine shop here, Mr Moorcroft, and you have been here as long as I can remember.'

Eric nodded. 'My grandfather had this shop first,' he said. 'His father used to have a stall in the market and he had been a fine saver, so I was told. So when he died, his son, my grandfather, was able to buy this shop – a wee huxter of a place it was then, and he built it up. When it became my father's shop after Grandad died, I was always in helping him, like my own son, Billy, used to do. He would have taken over from me.' Eric stopped and Angela saw tears glittering in his desolate eyes.

Then he seemed to collect himself and she saw his shoulders straighten, but his voice was husky as he continued, 'Billy won't be coming home from the war, though.' And he added bitterly, 'His body is littering some foreign field somewhere. Tell you something, though – it took some time for me to deal with that, the thought I'd never see him again. But it's got to be faced up to, hasn't it? It's what you have to do.'

'There was no alternative for me when I lost Barry,' Angela said. 'I had Connie to rear and Mary to see to as well.'

'Ah, that's the rub, you see,' Eric said. 'No one to follow on after me. No one to work hard for, so that my son would inherit a thriving business. We intended, when we married, Mabel and I, to have more than just the one son, but there was never any more after Billy. But he was enough, a fine boy I was mighty proud of.' He sighed and went on, 'Anyway, this morning I thought it was time to face facts and alter the sign. After all, the war has been over six months now.'

Angela glanced up, and the sign that once had read *Moorcroft and Son* was now just *Moorcroft*. She felt a lump in her throat and tears stung the back of her eyes. She willed the tears not to fall as she said, 'Mr Moorcroft, I think that was a very brave thing to do. I know how much you thought of your son, and you're right, he was a lovely young man and the loss of him must have been a dreadful one. My heart goes out to you and your wife.'

'Thank you, my dear,' Eric said warmly as he shook Angela's hand and added bleakly, 'Some days, you know, there doesn't seem any point to going on, for I have lost more than my son, because his mother has not been the same woman since we had the tragic news, and I don't think she ever will be.'

'It takes time,' Angela said. 'And some people take longer to come to terms with it.'

Eric nodded, 'I know, and if only she had something to focus her mind on, she might begin to recover, but . . .'

'She won't help in the shop again? I know she used to at the beginning of the war.'

'Aye, she did,' Eric agreed sadly. 'Not after we knew officially that our boy was dead, though. See, my lad died on that awful first day at the Battle of the Somme – July the 1st, 1916 – but the death toll was so colossal, it was nearly Christmas 1916 before we were informed. Till then I hoped. I mean, part of me sort of knew when the letters stopped, but we hoped. When we got the telegram, it was as if my wife died inside. Without our boy, nothing seems to have any point to it any more. I felt the same, God knows, but I had customers relying on me. I had to go on, and God it was hard, but Mabel hasn't set foot in the shop since.'

Eric suddenly picked up the ladder quite abruptly and took it through to the back yard, and Angela watched him go and knew he had hurried away because he was very close to tears. And not long after that Mabel Moorcroft developed Spanish flu and died, and Eric sold up the shop and disappeared, and was never heard of again. Now the shop was owned by Des and Molly Perks, and though they had been there seven years, many still referred to it as Moorcroft's.

Personally, Angela thought there was actually not anything 'great' about that war at all. It was supposed to be 'the war to end all wars' and all the men fighting in it were promised a land 'fit for heroes' on their return, when in fact those who returned had nothing but the dole queue and poverty awaiting them.

Angela often thought about George's words as the war raged on. Before her marriage she had worked in his shop for two years, beginning at the age of fourteen, when a neighbour visiting her daughter, who lived near Maitland's, saw a sign in the window asking for an assistant.

Angela remembered with a smile that George had been a little dumbfounded when Angela said she'd come about the job, for he'd never thought of a young girl applying, for he'd always had a young lad in the past. But he agreed to give her a trial, and by the time her probation period was over, George wondered what he had ever done without her. Angela thought George was such a kind man and a considerate employer, and she had become very fond of him. And George said it was like a breath of fresh air every morning when she entered the shop. She was polite to the customers and had a ready smile for all, a very cheerful disposition altogether. He had thought a lot of her too – so much so, that after he died she found he had left her his mother's jewellery that he had lodged in the bank with authorisation, saying it was for Angela alone and totally separate from his will. Angela had presumed he had left everything to his wife Matilda.

TWO

Angela knew the shop would be a different place with Stan at the helm. She was still a little nervous, so before her courage failed her completely, she opened the door. She blinked as she stepped into the busy grocer's shop, for the sun spilling through the big picture window brightened the whole place. Her brilliant blue eyes were fastened on the shopkeeper, Stan, the man she told herself never to think of by day, and who haunted her dreams by night. She was surprised he hadn't looked up when she heard the ping of the shop bell as she opened the door. Stan knew she was there though, she was sure, because their gaze had fleetingly met before she'd plucked up every ounce of courage she could summon, and stepped inside the shop that had once been so familiar to her . . .

For shopkeeper Stan it had, until that moment, just been a normal Friday morning. The sun was spilling through the big picture window, bathing the whole shop in warmth and light. His grocery shop was busy with customers stretching the last of their week's housekeeping to buy food for the weekend. Then he saw a figure making her way tentatively towards the shop door. Could it be . . .? Stan's heart sank. Yes, it was. Angela McClusky. Until he heard the ping of the shop doorbell, Stan kept a vain hope that she might walk on by.

Instead he felt a sinking in his heart when she pushed the door ajar. He purposefully kept his back to her, knowing he was being rude, but not trusting himself to turn and greet her. He listened to her footsteps drawing nearer to him with trepidation, wishing more than anything that he might never have to see or speak to Angela McClusky ever again. Angela had been his friend for years, but he had always harboured a hope that one day she would become *more* than a friend. Then his son Daniel had suggested it would be better to tell Angela how he felt and see her reaction. Stan had bolstered up his courage and told her, only to have his hopes dashed and his soul crushed when Angela had made it plain that she found the idea of being more than friends utterly repulsive. Humiliated and hurt, Stan knew beyond doubt that there was no place for him in Angela's life. They had both tried their hardest to avoid one another at all costs since that wretched day, so Stan wondered what on earth she was doing coming to his shop now.

There were a host of much nearer grocery shops to Angela's house, for his was a fair step from Bell Barn Road. He couldn't imagine what she might want, but he also couldn't bring himself to be the first to speak, so he kept his back to her.

Stan couldn't, or wouldn't, even look her in the eye, thought Angela, making her feel even more nervous than she had been on the walk over to his shop. But she knew she had to try and make peace with this man who had once meant so much to her. She'd spent weeks, months even, plucking up the courage to come and try one last time to extend an olive branch to him, playing the scene over and over in her head, her heart racing at the thought of being shot down once again. Summoning every ounce of strength she had, Angela said in a voice that shook with emotion, 'Stan – please, we need to talk.'

She watched, unable to breathe, as Stan turned slowly. His desolate eyes looked incredulous, as if he couldn't believe what he had heard. For a few moments he didn't speak, just stared at Angela, and she quailed inwardly at the look in his eyes that made her afraid to say anything further.

'Talk?' Stan eventually whispered into the strained silence. 'You want to talk?' His voice was getting louder now. 'The last time I tried to talk to you, I *disgusted* you. The time for talk between us is dead and gone.'

Angela had deliberately tried to push from her mind the details of the last time they'd met, because remembering it upset her so much. But they had been such good friends and she had found the months she had stayed away from him even harder than seeing him. So she tried again: 'Stan, please. Nothing you could say would ever disgust me.'

'No?' Stan asked, moving away from his browsing customers and lowering his voice once again to a haunted growl. 'Well, let's just say you have a funny way of showing it. When I tried talking to you, expressing my . . . feelings, you showed me plainly what you felt for me. Disregard and repugnance.' Stan's eyes were darker than Angela had ever seen them, and his words were like chips of ice in the air as he continued: 'My words of love caused you to shudder with disgust. So you see, the time for talking is well past. There is no need to pretend you have feelings that you don't really have.' He paused, then continued in a softer tone of voice: 'I am glad to see that you are all right, but now we must go our separate ways. I wish you well, Angela – you and your daughter. But this needs to be goodbye from me.'

'Stan.'

'Don't make this harder than it already is!' Stan pleaded, but as he turned from Angela, she saw the glint of tears in his eyes before he gathered his control and, his face implacable once more, he stepped into the storeroom behind the shop counter, shutting the door with a definite click.

Angela resisted the desire to hammer on the door. Stan had made it clear his ears and heart were closed to anything she had to say, and with a sad sigh she turned for home. The tears came as she left the shop. She wished there was some private place where she could go and cry, for she sensed she had irrevocably broken something beautiful, and all of a sudden the loss of Stan's friendship felt as heavy as grief, but there was nowhere private for her to go. She couldn't go home, for Connie would know something was up with her and would likely plague her with questions she didn't feel she would be able to answer. So she walked up and down those cold, mean streets for hours, scalding tears trickling down her face, keeping her head down, lest some well-meaning individual ask if she was all right. She felt so wretched, she doubted she would ever feel all right ever again.

Hours later she turned for home and she was barely in the door when Connie, in her bubbly, forthright way, exclaimed, 'Mum, you're home! Where on earth have you been all this time? You must be cold to the bone.'

'I've just been out walking,' Angela answered. But her voice betrayed her, and Connie looked at her in a concerned way.

'What's up?'

Angela gave an imperceptible sigh. She had obviously not stayed out long enough. This conversation was what she had been hoping to avoid. Determined to change the subject, she took a deep breath and said as brightly as she could manage, 'Nothing. What do you mean?'

Connie, who could see straight through Angela's cheery front, went on, 'Mum, it looks as if you've been crying. What has happened on this long "walk" to upset you? And don't say you haven't been crying, like you always do.'

Angela knew her daughter was concerned about her, but she just couldn't bring herself to talk about what had happened with Stan. Her stomach was still churning with the upset, and her heart ached so badly, it felt like a physical pain in her chest. She was incapable of saying any of this to anyone, even her beloved Connie, but she knew her daughter wasn't the sort of girl to let a thing drop. She had a split second before Connie's piercing stare reduced her to the tears she was determined not to shed, so she snapped out, 'Whether I have been crying or not is none of your business!'

Connie was taken aback and quite shocked. She shot a baleful look at her mother and flounced upstairs.

Connie was concerned because she knew it had to be something big that had happened for her mother to shed tears over it. She wasn't the sort of woman to cry at the drop of a hat. But she was also hurt that her mother couldn't, or wouldn't, open up to her. If she wasn't prepared to tell her what it was all about, there was nothing she could do. Neither of them spoke of it again, but all that day Connie was frosty with her mother, and both were glad when it was late enough to go to bed.

Once in bed, Angela relived the whole horrid experience with Stan. She didn't expect to sleep well, and she certainly didn't. It was almost a relief when it was time to get up again, and keep her mind busy rather than just replaying events over and over. One thing she was sure of, she would be too nervous of Stan's reaction to try and contact him again. He had made his feelings completely clear and as he had no wish to see her any more, so she must put him out of her mind.

Stan also went over the encounter again and again. He vowed he could never see Angela ever again. He had loved her so deeply and for so long that when he saw her, his body would betray him and he would have to fight the emotions that urged him to take her in his arms, which was obviously the last thing she would want him to do. If she was going to make a habit of turning up at his shop she would eventually destroy him, and for the first time he began to think seriously about an alternative offer of employment that he had been asked about a few days previously.

Stan, as a member of the Labour Party, was approached by a Labour MP, who told him some news he found shocking. During the Great War the outskirts of Birmingham had been blasted by bombs dropped from Zeppelins. The area they were dropped in was highly industrialised, with many factories, and a lot of these factories were making war-related goods. Often tall chimneys were attached to these black-bricked, grimy factories which constantly blew out dirty smoke into the already smutty air, so the whole area had been dubbed the Black Country. Stan knew that other places had been targeted too – King's Lynn, Great Yarmouth, Hull and, of course, London – but the residents of Birmingham and the Midlands generally thought *they* were safe from any sort of aerial bombing attack, as they were, after all, 200 miles inland. No plans had been made in the event of any air raids, so the whole area had been totally unprepared when Walsall had come under attack. Stan could remember it now as if it were yesterday, learning that eighty-seven people had been killed and over a hundred more injured. Stan hadn't been aware of these raids when they were happening, as he had been away fighting, but he'd been horrified to learn of them on his return.

The MP talked to Stan about all this, and he gazed at the MP in puzzlement. 'Why bring it up now, when it happened sixteen years ago?'

The MP didn't answer but asked instead, 'What provision do you think was made for these people who lost their homes, and in some cases, their businesses too?'

'Well, I don't know,' Stan admitted. 'But though it might have been inadequate at the time, surely to God that has all been corrected, sixteen years down the line?'

The MP shook his head. 'Alas, no,' he said. 'It cost a lot of money to fight a war and there were no funds for any form of house building planned for afterwards either. Those poor people who were made homeless bedded down where they could. Some had relatives willing and able to put them up, and they could be called the lucky ones. Others used the ruins of houses, warehouses, church halls, and in some cases they lived under bridges. The point is, many of them are still there. Recently, questions were raised in the Houses of Parliament about it. After all, so many of those who lost their homes and livelihoods were the very people who suffered four years of war: the men fighting, the women making weapons and running the country. They lost so much and now feel they have been abandoned by the government that took them into war in the first place. They are calling themselves the Forgotten People, because I suppose they feel they are. I would feel the same in their shoes. Personally, I think it's scandalous.'

'I agree with you,' Stan said. 'Scandalous is the only word, but what's to be done?'

'Well,' the MP answered, 'while some of these bombs completely destroyed some houses, others were made too unstable to live in, in their present state. The council have employed surveyors to check these out and see if they can be repaired to make adequate housing for at least some of the displaced residents, to try and get as many as possible under cover before yet another winter sets in. They also need an army of people to clear the site of rubble, sand and mounds of debris left from the demolished houses so that new houses can be built without delay. It seemed a good thing to get involved in.'

'I agree with that too,' Stan said. 'But I still don't see why you are telling me this.'

The MP said, 'Because I want *you* on board. At the moment all we have to do is clear the mounds left by the demolished houses. We need as many as we can get to clear the area. That's all for now.'

Stan stared at him. 'If all you want is a large workforce, you can take your pick from any of the unemployed hanging around our streets just now. Spoilt for choice, you'll be. I have a job. I run the shop.'

'I know, but hear me out,' the MP said. 'My suggestion is that you get a manager in for now and come and work for me. We want you because you are obviously good at leading men. You were a gaffer before you enlisted, and had your sergeant stripes after a few months in the army, and were then in charge of soldiers. Everyone speaks highly of you. These men are not in the army now, and they may not take kindly to people barking orders at them. I am assured you don't do that. I think they'll listen to you, and that's why I'm prepared to pay you more than you'd earn in the shop for your time.'

'That's really for others to say,' Stan said. 'In the army it maybe had to be a bit different, but I always think better results and a happier working environment comes from talking to people, not shouting at them.'

The MP nodded. 'That will be all to the good,' he said. 'We are drafting in lots of miners, and they can be problematic to work with.'

Stan was annoyed by the MP's obvious prejudice and said quite sharply, 'I'd say the miners are just the same as the rest of us – glad to be able to work for a living wage to provide for their families. They've had it hard, especially when you consider that coal exports have fallen since the Great War, and the miners' hours have been extended and their wages have been reduced. No one seemingly has given a thought to the families of these men, for you know as well as me that people have to eat in peace-time as well as during a war, and the rent has still to be paid. It's the newspapers that have coined the slogan, *Not a penny off the pay and not a minute on the day* – not the miners themselves. I'd say it's little wonder some miners have become frustrated and disgruntled. And I'm sure the majority of them will be glad of a job of any sort that pays enough for them to live on.'

'You're right,' the MP said, reluctantly. 'It's just . . . well, they seem so aggressive at times.'

'Like I said before, I find that quite understandable,'

Stan said, determined to try and open the Labour MP's mind to his own constituents. 'Hearing my children crying with hunger would tear me to shreds, as it would any decent father. And remember, many of these men were in the Forces, serving their King and Country.'

The MP nodded, and Stan hoped his words had struck a chord. 'Well, now the miners are needed again,' the MP said. 'The surveyors go around first and find out which houses could be made habitable, with some shoring up or reinforcing in places. Those renovations would be carried out by the workforce, but they'd only start any repair work when it's safe to do so.'

'And they will be well paid to do this work, I presume,' Stan said. 'They are taking more of a risk than the rest of us, crawling into half-demolished and damaged houses. They should be financially compensated for that. I'm telling you, if you offer them a pittance, they might well refuse to do it, and then where will the council be? If you're trying to do this on the cheap, you run the risk of annoying the miners, and you'll lose your entire workforce.'

'I told you they were problematic.'

'I don't find a man problematic because he is willing to work hard at what is sometimes dangerous work in order to provide for his family, but he wants a decent wage for doing so. I'd say a man like that is to be commended, and one I would be proud to work alongside.'

'Oh quite, *quite*,' the MP said, flustered.

Stan was barely listening to him, however. Had Angela not come into the shop, he might not have given the MP's proposal a second thought. As it was . . . well, maybe it would be better to be out of the area for a wee while. After all, it would not be forever, and he would welcome the chance for hard physical labour, for it might help him sleep better and not toss and turn in the bed, thinking of the loss of Angela.

'All right,' he said at last. 'Sadie Bradshaw took over the shop while I was in the army, and for some time afterwards, as her husband was numbered among those who never came back. It would be good to be able to offer her a decent salary, and if she's willing to do it for a few more weeks or months, then I will help for a short time.'

'Good man,' the MP said, shaking Stan by the hand. 'I will be in touch with instructions and directions to the area we're working in shortly. I believe we're starting in Walsall.'

'All right,' Stan said. 'If I were you, I'd go and ask some of the fellows outside if they are willing to work for a decent wage. But be careful, because you just might be killed in the rush. But it just may ease the tensions a little. Some of those unemployed are very angry, for they feel so little has been done to help them, it might boil over into violence any day, and without the slightest provocation.'

Stan was only too right. He knew groups of the unemployed were getting larger and there had been unrest about the lack of any sort of paid work since the war. The government had promised everyone 'a land fit for heroes', and it had all been eye-wash. Often the only one who got fed in a house was the man, so that if he should get a job, he'd be well nourished enough to take it. This meant that his wife and children often got by with bread and scrape, and not much of that, thought Stan. Resentment bubbled beneath the surface in many working-class homes at the lies the government had told them and the promises they had broken.

Bidding farewell to the MP, Stan walked home, noting the sense of relief he felt at the opportunity to be away from the shop, where Angela could appear at any time. He didn't share these thoughts with his son Daniel when he told him about the job that evening, and Daniel just hoped it might help his father regain his good humour, and even offered to come and help through the coming Easter holidays, when the school where he taught would be closed. *Yes,* thought Stan, *enough moping around.* This could be just the fresh start he needed.

Later that day Angela sat in her kitchen reading the local newspaper. 'There are so many on the dole already, it's so sad really,' Angela said to Connie as she read about the unrest. 'We should be thankful we are so much better off than many.'

'Yes,' Connie said, 'but we *could* be even more better off. Sarah's second sister is starting at the Grand Hotel next week, and she says she could get a job for me too if you weren't so set on me matriculating.'

'I thought we had discussed this, Connie. Nothing is more important than finishing your education.'

'But we never actually *discuss* it!' Connie burst out. 'You tell me how to live my life and if I ever disagree, you tell me that it's what my father would want. But how can you be so absolutely sure? This is a different world to the one Daddy left behind when he enlisted. Maybe he would feel differently if he was alive today.'

'You don't know that.'

'No, Mammy, but neither do you.'

'Connie, what on earth has got into you?'

'Nothing,' Connie said. 'I'm just growing up, that's all. I want to start living my own life, making my own decisions, and being able to live independently. Anyway, I could ask the same of you.'

'What d'you mean?'

'I mean, what's got into you that's causing you to go round with a face miserable enough to sour cream?'

'Connie!' Angela exclaimed, shocked and hurt, but knowing there was a shred of truth in her daughter's observations. 'You're being rude.'

'No, I'm not,' Connie retorted. 'I'm being truthful. What you mean is, you don't like what I am saying, and you probably have no intention of answering me, but that doesn't make what I said rude.'

Angela knew it didn't, and she couldn't answer Connie, because what could she say that would satisfy her?

'You'll probably just say that it's none of my business, like you did before,' Connie said. 'But if I said that to you, well that really would be rude! I would get it in the neck from you, for sure.'

Angela knew she couldn't argue that point. 'Connie, it's just too difficult to explain.'

'So that's that then, is it?' Connie asked, looking

pleadingly at her mother, hoping she might just open up and share.

Angela bit down the urge to share her heartbreak. Perhaps if she didn't talk about it, she might one day be able to pretend it had never happened. 'I'm afraid it is.'

'What on earth is the use of trying to talk to you about anything?' Connie cried, exasperated, and she left her mother standing in the middle of the room, and Angela felt suddenly bereft. She had seldom argued with Connie for almost all of her growing up, for Connie had been an unusually compliant child who was anxious to please, and in particular to please her mother. Angela was sad that Connie seemed to think she'd let her down in some way, as they had once been so close. After the unpleasant encounter with Stan in the shop, an altercation with Connie was the last thing Angela had the energy to deal with. She sighed and buried her head in her hands, not knowing how or if any of it could possibly be resolved.

Angela didn't know what to do with herself that evening, her conversations with Stan and Connie going round and round in her head. Eventually she went to see Maggie Malone, who ran a boarding house on Pershore Road with her husband Michael that they had inherited from Michael's parents. Maggie had been Angela's friend since their school days and the two kept nothing from one another. She was the only one who knew the darkest secret Angela hid from everyone else in her life, something so awful that Angela still woke wracked with guilt most nights. Twelve long years ago, she had had to abandon an illegitimate baby that she had just given birth to, leaving the child on the steps of the local workhouse. Maggie had stood staunchly at Angela's side through that whole time, and so Angela was confident Maggie would be able to advise her on what to do about Stan and Connie.

Maggie listened intently to Angela. She wasn't surprised Stan had expressed his love for her, for she had known how the wind blew for a long while and, like many other people, was just surprised Stan had taken so long to tell Angela how he felt about her. What she wasn't so pleased about was Angela's response, because she said she had shuddered. 'But why?' Maggie said. 'Whether you are going to admit it or not, I know you, and you are just as crazy about Stan as he is about you. Why didn't you grasp this chance of happiness?'

'You know why.'

'If you tell me that you can never be happy again because of what happened back then, I will be cross with you,' Maggie said. 'That decision was forced on you and is one you've lived with every day since. Had you confided in Stan, I'm sure he would have seen that for himself, but you didn't even give him the chance. Instead, when he told you his feelings, you *shuddered*. Can you imagine how hurt he would have been? It must have cut him to the quick.'

'I tried to speak to him in the shop – I told you.'

'And what did you want to say?' Maggie demanded. 'If he had asked why you recoiled, would you have told him the truth?'

'What shall I do, Maggie?'

'The only thing to do,' Maggie said decisively, 'is to find

Stan as soon as you can, apologise profusely and tell him about the baby you had to leave the way you did.'

'He will be disgusted with me.'

'No,' said Maggie thoughtfully, 'I don't think he will. But if he is, then he's not the man I thought he was and not the man for you. At least you'll have a better idea of where you stand, and that has to be less heart-breaking than the limbo you're currently in, that is making no one happy. You're torn apart by the guilt, and not only has it stopped you finding true happiness, but it's also driving a wedge between you and Connie. You make things right with Stan, and the troubles with Connie will fall into place, because you won't be carrying the weight of the world on your shoulders any more. You are very special to Connie, and seeing you unhappy makes her worry about you, and why she can't seem to do anything to ease your pain. Fixing things with Stan is the first step.'

Angela knew Maggie was right and thought about her words as she walked home, but Maggie hadn't seen the look on Stan's face when he told her he never wanted to see her again. And feeling that way about her, would he ever truly be able to understand her despair and desperation that had forced her to sacrifice her vulnerable new-born baby to save everyone else? She shook her head from side to side in agitation and fought back the threatening tears, because she really didn't think, with the best will in the world, that she could take that risk.

Over the following days Connie knew her mother was unhappier than ever and also knew it had something to do with the time she'd left the house early, dressed in her best clothes, and when she came home hours later she had been crying. Connie had no idea what might have upset her so and was well aware her mother had no intention of telling her, but she remembered that she and Stan used to get on really well, until that awful fall-out. But that had been years before, and surely to goodness it would all be forgotten now. Seeking only to find someone who might help jerk her mother out of the pit of misery she seemed to have fallen into, she said, 'Mammy, why don't we ever see Stan any more?'

'You know why,' Angela said through gritted teeth.

'Mammy, that was years ago,' Connie persisted. 'Surely if you were to see him, talk to him . . .'

Angela remembered the cold, bitter eyes Stan had turned on her in the shop, and said, 'Sorry, but neither of us will be seeing Stan any more.'

Connie's mouth dropped open and she said, 'Have you ever even tried to contact him?'

Angela thought of the hopes she had had that the argument between them would be more or less forgotten. Yet she had seen almost immediately that Stan certainly hadn't forgotten it, making it plain that he never wanted to see her again. That decision brought another problem to mind. It would be harder to keep well away from Stan if her daughter continued her friendship with Daniel. 'What is between me and Stan really is no concern of yours, but while we're on the subject, it might be better if you don't see Daniel any more.'

'What?' Connie was incredulous. 'What's Daniel to do with this?'

Angela sighed. 'It would just be easier, that's all.'

'Easier for who?' Connie asked accusingly. 'Easier for you, but not easier for me – or Daniel. We were friends once, and nothing in my life has happened to change that. If it is you that has a problem with Daniel's father that you refuse to discuss, then . . . Well, I just think you are punishing Daniel and me for something his father has done. That's hardly fair.'

Angela knew it wasn't, but could think of no answer to give her that would satisfy either of them. In the end she pleaded, 'Please can we leave it there, Connie? I won't insult your intelligence by saying you will understand all this when you're older, but please leave it for now.'

And Connie left it. She was frightened of the stricken look in her mother's eyes, and in her ashen face that filled with sadness. Connie saw the slight trembling of her limbs and was sorry she had caused her mother such distress. Angela had clearly decided that for now she would say no more. But it was frustrating, because, like so many conversations with her mother about the past, nothing had been resolved.

Just as Connie could sense her mother's sadness, Stan's son Daniel was noticing the same about his usually even-tempered father, who, despite the more physical job he was now doing, had continued being short-tempered. Stan regretted the years they had been kept apart because of the war, and knew that by rights he shouldn't be spoiling the time they had together now. Eventually, Daniel snapped back at his father after he had bawled him out about some trivial thing he had done. 'I don't know what's the matter with you, but whatever it is, it's not my fault, so stop taking it out on me!'

Immediately Stan felt contrite and said, 'You're right, and I'm sorry.'

Looking at his father's sad face, Daniel felt sorry he had been so blunt with him, and in a softer voice went on, 'Look, remembering back, this misery of yours seems to go back to the time I advised you to admit to Angela how you felt about her. *Did* you tell her then how strong your feelings were for her?'

Stan nodded. 'Oh yes, I told her, all right.'

'Well, it obviously didn't go down well,' Daniel said. 'I wondered at the time, felt quite guilty about it. I should never have interfered. After all, you know Angela much better than me.'

'Huh! I thought I did.'

'Sorry, Dad.'

'Oh, it's not your fault,' Stan said. 'After all, I didn't have to take your advice.'

'Maybe she wasn't ready for a declaration of love just yet?' Daniel replied hopefully.

'She certainly wasn't,' Stan said. 'But the point is, I don't think she'll ever be ready for a declaration from me.'

'Aren't you getting all this out of proportion?' Daniel said with a wry smile. 'Angela might not be ready for love just yet, but she thinks the world of you. You share a deep friendship, if nothing else.'

Stan nodded. 'We did, I grant you, but no more.'

'Surely not?'

'Worse than that,' Stan said morosely. 'Angela McClusky finds me repulsive.'

Daniel looked at his father disbelievingly. He had never known him lie to him, and yet he was talking about a woman he greatly admired, who had championed his father, said what a fine man he was. 'That's a bit over-dramatic, Dad,' he said. 'What makes you think Angela finds you repulsive?'

Stan didn't answer Daniel, but what he did say was, 'When your mother died, Barry and Angela, and Angela's mother-in-law Mary opened their hearts to me. With you living with your Aunt Betty, who had made it clear I was not welcome, the McCluskys made me feel valued and, well . . . loved, I suppose. However, some years later, when I began to have deeper feelings for Angela, I hid them and certainly never spoke of them.'

'Why not?

'Because she was married to Barry, who she loved to distraction. She never gave me any indication she thought of me as anything more than a great friend.'

'Is that why you tried to keep Barry out of the army?'

Stan raised his eyebrows. 'Who told you that?'

'Angela,' Daniel replied. 'How did you go about trying to do that?'

'Oh, Angela didn't tell you that, then?'

'No, she clammed up,' Daniel said. 'You know she doesn't like to talk about things that happened years ago?'

Stan nodded, for he knew that well enough. 'Well,' he said. 'The factory we both worked in made lots of things for the war effort. And when I enlisted, I recommended

Barry for my old job as supervisor. That meant he was in a reserved occupation and could have sat out the war in relative safety. I did that because he had a lot to live for – a beautiful wife, a child he adored – while I felt I had little in my life.'

'So how come he became involved in the war anyway?'

'He was bullied into it,' Stan said. 'The family were snubbed and mistreated by people they had known all their lives. Barry said he could understand it, for the casualty figures of those killed or injured made grim reading, and mothers who had sons in the thick of it were maybe understandably resentful of a young, fit man like Barry sitting pretty at home. Barry too was uncomfortable about it, and once said to me he had never let anyone else fight his battles before, and this was a particularly fierce battle that he appeared to be hiding from. He also did his very best to help out as many war widows in the local area as he could, stepping in to do any heavy lifting required, fixing up houses, playing football with the boys on the street. He felt it was his duty to be the man of the house for all those whose husbands were away on the front line. Never had a quiet evening in, did Barry – he was always out helping someone somewhere. But then the four white feathers arrived.'

'Four white feathers?' Daniel repeated, perplexed.

'White feathers for cowardice,' Stan said. 'Someone thought it their duty to tell Barry he was a coward. But he was no coward and enlisted straight away. His last act was to make a valiant effort to save me, and he lost his own life because of it.'

'Angela always said he was a hero.'

Stan nodded. 'He was, and so was every man who served at the Front.'

'And you are going to throw all that away? All that history you shared with Angela – over a stupid quarrel?'

'It wasn't a quarrel, but it became clear that Angela doesn't feel about me how I feel about her.'

'All right, what did she say when you told her how you felt?'

Stan paused, summoning up the courage to describe Angela's reaction out loud for the first time. 'Nothing.'

'Nothing?' Daniel repeated, incredulously.

'Nothing,' Stan said. 'She didn't give me the dignity of a reply, she just . . .' Stan hesitated, knowing he was already committed to telling Daniel the whole truth, '. . . shuddered.'

'Shuddered?' Daniel said, quite shocked.

'Yes, shuddered,' Stan said. 'I think that showed plainly enough that my love for her made her feel repugnance towards me. She can't help her feelings, but her reaction shows me plainly that there is now no place for me in Angela's life, or in her heart.'

Daniel was stunned. He could now understand how hurt his father must have been – and still was. He felt angry with Angela, and yet he would never have said she was a cruel person, but that reaction seemed a cruel one to have. She would have known how it would make Stan feel.

'Did you ask her for any explanation for the shudder?'

'What do you think?' Stan said. 'I had bared my soul,

and I walked away, wishing those words had been left unsaid.'

Over the next few days Daniel could not stop thinking about what his father had told him. His memories of Angela, her gentleness and kindness, did not seem the same person who would shudder when her great friend Stan spoke words of love, let alone allow him to walk away feeling humiliated. Eventually, he decided he would go and see Connie. Surely, if his father had been angered and hurt by what had happened, then Angela was probably upset too. Connie, he reasoned, might have brighter ideas than any he'd come up with on how Stan and Angela could at least become friends again – anything to stop his father looking so wretched . . .

Daniel knew better than to call at the house, fearing Angela might not let him through the front door, let alone have a private talk with Connie. He suspected she'd probably be at the library in the city centre where, he presumed, she still worked on Saturdays. So the following Saturday he headed there and waited outside.

Connie had been wondering for days how to talk to her mother, whose unhappiness was almost palpable. Despite this, she was still surprised to see Daniel waiting for her when she left the library in her lunch hour. 'Daniel, what are you doing here?' she blurted out, tripping over her tongue in surprise, feeling a blush tinge her cheeks. They might be family friends, but she was only fifteen, and Daniel was a very good-looking boy in his twenties. Connie could see other young girls giving him a second glance and felt proud that he had sought out her company, even if she didn't quite understand why.

'Waiting for you,' came Daniel's easy reply, his smile hiding the way his heart beat just that little bit faster the moment he saw Connie.

'You know our respective parents wouldn't like us to meet like this?'

Daniel shrugged. 'Then let's make sure they never find out,' he said.

Connie continued to look at him warily. It had been a long time since they'd seen one another, and he supposed, to her, he had appeared as if from the blue. *Best to lay all my cards on the table*, he thought. He continued, 'Look, Connie, my dad is going around like a bear with a sore head, and I would hedge a bet your mother is just as upset as he is?'

Daniel saw understanding settle in Connie's large, soulful eyes, and he carried on: 'I thought, together, we might be able to make them see sense. I have to say, my dad's attitude is making living at home almost unbearable at the moment.'

'Oh, I don't know . . .' replied Connie, cautiously. 'I agree with you, my mum is not herself at all at the moment.'

'It's worth a try, don't you think, Connie?'

'I suppose.'

Taking her arm, Daniel led Connie to a nearby café. 'Come on, let's have some lunch while we talk?'

Going out to lunch was a treat Connie wasn't accustomed to. Especially with a boy. Usually, at dinnertime she tucked herself away in the staffroom with whichever title she'd selected from the shelves to read that day, and buried her head in her book whilst munching on sandwiches from home. But there was a cold wind biting the air that afternoon and the thought of lunch in a warm café with Daniel was one that Connie suddenly found she didn't want to argue with. But however nice a change it was from homemade sandwiches, afterwards Connie found she couldn't really remember what she ate. Her mind had been too preoccupied with puzzling out what had happened between Stan and her mum. Looking at it all ways, neither she nor Daniel could think of any way to heal the rift between their parents, when they were confronted by the fact that neither would agree to meet the other, let alone talk.

'I don't know what to do,' Connie finally said in exasperation. 'Do you?'

Daniel shook his head. 'Not really,' he said. 'The situation seems as bad as ever. Worse, if I'm honest.'

'Yes,' Connie agreed. 'Mammy is definitely worse, and it all started again the morning she got up even earlier than she does when she cleans the pub. I didn't think anything of it until I spied her out of the window. She had the clothes on she wears for Mass. She wouldn't clean the pub dressed like that!'

'So you asked her, but she refused to tell you?'

'Not a word.'

'This recent business can't have anything to do with Dad,' Daniel said. 'To my knowledge, they haven't met for years.'

'Yes,' Connie said, 'it must all be to do with that quarrel they had years ago. Must have been some argument, that's all I can say. After all this time, instead of coming to terms with it and sort of burying the hatchet, if anything their differences, whatever on earth they are, have become more entrenched than ever.'

'Yes,' Daniel said in agreement, then he paused for a moment and then went on, 'mind you, I understand how humiliated Dad was, initially.'

'What do you mean?' Connie said. 'You mean you know what the quarrel was about?'

'Sort of.'

'You know, and haven't said after all this time?'

Daniel sighed. 'I didn't know if it was just that . . .' he went on. 'Look, I knew my dad truly loved your mother, and I advised him to tell her. I mean, she's an attractive woman and could be snapped up by another.'

Connie nodded, remembering her mother's mad period with a certain chap called Eddie McIntyre, whom she hoped she'd never see again.

'Anyway,' Daniel went on, 'that day we came to dinner and we went for a walk to see the canal and barges and that.'

Connie nodded again and Daniel continued, 'Well, that day Dad told your mother things he'd held in his heart for years . . .'

'And?' Connie asked.

'Your mother couldn't say anything back. Dad said she just shuddered at the thought,' Daniel said. 'Dad had obviously totally misread the way your mother felt about him. I often wished I'd kept my big mouth shut, because it was my urging that made him do it.'

'But,' Connie said, confused, 'I can't imagine any words Stan could say to make Mammy act like that. It was a cruel thing to do, and Mammy isn't cruel – not to anyone, and certainly not Stan. He was – is – so special to her.'

'It sounds to me,' said Daniel, 'that you need to ask your mother for her side of the story. Dad would hardly lie about such a thing.'

But Connie knew she couldn't do that, because then she would have to confess to seeing Daniel.

'Connie, it's been so good to see you,' Daniel said. 'I've been so worried about my dad, and you were the only person I could talk to about it. I'm glad we can continue to be friends.'

'My mum would have a heart attack if she thought we were meeting up,' replied Connie cautiously. But as she thought of Daniel, she realised she had missed him more than she had thought she would. Whatever had happened between their parents shouldn't be allowed to affect the friendship between her and Daniel.

He agreed, but said, 'Think about it. We are suffering the fallout from something that happened between our parents years ago, that we had no hand in. That's not remotely fair – so would you like to go out with me?'

Connie didn't have to think too hard before saying, 'Yes, Daniel. I would love to meet up with you.' She knew Angela wouldn't be happy, but seeing Daniel had been so unexpectedly lovely, she was already looking forward to their next outing.

'Will you tell your mother?'

Connie thought, and then shook her head. 'She might forbid it.'

Daniel paused and then said, 'All right, don't mention it yet, but she must be told soon. I don't like the idea of skulking round as if we were doing something wrong, running the risk of being spotted by someone who tells your mother.'

'That would be bad,' Connie agreed. 'But trust me. I know my mother well and I will know when the time is right to tell her.'

'I'll leave it to you then,' said Daniel with a smile. 'So, as we are in the town anyway, how about we see if there's a film we might both like to see?'

'Oh yes!' Connie cried, thinking it quite daring to be going to the cinema with a man her mother disapproved of, and without asking her permission.

It was like a proper date as well. Not just a casual walk in the park, where they could almost have accidently bumped into one another. Going on a date was something Connie had imagined she wouldn't do till she was much older, and she was incredibly excited.

'*The Thief of Bagdad* is showing at the Gaumont,' Daniel said. 'I've heard it's quite good. Have you seen it?'

Connie shook her head. 'Haven't managed it yet. Some of the girls from school have been and they said it was great.'

Daniel smiled. 'My friends said the same and I haven't seen it either,' he said. 'Shall we remedy that for both of us?'

'Yes please,' Connie said and took hold of Daniel's

outstretched hand for the first time. She stilled her conscience by telling herself Daniel was not responsible for the actions of his father, just as she was not responsible for the actions of her mother. She felt her heart flip as he gently squeezed her hand. Daniel smiled at her, a smile that suddenly seemed to have the power to make her feel weak at the knees, and a tingle of excitement began in her toes and travelled up her body as they neared the cinema.

They thoroughly enjoyed themselves there and Connie thought Daniel incredibly good company. They laughed at the same things, and Connie remembered their genuine friendship of a few years ago, which they had now rekindled with ease. She could barely remember ever being so happy.

On their way home Connie listened attentively as Daniel told her what his father was doing now to help the homeless in the Black Country – all those who had lost their homes, shops and businesses in the Great War when the bombs dropped from the Zeppelins had destroyed them.

Connie was astounded. She hadn't been aware of bombs dropping through the air and killing or maiming innocent people. That some of these had reached the outskirts of Birmingham was even more upsetting. Yet she said to Daniel, 'I thought your father already had a job in the shop.'

'Well, yes he has,' Daniel said. 'I mean, he's in charge and everything, but when he enlisted for the war, he employed a woman called Sadie Bradshaw to take his place when her own husband joined the army. She lives down one of the nearby yards and was known to be respectable and honest and had two young children. However, her husband was listed among the many who did not return from the war, and Dad was reluctant to tell her to go when she needed a job so badly, so she stayed on for a while. When he heard of this scheme to renovate bomb-damaged properties in the Black Country, he talked to Sadie and she has agreed to come back. Her children are grown up now, so she has more time and was at a bit of a loose end, and she said she will stay for as long as it takes. I have told Dad I'll give him a hand too.'

'What about your teaching job at the school?' asked Connie, who knew just how much Daniel enjoyed his profession.

'Well, initially I said I could help only through the coming Easter holidays,' Daniel said. 'I'm starting on Monday.'

'I could do the same. I'd love to be able to help out.'

Daniel was totally unprepared for Connie's reaction and answered cautiously, 'Yes, you could. But you'd really better ask your mother.'

Connie thought about asking her mother but rejected the idea almost instantly. It would mean telling her about meeting Daniel, and the mood Angela was in at the moment, she might forbid Connie to take any part in the whole thing. What if she banned her from seeing him? All of a sudden Connie knew that that didn't bear thinking about. She hadn't seen Daniel for so long, but now that she had, she realised just how much she was looking forward to seeing him again.

She shook her head. 'Not a good idea to tell Mammy

just yet,' she said. 'Let's get started on it first, and then I'll be able to give her a better idea of what it involves.'

Daniel really didn't feel comfortable about that idea. He wanted any friendship with Connie to be completely above board. 'Wouldn't your mother wonder where you went if you disappeared every day?'

'Not really,' Connie said. 'She'd think I was at the library, because it's where I usually work through the holidays. She's used to me not being at home.'

'Well, the library then,' Daniel said. 'You'd better let them know your change of plans for these Easter holidays, or they might worry.'

'Yeah, I will.'

'Even so . . .' Daniel said, '. . . in fact, the more I think of involving you, the more I think you must tell you mother what you intend to do, before you begin.'

'No!' Connie cried. 'What if she was to say I couldn't do it?'

'If she did, it would only be because she would be worried about you,' Daniel said. 'Not that it's meant to be dangerous – just hard work, I should imagine. I'm sure if you explained it to your mother, she would understand.'

'Well, I'm not sure she would understand, not at all sure, and I am not prepared to risk it. I'll tell you one thing I am sure of, though. My mother, when she was little older than me, made shells in a factory, six days a week. That was hard and dangerous work, all right, and though her mother, my granny, worried about her, she realised that she had to do it. Now this is something I need to do, but Mammy treats me like a hothouse flower.

No, Daniel, I am not going to risk telling her, and if she finds out some other way . . . Well, I'll cross that bridge when I come to it.'

Daniel still felt a little uncomfortable, though he had to concede Connie did have a point. 'Look, Connie,' he said again. 'Are you absolutely sure about this?'

Connie nodded her head vehemently. 'Absolutely,' she said. 'Now, are you taking me with you to help, or not? Because I'll tell you now, you could argue from now till doomsday, and not change my mind.'

Daniel held up his hands in surrender and gave Connie a rueful grin. 'All right, then. Point taken. See you on Monday morning at New Street Station at eight o'clock, and from there we'll take a train to Walsall.'

'I'll be there bright and early,' Connie promised, giving Daniel a wave as she made for the tram, a wide smile lighting up her pretty face all the way home.

THREE

It was cold and draughty standing on the station platform the following Monday, and Connie was glad that she had not worn the skirt and jumper she usually wore to the library. Leaving them folded on the chair by her bed, she had instead searched in the cupboard under the stairs for the dungarees her mother had worn during the Great War when she worked at a shell factory. Sadly, there was no sign of her rubber boots, which would have been useful, but regardless Connie put the dungarees on, as well as an old wind-proof jacket. She surveyed herself in the mirror, satisfied that she looked ready for a hard day's work, but also that the style she'd tied her hair in was both practical and flattering. She chided herself to stop thinking about Daniel and keep her mind on the job in hand. She was suddenly immensely glad her mother never got up before she left for the library where she usually spent her holidays, for if Angela had had one glimpse of how Connie was dressed that morning, she would have known she was not intending to go to the library, or anywhere else remotely respectable, dressed in such a way.

Connie, however, thought the dungarees were comfortable, practical and eminently suitable for the job she was going to be involved in that morning. She was glad they covered her legs, because it really was very draughty on the station platform, and she was walking up and down as fast as she could to keep warm whilst wondering where Daniel was. The station master said the train was on time, which meant there were just two minutes to spare. Connie was annoyed, because if Daniel missed the train, so would she, because she could hardly go without him. She wondered for a moment what she was doing, heading off to Walsall, a place she had never been to before, with Daniel on some harebrained scheme of his. She knew that had her mother known what she was about to do, she would be more than a little concerned. Would she have been worried enough to try and stop her going altogether? Connie thought she might well try to, at least till she found out what it was all about and what it entailed, and Connie couldn't enlighten her much about that. She imagined her asking Connie what she thought she knew of work like that. The answer would be, nothing at all, and for the first time she wondered if she would be any earthly use. Daniel had told her that machinery wasn't used – at first, anyway, because heavy lifting gear could damage the whole unstable structure or further demolish buildings that could be reclaimed. Instead they relied on manpower to earmark those that needed attention.

And what do I really know of work like this? Connie asked herself. *If the lifting proves too heavy for me, won't I be more of an encumbrance than any sort of help?* Might she be better going home to change and setting off for the library as usual? She was sure they'd have her back if she said she was available. And she really did love her job. Daniel was right when he said the librarians would be wondering where she was when she didn't turn up. They were lovely ladies, who had been so kind and generous with their time when Connie started working at the library.

Connie also loved some of the regulars that came into the library. There were some that came in almost every day, perhaps sometimes for the company as much as to exchange their books, Connie thought. Many of the children that came in were particularly fond of Connie. She had such a lovely way with them, as well as a real knack for recommending books that they really loved reading. There was one young girl in particular, called Chrissie, who always looked out for Connie. She idolised the older girl, and they'd spent a lot of time together, firstly talking about books, and then all sorts of things. Connie got the sense that this little girl didn't have any other friends, so she always went out of her way to say hello or put a particular book to one side on reserve if she thought Chrissie would like it.

The more Connie thought about it, the more she regretted not mentioning her new job to the librarians now; but she had hesitated because she would have hated it if word of what she was going to do somehow got back to her mother before she had a chance to mention it. She actually began to walk towards the exit when she saw Daniel hurtling at breakneck speed down the platform towards her as the train thundered into the station, grey smoke billowing out behind it as it began to draw to a halt with a squeal of brakes and a hiss of steam.

'You cut it fine,' she said to Daniel as he reached her and they boarded the train together. 'If you left it a minute or two later, you'd have missed it.'

'I know,' Daniel said, looking sheepish. 'I overslept.' And then he took in Connie's appearance and said, 'You're dressed for the part, anyway.'

'My mother's dungarees for when she worked in munitions during the war,' Connie explained.

'Those dungarees really suit you,' Daniel said quietly, and Connie blushed.

'Well,' she replied as quickly as she could, 'I thought, judging from what you said we'll be doing, dungarees would be more practical than the clothes I usually wear.'

'Oh, I'll say they will,' Daniel said as they found a compartment and sat down. 'It'll be much easier for you, climbing over the rubble. Anyway, you don't want your good clothes messed up, or maybe ripped. Your mother might have something to say about that!'

'Oh, she would, all right,' Connie said.

'Won't she miss her dungarees?'

Connie shook her head. 'No,' she said. 'She'd forgotten she still had them. I came upon them a few years ago when Mammy asked me to turn out a cupboard she said was full of rubbish. When I pulled out the dungarees, she was surprised she still had them. Anyway, I thought she'd say they were rubbish as well, but she said they'd be handy to put over her clothes when she was doing dirty jobs. To my knowledge, she never bothered with them again. I only remembered them myself when I started getting ready this morning. And even changing my mind about what I was wearing and having to search in the cupboard to find the dungarees, *I* managed to get to the station on time.'

'I'm sorry about that. It must have been worrying for you, thinking I wasn't going to turn up, and on your first morning too. It won't happen again. You know, I really did think it might be *you* that didn't turn up.'

Connie kept her head bowed to prevent Daniel seeing the telltale flush on her cheeks as she remembered her half-planned retreat back to the library. 'Why did you think that?' she asked.

'Oh, I don't know,' Daniel said. 'I suppose because you agreed so readily, almost as if it was a spur-of-the-moment thing. I couldn't tell you much about it either, because I only know what my dad told me, or even how long it will go on for – though you and I can only work as long as the Easter holidays last. I sort of thought, in the cold light of day, you might have changed your mind.'

There was no way Connie was going to admit to Daniel she nearly had done that. Anyway, now they were on their way, she felt her enthusiasm returning and said, 'No, I'm quite looking forward to doing something so completely different from anything I have ever done before. Something that will actually help people too.'

'I'm looking forward to doing something I consider useful for a change, as well,' Daniel said. 'Remember, I grew up not knowing my dad. The first time I met him was at your house, so the war had sort of passed me by. My aunt and uncle made sure the war wouldn't disturb their way of life in any way, and that included me too, of course.'

'Didn't they have a wireless to listen to the news?' Connie asked. 'Most people who could afford a wireless had one through the war.'

'If they listened to the news, they never did it while I was around,' Daniel said. 'Any papers we had were used for lighting the fire before I ever had a glimpse of them. Then your mother gave me papers to read about the first day of the Battle of the Somme, and I saw pictures of the soldiers involved in that battle. A good few of them were just boys, not much older than me. Some were dead or mangled. I didn't know why this news had been kept from me, especially as Betty and Roger knew my father might have been fighting in battles like that. I will always resent the fact that I was so protected from it all. Maybe I could have written to my dad, or even found something to do to help the war effort. What I'm doing now helps redress the balance a bit, hopefully.'

'I should say it does,' Connie said. 'Though you really have nothing to feel guilty about. You were only a child in the Great War.'

'I was nine when the war began and thirteen when it ended,' Daniel said. 'Dad said many kids of twelve or thirteen were filling up sandbags. Some went to hospitals to roll up bandages, push wheelchairs or anything else the nurses wanted them to do, and a few were drafted in for fire watching.'

'Daniel, you were away at school! Which is exactly where your dad would have wanted you to be.'

'I know,' Daniel said. 'War wasn't mentioned there either and my aunt and uncle weren't helping in any way. Children were evacuated, yet we didn't take in any, though we had a spare bedroom and Sutton Coldfield was one of the safest places in Birmingham, I would say. And there were girls travelling the country looking for war work.'

'Sutton had no industry,' Connie pointed out. 'That's why it was suitable for evacuees.'

'Sutton itself hasn't much,' Daniel admitted. 'But this train goes regularly to Birmingham and travels through Erdington, Gravelly Hill, Aston and Duddeston Manor before reaching Birmingham, and all of them are far more industrialised, with plenty of factories making war-related stuff back then. I'm sure they never even bothered finding out.'

'You're not responsible for what your aunt and uncle did or didn't do, Daniel.'

'I know that, but I can't help it, Connie – I do feel guilty when I realise what a dreadful war, with colossal loss of life, I was protected from. Many of these casualties were just out of boyhood, young men at the start of their lives, so when Dad told me what he was intending doing to help those made homeless because of that war, I decided to join him.'

'I'm glad you decided to do that.'

'Me too,' Daniel said. 'I'm really pleased to be here.'

Connie looked out of the window as the train left Birmingham. Walsall was where the Black Country really began and was no distance away by train. For the first part of the journey the train ran through the countryside. There were fields and fields of vegetables planted in ridges, with little green shoots peeping out of the soil. They saw cows being turned back into their fields after milking, horses galloping in one field, and in another, playful lambs gambolling near their watchful mothers, who continued to tug relentlessly at the grass. 'The countryside is full of growth and new birth,' Daniel said. 'Springtime is my favourite season.'

'Mine too,' Connie agreed as she watched the countryside flash by as the train ate up the miles. Eventually, the farmlands began petering out and there were more houses, shops, offices and a few small factories and warehouses. Connie watched as the train crossed a bridge. There were canals on either side and almost immediately, there were far more houses, and they seemed very squashed together. In among the streets were some small factories and all kinds of shops and a couple of pubs. 'Looks cold out there,' Connie commented. 'It was freezing in the station. It's hard to believe it's late March.'

'It's early days yet,' Daniel said. 'And stations are notoriously draughty places. No doubt we'll soon warm up when we're working. I can hardly wait to get cracking.' His enthusiasm was evident and infectious, and Connie felt her own enthusiasm returning as she said, 'The more you tell me about this, the more anxious I am to get started on it.'

'Haven't time to tell you much more,' Daniel said. 'We're coming into Walsall now. Look. See all the disused factories and warehouses? Still sitting untouched, and the war has been over for years.'

Connie nodded and said, 'Are they all being demolished?'

Daniel shook his head. 'Not necessarily,' he said. 'A lot depends on the state of them, of course, but if we can make those buildings safe without too much outlay, Dad said the plan is to turn them into hostels for the homeless people.'

'That's a good idea.'

'I thought so too,' Daniel said. 'Anyway, not long now. Ours is the next stop.'

As the train stopped Daniel took Connie's arm, led her out of the station and down the dusty streets to the site where most of the damage was. Arriving at the scene, Connie felt overwhelmed by the gargantuan task ahead. She was astounded and heart-broken at the devastation. How had she lived so close to this, but never really known how bad it was?

As well as shocked, Connie felt a bit shy, meeting all the others there. But Daniel stayed close by her side and introduced her to everyone. As they began work some of the locals wandered onto the streets to see what they were doing.

There were a fair few children about, with it being the Easter holidays. 'Those are the ones to watch,' Stan said.

'For some reason building sites attract children like the very devil, but it's not at all a safe place to play.'

Connie looked about her and said, 'No I wouldn't think so.'

'Keep your eyes peeled and make sure they're not up to some mischief,' Stan said. 'The boss has ordered fencing but till it comes we'll have to be careful. The last thing any of us want is for one of the children to be hurt.'

As well as keeping a weather eye on the kids, Connie toiled as well as anyone, lifting bricks and wood and shards of glass and the assorted debris from people's homes. It was tedious and tiring work, but Connie didn't complain once, the task at hand making her acutely aware of how much the people of Walsall had lost. When a halt was eventually called at the end of that first day, she stretched her limbs gratefully and yet had a smile on her face. 'I ache all over,' she commented, 'and yet I have really enjoyed the day. I feel as if I've achieved something worthwhile. I'll tell you something else as well. I've never been in an area blown to bits by bombs before, and let's just say I like the thought of the miners checking the stability of any structure before any renovations can start.'

'It's a sensible precaution, right enough,' Daniel said. 'I'm sure your mother would agree too, if you were to tell her that.'

'Well, she won't know, will she?' Connie retorted. 'For I have no intention of telling her.'

'I really think you should.'

'Worry-guts,' Connie said to Daniel with an impish grin. 'I'll think about it.'

That evening Connie felt completely exhausted and fell into bed as soon as she'd finished her hot meal. And the next morning, although she was stiff and tired, she felt invigorated by the thought of the day ahead.

As the days passed, more and more locals had wanted to know what Stan's team were doing. Sometimes a cheer would go up when they arrived and others set to and began to help clear the rubble. Now and again women would come out with trays of very welcome tea. This was a town that couldn't believe they were getting some help at last. Connie was moved by the stories they told her. One young mother's words really stuck with her. She'd said that though the bombs falling was terrible, just as bad was the aftermath, when she returned home to find that her house was no longer there.

'Everything had gone,' she said. 'We had nowhere to live, no food to eat, certainly no money to buy anything, and the only clothes we owned were those we stood up in.'

'We thought the government would step in eventually,' another told Connie. 'Thought they'd have something in place, like – some sort of plan. But there was nothing. I had three kids and a husband in the Forces. We took shelter in a nearby church hall and we was just forgotten about, like. I mean, I'm real glad you're here and it ain't your fault, like, but it's taken the government a bleeding long time to remember we're still here and we all still need things. My constant headache has been, and still is trying to find enough food for the kids. Tears you apart to hear your kids crying with hunger, unable to sleep because of the gripes in their stomachs.'

Connie was appalled and felt further sickened when she realised that the women's stories were not unique. Many of the other workers had heard similar tales from others, and she thought, *No wonder they are so pleased to see us arriving and actually trying to help.* It made everything worthwhile suddenly and she certainly worked a little harder and longer than she had previously. Her respect for her mother, working in the shell factory through the Great War, grew as she laboured on. Her granny had told her she had done it to provide for them all. And she had, Connie thought with a hint of pride, because she couldn't ever remember a time when she was hungry or cold. She'd always had a warm coat and warm boots to wear, with hats and gloves for cold winter days. Suddenly she felt dejection and a hint of anger that – after a war of such magnitude, when so many, like her own daddy, would never come home again – fourteen years after the armistice was signed, these women still struggled to provide for their children.

She often went home at night wishing she could discuss this with her mother. She knew she would be interested because, not only was it a time she'd lived through, but Angela hated injustice. And it certainly was unjust to leave those poor needy people to fend for themselves. It really felt as though her father and plenty more fathers had died in vain. She needed her mother to talk to her about it all, and maybe together they could think up a sort of plan to help. However, Connie knew if she told her about the destitute people, it would have to all come out about meeting up with Daniel again. Connie really thought she was a bit feeble not mentioning it, though – especially when she reminded herself that Daniel had already crossed that first bridge and told his father they had met up. But somehow the thought that it might all get pulled out from underneath her – this important work, and the time she spent with Daniel – stopped Connie from uttering the words out loud to Angela, however many times she'd steeled herself to tell her mother the truth. She had to go back, she was determined to finish what she'd started.

Stan had been surprised when Daniel had asked if he'd mind Connie helping out too. Stan's reply was that he was more than happy for Connie to help, as long as that was what she wanted to do. Of course, he was concerned about a link back to Angela, but he reasoned that he couldn't dictate who Daniel's friends were and that his best bet was to stay well out of it.

'She does want to help,' Daniel assured him. 'And there's something else. I really like her, you know. I'd like to ask her out a time or two. I know how old she is, don't worry, but I mean, I'm over twenty-one now.'

'And should be able to choose your own friends.'

'Well yes, I should.'

'I agree you should,' Stan said. 'And I am not going to police either of you. If you and Connie want to see one another, it's fine by me.' Then he added, 'I've never had any animosity towards Connie, but just remember that I don't want to see her mother, and you must take that on board if you go out with Connie. Any sort of friendship between me and Angela is dead and gone, and you must accept that, as I have to.'

Daniel was upset to hear his father talking so resolutely about the end of the friendship he had with Angela, but he told himself he had interfered enough by suggesting his father open up to Angela in the first place, and look where that had got him. But he was delighted that his father had agreed that he could see Connie. But he felt he had to tell his father the whole story. After all, Stan was also the Gaffer, and should be aware of the circumstances of those working for him. 'Angela doesn't know what Connie has been doing over the Easter holidays, and who with, by the way.'

'Why ever not?'

'Connie's afraid she might stop her.'

'Is she likely to do that?' Stan asked, knowing that if she made difficulties with Connie working clearing the site, it would probably be because she had heard somehow he was involved in it. He thought it was monstrously unfair to involve the children in any problems they had, but there wasn't much he could do about that.

'I don't know,' Daniel said. 'Connie thinks she might.'

'Her mother should at least know where she is and what she's doing.'

'I've said all this.'

'And she's taken no notice?'

'No, none at all.'

'Well,' Stan said. 'You can't make her listen to you and do the right thing. I remember she always had an independent and determined streak in her. Gets it from her mother.'

'So, what shall I do?'

'Let her come and try, and we'll both keep an eye on her,' Stan said. 'And remember how old she is. I won't tell Angela, never fear. Like I said, I have no wish to speak to her ever again, but I don't want her coming to my door demanding to know where her daughter is.'

'All right, I'll do my best,' Daniel said, knowing Connie wouldn't be likely to listen to his father any more than she had listened to him.

So Daniel told Connie his dad was fine not only about her helping, but also about them going out a time or two as friends. Connie was glad Stan obviously didn't hold her responsible for whatever had gone wrong between him and her mother. But she imagined Angela would react totally differently, so she decided to let sleeping dogs lie and keep quiet for the moment . . .

After talking to his father Daniel began a light courtship with Connie. They found out a lot about each other as they travelled back and forward to Walsall each day, and in the evening they would go for a walk or perhaps visit the cinema. Once Daniel took Connie to the Bull Ring in the evening. It was now restored to its pre-war glory, with the spluttering gas flares lighting up the stalls like fairy land, and entertainment on every corner. Connie was enchanted by the men on stilts effortlessly striding down the cobbled streets between the stalls, as well as the man tied up in chains, or another man who lay on a bed of nails as easily as if he'd been lying on a feather bed, encouraging the watching girls to stand on his bare, gleaming chest.

'You hungry?' Daniel asked as they turned away from the stalls.

'Mmm, a bit, maybe.'

'Ever had jellied eels?' Daniel asked Connie with a wide grin as he dragged her over to the fish stall.

He expected her reaction. 'Ugh, no I haven't, and I have no intention of trying them now, either!'

'How d'you know you don't like something unless you try it?'

'I just know! They look disgusting. Why would I want to try them?'

'Lots of people like them,' Daniel pointed out.

'That's all right for them,' Connie said, 'but I'm not one of those people.'

Daniel laughed and said, 'All right then. I'll buy some for me and you can have a little bit to try.'

'Why should I?

'To please me,' Daniel said, 'and to say you've tried it, and therefore are allowed to pass judgement. You might even get to like them.'

'I doubt that very much,' Connie said, and not giving herself time to think about it much, she took the morsel Daniel offered her and put it in her mouth.

Daniel laughed at the look of disgust that flooded over Connie's face, for the jellied eels tasted just as slimy and disgusting as she thought they would. Only good manners prevented her spitting them out. 'I'll pay you back for that,' she said to Daniel when she had eventually swallowed the offending fish.

Daniel didn't seem the slightest bit worried and had a big grin on his face as he asked, 'How?'

'Well, I don't know yet,' Connie admitted, 'but I'll think of something.'

That made Daniel laugh even louder. 'Come on,' he said, 'I'll make it up to you. Let's have a baked potato.'

'Oh, yes please,' Connie said. 'I like those.' And they bought the potatoes from a little man standing in front of something that looked remarkably like the picture of Stephenson's *Rocket* that Connie had seen in one of her books. The man dropped the potatoes in little triangular bags he'd made out of greaseproof paper, and Daniel and Connie tossed them from hand to hand till they were cool enough to eat.

Connie could never remember feeling so happy. She lived for Sunday, for there was no work, and the day was theirs after Mass. Sometimes they went further afield, taking a train to Sutton Coldfield and exploring Sutton Park or crossing over the town and taking a Midland Red bus to the Lickey Hills.

'Where does your mother think you are?' Daniel asked Connie one day. 'As you are forbidden to see me, it couldn't be the truth.'

'She doesn't always ask,' Connie said. 'If she does, I tell her I'm out with friends from school.'

'Does she believe you?'

'I think so,' Connie said. 'Till we started going out together, I wasn't in the habit of lying to my mother.'

'You saying I'm a bad influence?'

'If the cap fits,' Connie said with a smile.

'Maybe then we should do as your mother wants and I won't see you any more?'

'That wouldn't please me one bit,' Connie said. 'Let's say I like you being a bad influence.'

And Daniel gave a whoop of laughter and put his arms around Connie and held her tight.

FOUR

Daniel met Connie on the road one morning to tell her the first job that morning was clearing out a shell factory. They had done this a few times before, but he said, 'This one is a little bit different. As you know, usually all dangerous machinery and materials are carted away before we start, but Dad said this factory must have been missed, so there are likely to be a fair few shells still in there. Obviously, our first priority is to get them all out, and carefully, because some might well still be active. I don't want you involved in this, Connie. Leave this factory to the rest of us.'

Connie remembered the pride she felt for her mother and the way she had provided for them all and her granny too, choosing dangerous work making shells because it was the best paid. She wondered if she was a lesser woman than her mother, the sort to scuttle away at the first sign of danger. No, she wasn't, she decided, and she turned to Daniel and shook her head. 'Are you mad? There is no way I'm going to stay away from that factory.'

'You must,' Daniel said. 'You're too young. I mean, it really might be dangerous.'

Connie knew her mother's work had been deadly dangerous, not that her mother said much about it, but her granny had told her how Angela had never flinched from danger. 'Dangerous?' she said to Daniel. 'Working with live shells – you mean, like my mother did throughout the war? I'm sure I can cope.'

Daniel shook his head. He remembered what his father had said about keeping an eye on Connie, and knew he would more than likely not approve of him letting Connie get involved, so he said, 'I can't let you do this.'

'You can't stop me.'

'Maybe,' Daniel said, 'but my dad can. He's the Gaffer and you've got to do what the Gaffer says. He told me you're not to do stuff like this. If I tell him . . .'

Connie fixed Daniel with a gimlet eye as she said, 'You tell tales to your father, and I won't ever speak to you again. Anyway, have you time to look for your father? Thought you said the factory was high priority, no one can do anything till we take out the shells and make sure the place is safe.'

Daniel bit his lip in consternation and might have argued further, but he recognised the stubborn note in Connie's voice and knew he'd be wasting his time. And she did have a point about emptying the factory quickly. 'All right, but for God's sake take care!'

Connie suddenly remembered what her mother had said on the rare occasions when she'd spoken about her work in the shell factory: 'We had to wear dungarees and rubber boots to prevent a spark igniting the shells and causing an explosion. And a spark was all it took sometimes. Live shells have to be treated with respect. Every bit of metal on our person had to be removed before we went on the factory floor, even wedding rings and Kirby grips.'

Connie looked round, and though she was wearing dungarees, like she had every day since working with Daniel, she saw that none of the other safety precautions were in place. But she was the youngest worker, and one of the few women, so she didn't want to be the one to make a fuss. Besides, Daniel might say again that it was too dangerous for her and, despite what she'd said, send for Stan. And anyway, she realised it might take some time to get protective clothing and rubber boots for everyone. Daniel had advised her to take care, and she thought grimly, *I'll make damned sure I take care.* She shouted back to him, 'Don't worry, I'll keep my wits about me. Now let's get on!'

Working with the miners, she and Daniel carefully moved the heavy, dirt-encrusted, greasy shells out of the factory, one by one, loading them onto a truck outside. After hours of this work, Connie was hungry as well as tired, but she said nothing about it. Suddenly Daniel was aware of a crackling sound and said urgently to Connie, 'Put that shell down very slowly and carefully.'

Something in Daniel's tone alerted Connie and she replaced the shell very cautiously, but just as she did so, the shell started to spark and wisps of smoke came out of the top of it. Connie felt paralysed with fear. She knew she had to move, but her legs seemed frozen to the ground.

Then she saw Daniel lean over a railing and shout to the miners below, 'Run, run for your lives!' She felt herself being hauled to her feet as he spoke and pulled towards the stairs. Connie could see in his eyes that he didn't think they had a hope of reaching safety in time. She knew it too and gave a whimper of fear as she watched, horrified, as a smouldering shell shot upwards and exploded as it reached the roof beams.

Masonry hit Connie from all angles as she felt herself falling as if into the pit of Hell. She opened her mouth in a scream, but the scorching heat burnt her throat as her mouth filled with brick dust, and little sound came out. Eventually she stopped falling and she landed on a heap of assorted rubble. For a while the world around her went from scorching red to black as the darkness of the smoke engulfed her.

Connie's eyes fluttered open, but she couldn't see a thing. She was frightened, very frightened, but gradually what had happened came back to her, and from what she could hear it seemed, she thought, that the worst was over. All she had to do was wait for rescue, and she focused her breathing on trying to control the panic that threatened to overwhelm her. Then suddenly she heard a roar from above her. She could see very little, the only light was from the flickering flames of the burning debris, but she feared the whole roof was about to collapse on top of her. Instinctively she wrapped her arms around her head and began to sob in fright. Her last thought was about her mammy, and how terrified she'd be for her beloved daughter, if only she knew where she was . . .

The workers outside the building heard the roar too and saw the whole structure drop down a few feet. They looked at one another in shock and alarm, fearing that anyone who had managed to stay alive so far wouldn't survive the collapse of the building.

'What are we doing just standing here?' one of the miners asked.

'You saw the second fall,' another said morosely. 'No one could be alive after that!'

'Let me tell you,' the first miner said, 'I've worked in mines where there have been more than two falls, and we still found people alive under them. So are we going to dig down and try to reach these people, or are we just going to give up?'

A murmur of support went around the waiting crowd. 'Hear, hear!' said a fellow miner. 'Ted's right. We've never given up on our mates, so let's put our backs into finding anyone trapped in this little lot.'

The miners' words galvanised the men, and they began shifting the wreckage with vigour.

Below them, inside the factory, neither Connie nor Daniel could hear a thing; it was as if they were enclosed in a dark and silent tomb. Connie was almost consumed by a terror such as she had never felt before, forced to lie silent and rigid, pinned down by a roof beam.

Daniel thought she must be dead, for since that first strangled scream, he had heard no sound from Connie. Aware of the charred and fractured roof beams, slates, shards of glass, broken bricks, and brick and plaster dust that had rained down on them, he knew it was very unlikely she would have survived. Until his ringing ears picked up a sound that he thought might have been sobbing, although he told himself he could have imagined it. Clearing his throat as best he could, he croaked out in a low, scratchy and hesitant voice, 'Connie?'

Connie was drifting in and out of consciousness and she wasn't sure if she'd heard right either, so her voice, husky from the dust, was little more than a whisper as she asked anxiously, 'Daniel? Are you in here too?'

The relief when she heard Daniel's voice was immense, for it had been horrible to think that she was buried in the rubble all on her own. Yet she wondered how she could be glad Daniel was there too, because she'd never want anything bad to happen to him.

But when she admitted this out loud, Daniel seemed surprised. 'Wouldn't you?'

'Of course I wouldn't want anything bad to happen to you, Daniel,' Connie said. 'You must be aware of how much I care for you?'

'As a big brother?' Daniel said. 'You referred to me as that once.'

'I was a child then.'

'You're not much older now.'

'I will be sixteen in May.'

'And I am ten years older than you,' Daniel said. 'And I should never have let you get involved with this shell factory clear-out, whatever you said.'

'Too late to worry about that now,' Connie said, trying to make light of the situation. 'And anyway, what do years matter?' She paused as if gathering both strength and courage to speak her next sentence. 'I am old enough not to think of you as a brother any more,' she said, and then went on: 'I told you that because we might die in here, and then you'd never know.'

'Well, I'm very glad you told me,' Daniel said, and added, 'How are you feeling? I know you must be worried, but at least we're in this together and we can keep one another company whilst they send in people to look for survivors. After all, at least they know where we are.'

'Yes,' Connie said doubtfully, 'but there's a lot of stuff over us.'

'They have teams trained for rescuing people,' Daniel said. 'Dad said there were a fair few explosions in the munition factories during the war years.'

'Were there?'

'Didn't your mother tell you? I'm sure she'd have heard about things like that, working in a shell factory all that time.'

'No, she never told me anything like that,' Connie said. 'I often asked her about what she did in the war and things like that, but she always said the past should stay in the past. I mean, I never knew you even existed. I overheard people talking of the tragedy, your mam dying whilst giving birth to you and everything, but no one talked of what had happened to *you*, so I thought you must have died as well. Not even Granny told me you had survived, and then Mammy opened up and told *you* about things I had wanted to know for ages.'

'I should say she probably told us because she felt her

past coming to meet her,' Daniel said. 'You know, finding my father when she thought him dead, me turning up on her doorstep out of the blue. I mean, she started telling me all about my father and how it was that we had been separated, so I suppose the memories she might have tried to bury rose to the surface.'

Connie sighed. 'I suppose you're right. It's just that Mammy is so open about most things, except her past . . . Sometimes I wonder if she has some murky secret!'

Daniel gave a wry laugh. 'Oh Connie, how can you think that about your mother? I would say that it's just that thinking about those dreadful war years could easily drag up painful memories she'd rather not dwell on. And really, who can blame her?'

Connie thought again Daniel was probably right. Thinking about her mammy had distracted her momentarily from their situation, but it all suddenly came flooding back, and she fought the feeling of panic that threatened to engulf her again. 'Do you really think we might get out of here alive?' she asked Daniel in a voice so quiet, he had to strain to hear.

Daniel knew Connie was no child to be given false reassurances, and so he answered, 'I don't really know, Connie, but like I said, I hope so.'

'I don't want to die,' Connie said, choking down a sob. 'Do you?'

'Of course not,' Daniel answered. He had always intended to take it slowly in moving things forward with Connie, but now they were entombed in this wreckage, and it might be his last chance to confess his feelings for her. So he took as deep a breath as his smoke-filled lungs would allow and went on: 'The fact that we might never get out of here has forced me to tell you how I really feel about you now. I have held back for so long because I didn't dare think you felt the same, and also because you are still so young, but I have loved you for years. I can't remember when it changed from the love a brother might have for a young sister, to the deep abiding love a man has for a woman who he wants to share his life with, always.' Daniel snaked his hand across the littered ground as he spoke and eventually his fingers entwined with Connie's, and then his hand was grasping hers firmly and he heard her sigh, and they lay together and listened, hoping to hcar sounds of rescue, but they could hear nothing.

Daniel thought time seemed to have no meaning, in that deep intensely dark grave. Sometimes he could hear Connie's even breathing and sometimes he could not. The first time she had grown silent he had been worried that she had died, but there was no way of checking, for it was far too dark to see anything clearly, and so he lay as near to her as he could and held his own breath until she began to breathe again. Sometimes he was overcome by weariness himself, but he fought it valiantly, for he did not want to leave Connie alone. But eventually his eyes began closing despite his efforts to keep them open, and he fell into a deep sleep.

Stan had gone into shock when he was told that Connie and his son were among the people who had not been accounted for. He looked at the mangled structure and his heart sank. He could scarcely believe he might lose the son he'd only recently found and loved dearly. He knew if his son had died his heart would break. Stan had seen enough death to last him a lifetime in the Great War. Most were lads as young as or even younger than Daniel, and he had grieved for each and every one. As an NCO, it was often his job to write letters of condolence to grieving parents, who were told only the stark details of their son's death by a telegram or letter from the War Office. He told the parents what they really wanted to know: what kind of man their son had been, and that the manner of his death meant he had given his life for King and Country. Stan always hoped his letters gave grieving parents some comfort in the bleak days that would lie ahead.

He thought he understood death, but the possible loss of his own son crushed his very soul and caused a pain so sharp, he struggled not to cry out against it, for it seemed to pierce his heart. Then he thought of Angela and how she would cope when she learnt that her daughter might be lying there buried too, presumed dead, in the ruins of the collapsed factory – and he felt guilt wash over him. He had known Connie's age and he shouldn't have allowed her anywhere near the site.

What in God's name had he been thinking of? He knew that if Connie was injured – or Heaven forbid, dead – he would never forgive himself, and if Angela ever found out, she wouldn't forgive him either. He wouldn't blame her one bit. He groaned as he realised the hammer blow about to be inflicted on Angela when she found out what had happened to her daughter. Connie was all she had to live for.

Bobby Gillespie was a young miner who was small for his age but strong and wiry, and he looked at Stan's face and said, 'I know where Connie lives. I'll go and tell her mum, if you like.'

Stan hesitated, because Daniel had told him Angela had no idea what Connie was doing, but he knew he couldn't protect Connie any longer, her mother simply had to know what had happened to her daughter. 'All right,' he conceded to Bobby at last. 'Don't say anything to Angela about Connie being buried. Just say that there was an explosion in the shell factory they were working on in Walsall. We don't want her worried unnecessarily until she gets here.'

'Right-oh,' Bobby said before scampering off as quickly as his legs would carry him.

Angela, of course, thought Connie was safe and sound, working at the library, so when a young boy arrived at the door to say there had been an explosion in the abandoned shell factory her daughter had been working in, she initially thought he must have the wrong house.

'There must be some mistake,' she said. 'My daughter is working in the library.'

The boy shook his head. 'No she ain't,' he said. 'I know it's Connie. She's clearing the bomb sites. Been doing it for days now.'

Angela's senses were reeling, and she felt a constriction in her throat. She didn't even know about any bombed sites. However, she didn't question the boy further. Instead, she remembered the words he had blurted out when he first came to the door, and in a voice that shook slightly, she said, 'You said something about an explosion. Is my daughter hurt?'

Bobby, remembering his instructions, shook his head. 'They just said there had been an explosion, and the man said to come and tell you.'

'What man?'

'The Gaffer,' the boy said. 'The one in charge, like. His name is Stan summat.'

Angela felt an icy-cold shiver wash over her body. 'Stan Bishop?' she asked urgently.

The boy, however, shrugged as he said, 'Dunno. Could be?'

Angela's mind was teeming with questions, but she guessed the boy knew little more than he had already told her. After that awful encounter she had with Stan in the shop, she had no desire to ever see him again, but far more important than how she felt about Stan was the need to find out if her daughter was all right, so she said urgently to the boy, 'Can you take me to this place?'

'Yeah,' the boy said. 'I just come from there, but it's in Walsall, so we'll have to make our way to the city centre and take a train out, and the thing is, I ain't got no more money.'

'Oh, that's all right,' Angela said. 'I'll pay for us both. Can we go straight away?'

'Yeah, 'cept I got to pop in and tell my mum what's happening. Won't be a jiffy.'

'Hurry,' Angela said, lifting her coat from behind the door. 'We'll go as soon as you've done that.'

While Angela and Bobby were hurrying to the tram stop, news of what had happened to Connie McClusky was flying around those mean streets. Bobby had been overheard talking to Angela on her doorstep, and everyone wanted to help, though there was little that anyone could do, with Connie still trapped under the piles of masonry, while Angela waited for news, not knowing yet if she was alive or dead.

On the train out to Walsall, Angela was completely quiet, and Bobby gave her a surreptitious glance and thought her face was very white. 'You all right?'

'Not really,' Angela said. 'I will be, though, when I have found my daughter is uninjured.'

Bobby recalled the huge mound of debris he had left earlier that this woman's daughter was buried beneath, and he felt sorry for her. He couldn't tell her anything more, the Gaffer had been adamant about that. Really he thought it would be safer all round if he said nothing at all.

So, the journey was taken in virtual silence and Angela was almost glad of it. She tried to push from her mind the explosion in the shell factory she had worked in. She had been out on the road driving the truck when it happened, but she remembered Maggie had been trapped for a while and it had been horrifically worrying at the time, but eventually she had been rescued. They had a system in place to organise the rescue crews, or at least they had in the war. But the war had been over for years now and she felt her heart banging in her breast, and she forced herself to calm down. Whatever had happened, she would be no use to Connie if she went to pieces, and instead she concentrated on the journey and wished the clanking train could go faster.

When Angela and Bobby reached the factory, she saw the gigantic mound of masonry and assorted debris, and her heart froze. If her daughter was buried under that, there was virtually no chance she would have survived. She spotted Stan in the far end of the factory, but before she could head his way, she overheard that a number of people were unaccounted for. 'Amongst them is the Gaffer's son Daniel, too,' one of the miners said.

For a time she stood where she was, seemingly rooted to the spot in shock and horror. She watched the miners tirelessly moving debris from the stack. They worked to a rhythm, knowing that while time was of the essence, any sudden movement might dislodge the structure, which would likely be fatal to anyone trapped underneath. Suddenly one of them spotted Bobby and gave him a shout and a wave. Bobby rushed over to see what he wanted, with Angela close on his heels.

The rescuers had uncovered part of the roof of the factory, and there was a small hole to be seen between the piles of masonry. 'Could you squeeze through there, lad?' one of the miners asked, adding to Angela, 'Don't you worry, missus. If anyone can get through that lot and tell us what's happening, it will be Bobby Gillespie.'

The boy, after scrutinising the hole, said, 'I reckon I could climb down there.'

An older miner came over and shook his head. 'I don't know, lad. The whole stack is unstable. This time it could be just too dangerous.'

'Look,' the young miner said, 'my brother might be down there!'

'But he's just a child!' Angela cried.

The boy's worried eyes met Angela's anxious ones. Then he said, 'I stopped being a child when we lost Dad, a few years back. There's just me and my brother to look after my mum and my younger sisters, still at school.'

'So what if she was to lose you too?'

'It would be far worse if she lost our Len,' the young lad retorted. 'I'm only young, see, so I don't earn enough to keep my mum and my sisters, and pay the rent and everything.'

'They still shouldn't let you risk . . .'

'Look, I can go down roped up and see if I can find out if there's anyone still alive, and where they are, and how difficult it will be to get them out,' Bobby said. 'And you needn't worry. I can't fall because of the rope, and they can pull me up if I am in any danger. Safe as houses, it will be.'

The boy was so confident and Angela was so desperately worried about Connie that she didn't argue further, and she watched Bobby being securely roped up before being lowered into the hole.

'Has he done this type of thing before?' she asked a nearby miner.

'Oh aye,' the miner said. 'When there is a fall, young Bobby Gillespie is invaluable, because he can wriggle into spaces other miners can't reach. And he has his head screwed on – good at sizing up a situation, you know?'

Angela thought it monstrous that such a young child should be down a mine in the first place. 'Isn't that extremely dangerous?'

'Life is dangerous,' the miner said. 'Every time the lift drops down the shaft, or I am trudging to the coal face, I think if there is a fall that I am trapped behind, I'd like to think there would be someone like young Bobby to locate me quickly, so they have a chance of getting me out alive. I have a wife and three young ones at home.'

'I'm sorry.'

'Don't be. If there was the possibility of my daughter being buried under that lot, I'd likely feel the same. Let's wait and see what Bobby finds, shall we?'

It was suddenly too much for Angela. She didn't understand any of it. Connie was trapped under the bomb-damaged wreckage of a derelict factory. How had it happened and what was she doing there in the first place? The thoughts were whirling in her brain, and she tried to stand, aware that the wall seemed to be tilting and her head was fuzzy and an ache pounded in the side of it. Suddenly a wave of blackness seemed to enfold her, like a cloak thrown over her head, and she felt herself falling . . .

When Angela came to, Stan was by her side. He had put a pillow someone had brought beneath her head, and laid his coat on top of her. Despite the angry words he'd spoken in the shop, he wanted nothing bad to happen to this woman that he loved beyond reason. It was just immeasurably sad that she didn't feel the same about him. Angela opened her eyes and found herself looking straight into Stan's deep, dark eyes that were full of concern.

'Are you all right?' Stan asked, and his voice was soft and gentle, just as if the altercation in the shop had never happened. She didn't know how to react to this different Stan. But concern for her daughter overrode everything else, and according to young Bobby, Stan might be able to answer her questions, so she said hesitantly and in a voice little above a whisper, 'They say . . . they think Connie is under that lot.'

Stan nodded, 'Daniel too.'

'But . . . but what are they both doing here?'

'Helping me.'

'Helping you?' Angela repeated. 'How? Why? Connie hardly knows you.'

'She knows Daniel.'

'Hardly. She hasn't seen him for months.'

'They have been seeing each other a little bit of late.'

'Seeing each other? You mean . . .?'

'Going out together.'

Angela could hardly believe that the daughter she thought she was so close to should be seeing a boy she knew her mother wouldn't approve of, and seeing him behind her back. Now, though, that hardly seemed to matter. What mattered more than anything else was that Connie should survive, for without Connie, Angela knew her life would have no meaning. She summoned the courage to choke out the question she hadn't been brave enough to ask until this moment: 'What are their chances of getting out of there?'

Stan shook his head. 'No idea, really,' he said. 'Young Bobby might have some news for us eventually.'

'So, we can do nothing but wait?'

'That's about the strength of it,' Stan said. 'Are you strong enough to sit up?'

'I . . . I think so.'

'I'll get us a couple of chairs and tell you what I have become involved in, that has further involved our youngsters, while we wait for news.'

Stan told Angela all about the proposal put to him by the Labour MP, and how Connie became involved.

'She didn't say a word about it to me,' Angela said.

'Yes, sorry about that,' Stan said. 'Both Daniel and I encouraged Connie to tell you.'

'So why didn't she?'

Stan shrugged. 'According to Daniel, she thought you might not approve.'

'I thought she knew me better than that,' Angela said. 'I think it's a splendid idea. Might have become involved myself, but did you know it was so dangerous?'

'No, indeed I didn't,' Stan said. 'All the dangerous materials should have been removed before we were sent in to clear out the rest. Apparently, according to some of the other chaps, when Daniel heard about the live shells, he was adamant Connie shouldn't be involved.'

'But she wouldn't hear of dropping out?'

'No, she wouldn't,' Stan said with a grim smile.

'Oh, don't worry,' Angela said. 'I do know how stubborn Connie can be.'

There was a pause and then Stan sighed and said, 'Angela, it was all my fault. I'm so incredibly sorry.'

'How can it be your fault?'

'I'm the Gaffer,' Stan said. 'I should've checked Connie wasn't involved in anything dangerous.'

'She would have hated that.'

'Maybe, but she would have been safe,' Stan said and added, 'I'm surprised you don't hate me. If your daughter is hurt, I will never forgive myself.'

'I don't hate you,' Angela said. 'I don't think I could. Nor do I hold you responsible. It was a terrible, tragic accident, so let's just hope and pray Bobby has some news for us soon.'

'Yes, let's hope so.'

FIVE

While Stan and Angela sat in the bomb-wrecked factory in England waiting for news from Bobby, in New York a man whom those in the Black Country had tried hard not to think about for many a year, was pacing up and down in the poky front room of the small house he rented with his uncle.

Eddie McIntyre was facing said uncle, one furious Sam Winters. Eddie had involved himself in Angela's life some years back, but when he returned from England he found his uncle had become much frailer in his old age. Sam had been glad to hand more and more of his business to his young nephew, even giving him a fair amount of financial control, so that it was Eddie making many of the decisions, the boss in all but name.

He dabbled in stocks and shares, something his uncle has steered well clear of. At first, though the shares went up and down, he had made a considerable amount of money. But instead of investing in the company, he had used the excess to buy more shares, and eventually used the house and cars as collateral to buy even more. Then three years before, in October 1929, there had been the Wall Street Crash. Eddie hadn't seen the danger in time, for he was used to the variable prices of the shares. When he saw them reach their peak in August and then begin to drop in September, he thought they would come back up again, as they had done in the past.

When the prices continued to fall more rapidly in October, many sold their shares at a loss. Eddie did not, and had to eventually admit to his uncle just how involved he was. Sam had been unaware until then that Eddie had risked not only the fancy cars, but also the large house and the horses and carriage in the stables as collateral to buy more shares. When, listening to the news on the wireless on what would later be dubbed Black Tuesday, Sam realised he was ruined, Eddie thought his uncle might be having a heart attack. It was clear that their privileged lifestyle would be no more. The cars were sold for less than half their value and so were the house, the carriage and the fine horses in the stables.

The servants had seen the writing on the wall. Most had made contingency plans and, knowing there would be no more wages, left even before the house sale was completed.

Still the creditors were hammering on the door, and Sam sent for his nephew. Eddie hated poverty and detested the mean house his uncle had rented while he tried to find a route out of the mess. His uncle was angrier than he had ever known him and he stared at Eddie with hate-filled eyes and his chest heaved up and down like that of an enraged bull, but Eddie was totally unprepared for what Sam had to say. His mouth dropped open.

'England? Why do you want me to go to *England*?'

'Because,' Sam said in clipped tones, 'I don't know how else we will survive. I have sold everything of value, but we can't eat without money. I can get no credit anywhere and I'm constantly receiving bills – sometimes sizeable ones, too – for goods ordered before the crash, and I have no funds to pay any of them. Now, I don't know how you did it, for you are an irresponsible nincompoop, but you developed some valuable trade links and good solid orders last time you were in England. I want you to go back, check them out and maybe keep us afloat that way, for a while at least.'

Eddie looked at his uncle with resentment. Initially, he had no desire to go back to England. He'd been glad enough to reach England some years before to escape the consequences of a dreadful act of violence he had inflicted on a man called Tom Goldsmith. An image flashed into McIntyre's mind of the man he'd beaten and kicked senseless before he'd fled to England. He had been seeing the man's daughter, Susan, and her father had just discovered her pregnancy and had been told that Eddie refused to take any responsibility for it. Susan's father had come looking for Eddie, prepared to 'do' for him if necessary, for disgracing his daughter.

All the streets round the docks had been black as pitch. As prohibition was ruling America, under cover of darkness Eddie had been offloading a consignment of bootleg liquor from a boat onto lorries to supply the speakeasies, and he was unprepared for the attack. However, just as Susan's father raised the chunk of wood he'd found on the ground and prepared to strike McIntyre's head, a ship's hooter sounded. The man gave a start and Eddie spotted him out of the corner of his eye, catching sight of the raised weapon. He jerked out of the way so that it slammed into his left shoulder rather than his head. Eddie wrested the bar from the older man and cracked it into the side of his skull.

Eddie remembered staggering to his feet and hurrying home, hoping that his mother was there and his uncle was not. He went round the side of the house and so, with relief, saw his uncle working in his study. He found his mother in the kitchen and she gave a cry when she saw him holding his arm. 'What happened?' she said, easing his jacket off, and she listened dispassionately to Eddie's account of the encounter. 'He started it, not me,' he added at the end.

But his mother knew him well and she said, 'What did you do, for him to attack you? Most probably it was something to do with a girl – his daughter, perhaps?'

Eddie shrugged. 'Like mother, like son, maybe.'

His mother's face flushed crimson. As a young child, Eddie had been aware that his mother had slept with his uncle, even though he never married her. But his uncle wasn't the only one she took to her bed, though Sam had been unaware of that. But the fact that Eddie had found out meant that she could hardly chide him for doing something she did herself, so she just said, 'Did you kill him?'

'No . . . well, I don't know. He was alive when I left him, I think.'

'If you've left him alive and if he recovers enough to tell them who attacked him, the police will be feeling your collar before you're much older,' his mother said. 'Even if he's dead and he told anyone of his intention when he left the house that night, they will come for you, so the only thing to do is get you away from here – fast. You were due to go to England anyway, and this just means going earlier than planned. I will cover for you here.'

So that was how Eddie had found himself on the next available ship bound for England. It had been the kind of ship captained by a man who asks no questions if you are prepared to pay enough money for the privilege. And it was then, on his first trip to England, that he met Angela McClusky.

A frown now darkened his brow at the memory of Angela. He didn't think he behaved very well with her, or at least that's what she would have everyone believe. And what a tease she turned out to be! She looked like an angel and promised a man the earth, with her luscious body willing and more than ready for sex – and then she slammed the brakes on when the mood suited her.

He had to admit, though – when he did manage to take her to bed, it had been mind-blowing. A smile curled around his lips as he wondered whether he still had the same pull he once had. He would love the chance to get her into his bed at least once more. *Oh yes,* Eddie thought, *maybe there could be some benefits to a return trip to England, after all . . .*

Sam told him there was also a slump in England, but it was nothing compared to what was happening in America at that time. 'If you fail to secure orders and develop trade links for us,' his uncle threatened, 'then on your return, you and your mother will be on the street. Your greed caused this disaster to befall me, so any responsibility I may once have felt for you *has now ceased*. I can no longer support either of you, and have no wish to do so, either. This is your very last chance.'

Eddie felt a coldness in the pit of his stomach and there was a tremor in his limbs, for he didn't doubt that his uncle meant every word. If he and his mother were out on the streets of New York, he didn't know how in God's name either of them would survive, because the whole country was in the grip of the biggest slump America had ever known. He had to make a success of this trip, or his very life and that of his mother were in grave danger. Maybe on this trip back to England he might be well advised to steer clear of the whole area where Angela lived. He had enough to do and would do well to keep away from any distractions, tales of which might easily reach the ears of his uncle and scupper his chances of redeeming himself in any shape or form.

In the cold light of day, however, Eddie dismissed the misgivings he'd had in the night. He remembered the feel of Angela's body as he ran his hands all over it, and he decided it would be mad to go back without even trying to see her. The area, he was sure, would have changed over the years. People living there now would probably not know him at all.

Eddie was right about the area changing. Many had aged and died or retired and moved away, including Breda and Paddy Larkin, who had owned the pub. After a lifetime pulling pints, they had decided enough was enough. Breda's arthritis had worsened with age and they had moved down South, where they had family living. Angela had been sorry to see them go, because over the years they had become good friends and Breda had been her confidante and always supported her. Angela had the address of where she had moved to, so she could and did write, but letters weren't the same thing. The pub had been taken over by another married couple, Muriel and Noel Lampeter, who were very pleasant, but they knew nothing about any past history between Angela McClusky and Eddie McIntyre. And no need for them to be told either, Angela thought, especially as Eddie had disappeared out of all their lives, thank God.

Daniel was wakened by brick dust falling on his face, making him cough as he realised where he was and that someone was moving above him. Daniel's coughing alerted Bobby as he was climbing down the structure. He peered into the hole but could see nothing. He opened his mouth but closed it again when he realised he was about to ask the man if he was all right. It was what people said, but in this case, it seemed meaningless, so instead he called out, 'Don't think we'll be able to get you out for some time yet. Do you want anything I could lower down to you?'

'Water,' Daniel pleaded. 'I'd love some water. There's at least two of us down here.'

'Righto,' Bobby said. 'I'll have to climb up to get some, but I'll be back as soon as I can.'

'All right, do your best,' Daniel said and he heard the scrabbling of feet as Bobby pulled himself off the rubble and began his ascent.

'Connie . . . Connie, did you hear that?' Daniel said into the darkness. 'They're coming to get us.'

But there was no reply.

Stan and Angela had been sitting for hours. She had almost fallen asleep, her head dropped sideways to rest on Sam's shoulder. She felt embarrassed as she woke up properly, but when she mumbled an apology, Stan told her not to worry about it.

Her entire soul was consumed with thoughts of Connie. What must she be going through at the moment? Was she still alive, was she frightened, had she been calling for her mammy, who couldn't get to her? These thoughts went round and round in Angela's head on a never-ending loop. Her stomach was churning with anxiety, and all she could do was pray for the safe return of the daughter she loved beyond anything. Was this God's punishment for what she'd done in her past? She'd given away one beautiful daughter, so she didn't deserve to keep another. Angela was wracked with guilt that this was all her fault. She knew one day she'd really have to pay the price of the terrible deed she'd done, and perhaps now that day had come? These were all thoughts she couldn't share with Stan, couldn't share with anyone. *Dear God,* thought Angela, *what have I done . . .?*

And as if in answer, Angela looked up to see something she'd thought about almost every day with equal parts horror and joy. Her heart, which had been racing ever since Bobby Gillespie turned up on her doorstep, now almost stopped beating.

Just opposite to where Stan and Angela were waiting, a young girl walked onto the factory site. Beside her were a priest and a woman. Angela felt the blood running like ice in her veins. Her mouth seemed unaccountably dry and her head swam. Her innards were gripped by the panic flowing through her.

Stan didn't know what had happened to Angela, though he was aware something was wrong, for the look on her bleached face expressed pure anguish. 'What is it, Angela?' he cried.

She couldn't answer Stan, for her eyes were riveted on the child. Angela knew she was looking at her own daughter she had abandoned on the steps of the workhouse all those years ago. She had never imagined anything like this happening. She didn't know what the child was doing there, and she had no right to ask her. It was far too risky to acknowledge her in any way, but the memories were reverberating in her head and she had the urge to run from the place. But she knew she couldn't do that either, not while Connie needed her.

Chrissie had come to the factory because she was worried about the girl who had become her only friend. She had gone to the library to get a book to read during the Easter holidays, and she was surprised not to see the girl with the golden ringlets there. When she had made a second visit a few days later, the girl was still missing. Chrissie had asked where she was, but neither librarian knew. One had mentioned that they were a little concerned that she might be unwell, as she had always let them know in the past if she couldn't come to work at the library. 'I could go and ask, if you want me to?' Chrissie said. 'But I don't know exactly where she lives.'

'We can give you her address,' said the older librarian. 'You don't mind going?'

'Not at all,' Chrissie said. 'I'd like to see how she is, anyway.'

However, when Chrissie arrived at Bell Barn Road and hammered at the door there was no answer, and the woman next door came out and told her there was no one in. 'They're all right though, aren't they?' Chrissie asked. 'Not ill or anything?'

There were few secrets that could be kept in those back-to-back streets, and the neighbour knew all about the young boy coming to the door and what he had said to Angela. She told Chrissie what she knew.

Chrissie ran home, via the library, to tell Eileen and Father John what she thought might have happened to her friend from the library. Eileen and Father John (Eileen's brother), who were the people who had taken her in, knew all about Chrissie's fascination with the girl with the golden ringlets whom she had met at the library. They were extremely concerned when Chrissie told them what the neighbour had said.

'Apparently it's a factory in Walsall,' Chrissie said. 'Can

we go and find out what's happened? I won't be able to stop worrying until I know what's happened to my lovely friend Connie.'

Eileen had a list as long as her arm of things to do that day, but she saw Chrissie was really concerned about what had happened to the girl she had befriended at the library, and she too was quite anxious about her, so she nodded her head.

'Let's ask John if he wants to come too. There might be some there looking for reassurance from a Father. I just hope the news is good, and this girl with the golden ringlets is all right.'

They found Connie was far from all right. Her mother was in a right state too – and no wonder, Eileen thought. She was very agitated, she had difficulty meeting Chrissie's eyes, and her face was flushed scarlet. It looked as if she was being consumed by shame.

Eileen recognised Angela as a woman she had seen occasionally at Mass at St Chad's. Every time she had seen Angela at Mass she'd had her head covered, but now that Angela had removed her scarf, Eileen felt trepidation flood over her body, but didn't know why.

The strained silence between them all was broken by a shout from underneath the rubble from Bobby. He had shouted up before and asked for water, which had been lowered down to him, but this time he tugged on the rope and began to climb up, and they all dashed over to hear the news he might have. Bobby said not everyone had been crushed, as most people had thought, because they had been protected by the angle of the roof. Angela let out a sigh of relief and she didn't know whether he heard or not, but he shook his head. 'We have to get them out real quick though,' he went on, 'because the roof won't hold much longer, because it's creaking and groaning above them. If it collapses . . .' He didn't need to go on.

'Can we reach them?' one of the miners asked.

'Not easily,' Bobby answered. 'I couldn't get any nearer than I did without dislodging stuff. I lowered that canteen of water down. And they need torches – it's pitch black down there. Nobody will be able to do anything if they can't see.'

'How are the survivors doing down there?' asked one of the miners.

Bobby shrugged. 'Hard to say. Some could be alive but unconscious. One man's definitely alive. He's the one who asked for the water, but he said the lady beside him is in a bad way – but I'm not saying she's dead, like. We need men to shore the structure up as secure as they can make it, so we can get all those people out as quickly and as carefully as possible, I'd say.'

Angela knew that there was nothing else to do, except anxiously wait while those trained in this type of work organised teams to rescue as many of those trapped as possible. Anyone still alive had been lucky so far, but they were still at risk, for any sudden movement, especially the removal of blockages, could bring the whole thing down. Bobby said the roof had protected them so far, but to Angela it seemed such a flimsy roof to hold so much weight. She could only hope and pray that it might hold out a little longer till everyone was freed. But just how likely was that? A feeling of dread and terrible sadness filled her being as she faced the fact that in all probability, she would never see her daughter again.

Many excruciatingly worrying hours later, Stan, who had gone to see if there was any further news, came to see Angela. 'I have news of Connie.'

Angela's mouth suddenly went bone dry. 'Bad news?' she croaked.

Stan didn't answer directly but said, 'She's alive, Angela. Connie is alive.'

'Oh, praise the Lord! But what's the problem?'

Stan replied gravely, 'She's very weak and they need to get her out and into hospital right away. But before they can do that, they need to lift a beam off her. They're putting chains on it now, but it will be a dangerous procedure and might take a long time. The beam is supporting a huge amount of debris, so they'll have to have the miners down there, reinforcing it bit by bit as they start to lift it.'

'Is there a chance the whole lot might fall on her, burying her again?'

Stan knew that was the very thing the whole crew were worried about. He also knew that the rescuers and miners were risking their own lives to release Connie safely. His own son Daniel was one of the lucky ones who had been rescued with relative ease. The relief Stan had felt when Daniel had been lifted out of that hole was immense, but Angela was far from experiencing that joy.

'It will take some time, as I said. But she's alive, and you must hold on to that just at the moment.'

The wait this time was different because, as they

struggled to free Connie, Angela could hear the clanking of chains, and the miners calling out to one another, and the dull thud of the pit props being hammered in, prior to moving the beam, as well as the awful sound of sawing. At each noise emanating from the hole, Angela jerked slightly in her chair. She felt as if her nerve endings were raw, exposed. Her limbs trembled and her ears were attuned to any sounds that might spell disaster. Any crash, clatter or crunch made her flinch, as if she were experiencing physical blows. Angela remembered how the Moorcrofts felt at the loss of their son Billy. No wonder his mother had lost the will to live without him. She watched the clock on the factory wall. Surely it had stopped or was running slow, for never had she known time to pass so slowly.

Stan watched as Angela sat on the chair, shrouded in misery and foreboding, as worry for Connie filled her whole being.

By the time Connie had eventually been gently lifted out of the hole, strapped to a stretcher, the flicker of hope Angela had once had, that Connie just might have survived against all the odds, had been completely extinguished. News of the explosion had leaked out to the general public, and as Angela followed her daughter's stretcher, she was subjected to the pop and flash of cameras securing pictures for the papers, and journalists were there with notebooks at the ready, collecting human-interest stories. The police and medical staff tried to protect Connie and Angela from this intrusion, but

Angela, almost out of her mind with anguished worry, was almost unaware of it. Connie lay on the stretcher covered with thick grey dust, which still couldn't disguise the dark bruises that covered her body or the gash on her head that had seeped rust-coloured blood onto her hair. An ambulance had been summoned, and as Connie was being lifted into it, Angela, who thought she must be dead, wondered why the blanket they had wrapped around her wasn't covering her face.

It was the doctor who said, 'Your daughter is not dead, Mrs McClusky, but unconscious and in a coma – a kind of deep sleep.'

Angela reeled backwards in relief and shock, and gave a half-cry at the news. 'Will she wake up?'

'We hope so, in time.'

'How much time?' Angela managed to choke out, her mind still processing the news that her Connie was still alive.

'That very much depends on the severity of the injuries to the brain and the tenacity of the patient,' the doctor said. 'The quicker we can get her to the hospital, the better we can treat her. So, Mrs McClusky, jump into the back of the ambulance with your daughter, and let's get her to the safest place for her right now.'

Just behind the ambulance, Angela could hear Chrissie talking to Eileen.

'Can we follow the ambulance to the hospital, Eileen?'

Angela had almost forgotten the child was there, her attention had been so fully centred on Connie. She was about to boycott the girl's request when one of the nurses who had come with the ambulance said, 'A friend talking to Connie might help bring her out of her coma.'

'But they're not friends, not really,' Angela protested.

'Maybe not best friends,' Eileen conceded, 'but they knew each other quite well through the library. Chrissie really admires your daughter, and I think they have got quite close. She was dreadfully upset when news of the accident reached her.'

'How did she know?'

'She had gone to your house to see if Connie was all right. The librarians had been wondering if she was unwell when she didn't start at the library as she usually does in the holidays. One of your neighbours told Chrissie what had happened, and she came home quite distressed. Nothing would calm her down except coming here to see if Connie was all right.'

SIX

At the hospital Connie was immediately whisked away to be examined by the doctors. Angela found herself alone in the waiting room, her head spinning with the events of the day. Was that little girl Chrissie really the baby she'd abandoned? Angela knew it was so; she supposed it was a mother's instinct kicking in after all these years. She just knew. What on earth was she to do now? Angela couldn't properly think about this, whilst so consumed with worry for Connie. What if she never woke up? Angela had heard stories of people that lived out their lives in these comas. *Please, God – don't let that happen to Connie!* She'd do anything it took to get Connie to wake up, anything at all.

As she was pacing around the waiting room, a kindly nurse came over to Angela. 'Please try not to worry too much, Mrs McClusky,' she said. 'Let the doctors do their job, and you'll soon be back by her side. And when you are, sometimes it helps to talk to people in a coma. You could try that, or singing a familiar song – anything at all that might break through the fog surrounding her brain at the moment.'

'Will she be able to hear it?' Angela asked.

'Many of my colleagues think she might be able to, even if she's unable to respond.'

'And you, nurse? What do you think?'

'I think, Mrs McClusky, it's far better to talk or sing to your daughter than sit by her bed in silence, whether she hears it or not.'

Angela knew by the nurse's evasive reply that she didn't totally believe Connie would hear any words said to her, but it would do no harm to try.

And Angela did try. At Connie's bedside, she told her over and over how much she was loved and needed, and stroked her hand.

Hours passed, and still she sat there. Then Eileen, the priest's sister, popped her head round the door with a cup of tea. 'I thought you might like this,' she said.

Angela took the cup gratefully and drank the scalding tea. 'Thank you, that really was most welcome.'

'Could you do with company?' Eileen asked. 'Or would you prefer to be alone with your daughter?'

Angela was touched by Eileen's thoughtfulness and understanding, and said, 'I was glad to be on my own before. I was trying to make sense of everything, you know, but now I think I might value your company, if you're sure you have the time?'

'I'll make time,' Eileen said with a smile. 'If I waited till I had the time, I'd never get anything done. And can I bring Chrissie in, too I left her with the nurse, but she is so anxious about your daughter. They often met in the library, and the nurses seem to think a friend talking to her might help.'

Eileen noticed how pale and tense Angela looked. *Best to keep her talking,* thought Eileen, *keep her distracted from the worry.*

'This must have come as such a shock,' said Eileen.

'I just thought Connie was at the library, as usual,' Angela said.

'She didn't tell you she'd changed her plans, then?' Eileen asked.

'No, not a dicky bird.'

'Mothers are often the last to know,' Eileen said. 'According to Chrissie, she also has a young man. Daniel, I believe he's called. Was he also hurt?'

Angela was surprised at that news. From what Stan had said, they had gone out a few times. In her mind there was a difference between Connie going out a few times with a boy she knew quite well, and having a steady boyfriend, when she wasn't yet sixteen years old.

Eileen saw the shocked surprise on her face, and she asked, 'Do you know him?'

'Oh yes, I know him,' Angela said. 'I just didn't know Connie was seeing him, that way. I mean, I thought her a little young for that sort of thing.'

'I think the war made girls grow up quicker, doing things they'd never done before in factories all over the country.'

'But that surely wouldn't affect Connie. She wasn't born till 1916.'

'I know, but what the women did, were often forced to

do, changed Britain's perspective on women forever,' Eileen said. 'They have more freedom now.'

Angela was slightly aggrieved that Eileen seemed to know more about her daughter than she did. She knew she was being totally unreasonable to feel that way. Eileen seemed to know so much about Chrissie, that she even showed an interest in the girl's friends. She also clearly shared her passion for the library, and Angela felt a pang of guilt at the times she had barely listened to her daughter talking about her work, seldom asking her any questions. To Connie she must have seemed totally disinterested in her life. No wonder Connie didn't confide in her about meeting Daniel or her involvement in clearing out the bomb-damaged buildings.

Eileen had watched the slight resentment slide across Angela's face just for a second or two, before Angela managed to brush it to one side.

Angela decided to find out more about the relationship between Connie and Daniel, and she asked, 'Where did they meet up, this young man and my daughter?'

'Well, that's just it,' Eileen said. 'He used to meet her at the library, and the librarians felt a bit responsible, and so they made some discreet enquiries and found he lives locally with his father, who seems eminently respectable.'

'Yes, he is,' Angela said, and went on: 'Daniel's mother died when he was born, and his father and I have known each other for years. He served in the army with my husband – in fact, my husband died trying to save him.'

'Oh, my dear! What a history your two families have between you.'

There was a slight pause and then Angela asked, 'Did the nurses really think it might help Connie to have the child in here?'

Eileen nodded. 'They did, and they asked the doctor, and he was all for it as well.'

So, although Angela didn't want the child in, she hadn't any right to veto something that might help Connie, so she said, 'Please fetch her, Mrs . . .'

'Eileen, that's what I'm called,' said the priest's sister, getting to her feet.

'I think you might need some time alone with your daughter,' Eileen said. 'How about you have an hour or so with her on your own, and then perhaps Chrissie can pop her head in to say hello?'

Angela realised that these two girls, who had met because both of them loved the library, were sisters, though neither knew that. Chrissie obviously cared for Connie, and as her sister had almost a right to be there.

A little bit later Eileen came to Angela at Connie's bedside to ask if Connie's little friend might come in to say a quick hello now. Desperately not wanting to let her, Angela bit back her refusal, remembering the nurse's previous recommendation that close family and friends talk to Connie to try and pull her out of the coma.

When Eileen brought Chrissie in, Angela forced herself to look her full in the face for the first time. Her brown eyes looked large in her pale face and so sad, they were like pools of sorrow, and she realised this child she had abandoned was anxious about Connie too.

But now that they were in a room together, Angela didn't know what to say to the child sitting on a chair beside Connie's bed, watching her intently. The child herself was utterly still and silent. Father John could have told Angela that the day he had fetched her from the workhouse, he had been struck by the way she could sit so still and for so long. Chrissie had later told him that it was her survival technique in the workhouse. 'If you sit still and quiet for long enough, people more or less forget you're there,' she'd told him. 'It's the next best thing to becoming invisible.' Now she was doing it again because she had promised not to bother the Connie's mum. She thought if she did, or if Angela even noticed her in any way, she might send her away . . .

Angela, though, was well aware of the silent child in the chair and felt the deep silence between them was becoming awkward, so she steeled herself to speak to Chrissie. 'I didn't know you were so friendly with Connie.'

'I'm too in awe of her to be really friendly with her,' Chrissie admitted.

'In awe of Connie?' Angela repeated with a smile. 'I'm sure there is no need for you thinking that way.'

'Maybe not,' Chrissie agreed. 'She is always kind, but she's older than me, and so pretty. It was her hair that attracted me first. I had never seen hair like it. She said she took after you and she does, you have both got the loveliest hair.' And then Chrissie went on wistfully, 'I wish I knew what my mother looked like. I suppose I could look a little like her, couldn't I?'

Angela felt as if her heart was breaking in two at the

anguished longing in Chrissie's voice. She spoke slowly and hoped Chrissie wouldn't guess how close she was to tears as she said, 'Possibly Chrissie, though it's not always like that. Some daughters don't look like their mothers at all.'

Chrissie knew Angela was right because she had seen it herself in her friends' parents, but when Angela said, 'Would that upset you, if you found that you didn't look that much like your mother?' she shook her head vehemently.

'Oh no,' she said. 'I would just like to know what my mother looks like, for my own sake.'

'And you really would like to know what she looks like?'

Chrissie nodded, 'Oh yes. More than anything in the world.'

Angela could hold the tears back no longer and they trickled down her cheeks, yet she wiped them away with her hands impatiently.

She was unaware Stan was approaching the side room at the bottom of the long ward. He'd come from visiting Daniel to check up on both Connie and Angela. He had had a word with the nurse on duty, who had told him that there was no change, but that the young girl's mother was talking to her a lot, which was good. As he got closer to the side ward, he could hear the murmur of voices because the door had been left slightly ajar, but he couldn't distinguish any words because they were speaking so quietly.

In fact, Chrissie's voice had dropped to little above a

whisper, and she began to unbutton her coat as she said, 'And anyway, whatever my mother looks like, she left me something special. Father John said she told him in Confession that the gift she left with me was the most precious thing she owned, and that she gave it to me to show me that somewhere out there was a mother who loved me but couldn't look after me. Apparently, she put it in my hand when she left me on the steps of the workhouse, and when they found me, I still had it in my fist.' Chrissie suddenly lifted her jumper, and round her neck was the original silver locket Angela thought she would never see again.

She gave a cry of dismay and saw Chrissie's eyes open wide with alarm, and all of a sudden, she knew she had to tell Chrissie the truth. There was no one left to hurt now but Stan, and he was lost to her anyway. Was she ready to open up her deepest, darkest secret to the one person she had hurt most of all? Angela wondered if this was God sending her a sign that this was the time to make things right, to set things on the right course.

She first glanced over to Connie's bed and saw that she was comatose and totally unresponsive, and gave a surreptitious sigh of relief as she turned to look into Chrissie's deep, dark-brown eyes. She saw those eyes darken in slight bewilderment as, dropping her voice to a whisper to match Chrissie's, she said, 'I am going to tell you something very important. Not many people know it.'

'Is it a secret?'

Angela gave a sigh. 'It has had to be for many years, but now it is time to tell you the truth, because it concerns you.'

Daring rejection, she put a tentative arm around Chrissie's shoulders as she continued: 'Father John was right when he said your mother gave you that locket, which was the most precious thing she had ever owned, and I know that because . . .'

The lump in Angela's throat threatened to choke her and she swallowed, knowing that if she didn't go on now, she might lose her nerve altogether. She really didn't know if telling the child there in that hospital room was a sensible thing to do. It was certainly something she had never envisaged having the opportunity to do; but then, she had never expected to ever see the child again. She certainly never thought for one moment that she'd come face to face with her in this way. Had she any right to deny Chrissie the knowledge of who her mother was? Angela reasoned that if she didn't confess to Chrissie, she would be keeping her secret for her own sake, not for the sake of this innocent young child.

Taking a deep breath, Angela spoke at last, her voice choked and haunted: 'I know it was your mother's most precious thing because . . . because the locket used to belong to me. I am the one who left you on the workhouse steps.'

Chrissie sprang from Angela's tenuous hold and stood up facing her. She had never thought she would discover who her mother really was, never allowed herself to imagine how she would feel or react. But now, hearing it from Angela's own lips, the girl felt complete shock, mixed with white-hot fury. In a flash she remembered her harsh, loveless life before Father John rescued her. She remembered feeling so lonely at Christmas, when some children had had visitors, and some even went off to spend Christmas with their extended families, but no one came to visit Chrissie. The first birthday she ever commemorated was her eleventh, celebrated in Father John's house, where Eileen made it special. The life she'd had to endure until Father John took her into his home was due to this woman in front of her.

'Father John said the woman who gave me the locket was my mother, so that was you?' she asked incredulously. 'And after dumping me on the steps of the workhouse, you gave me the locket to make you feel better, not because you loved me at all. I expect that's what you told Father John so he wouldn't see what you're really like, because you are bad through and through. Well, I am telling you now, a silver locket, however pretty, or even valuable, is no substitute for a family, a mother of my own.'

Angela was crying in earnest now. 'No, Chrissie – it wasn't like that!' she spluttered.

'Yes, it was exactly like that!' Chrissie snapped, and she had the desire to leap on this horrible woman, this excuse for a mother, and score her nails down her face.

Hearing the commotion, Eileen came running to Connie's bedside. When Chrissie told her the news, she too was shocked, for she hadn't any idea that Connie's mother was also the mother of Chrissie, whom she'd abandoned on the workhouse steps. But if this was an overwhelming surprise to her, Eileen could only guess at the distress it must be causing her beloved Chrissie, who she thought of as her own daughter and loved beyond anything. She put a gentle but restraining hand on each of Chrissie's shoulders, squeezing them kindly as a gesture of support.

Eileen turned Chrissie towards her and enfolded her in her arms. Chrissie said to Angela, 'I cried often too, but I had to stop in the end, because I was beaten if I continued to get upset. So I learnt to stop crying, but the hurt never went away. Did you have the least idea of what you were condemning me to?' Chrissie too was sobbing now. 'I hate you! All my miserable life I've hated you, and I probably always will.'

Stan had clearly heard Chrissie's anguished outburst, and he had been totally stunned by what she was saying. In fact, he had been so stunned that he had staggered, and nurses came running, thinking he was going to collapse. He assured them he was all right, but he wasn't. He wanted to burst into the room and demand an explanation, though he had no right to do that. Stan desperately needed to hear Angela's response, and so he moved as close to the door as possible and listened intently.

There was someone else in the room as shocked as Stan had been, who was also listening intently, and that was Connie. The soft voices of Angela and Chrissie had not disturbed the fog surrounding her brain, but Chrissie's angry, hurt-filled cry had punched a small hole in it. Everything was still vague and she felt very disoriented and had no desire to open her eyes in any case, so she lay there, able to half-listen to someone saying awful things about her mother that couldn't possibly be true.

Then, piercing the fog, her mother's voice came through

clearly, and she heard Angela say in a voice husky with unshed tears: 'Yes, Chrissie, I am your mother, and I'm sorry to the heart for what I had to do that dreadful, awful day. I don't think I'll ever be able to take away the pain I have caused you, but I would like to tell you why I was forced to do what I did.'

'Give me one good reason why I should listen to you!' Chrissie demanded angrily. 'You abandoned me, and left me to the workhouse. It's all cut and dried as far as I'm concerned, and I am certainly not prepared to listen to a list of excuses. I can't believe I've spent so many years wondering about you. I have seen what you look like now and the type of person you are, and I don't really want anything more to do with you.'

Angela gave a cry of anguish and pain, for Chrissie's hate-filled words pierced her very soul. They reflected everything she'd ever thought about herself since the day she'd had to make that heart-breaking choice. She bitterly regretted telling Chrissie everything. She wished she could unsay the words that had hurt the child so much. What had she been thinking, just blurting them out? Chrissie was still so young; there was no way she was emotionally ready for the whole truth just then.

Risking further rejection, for Angela couldn't just leave it there, she tried again. 'Every word you said is true, Chrissie,' she said. 'I did leave you on the workhouse steps, and I fully understand your anger and resentment, for there isn't a day goes by when I am not ashamed of what I had to do. But I beg you again, will you let me try to explain why I had to do it?'

Chrissie was going to refuse again but realised she really did want to know why she had done it. At the workhouse they had told her that her mother had dumped her on the steps because she didn't want her, and no one else would want her either, because she was unlovable. When Chrissie told Eileen what they had said, she said they were talking rubbish, but Chrissie knew Eileen was a very special, very kind person. Chrissie wanted to hear what her natural mother had to say about it.

The nod Chrissie gave was almost imperceptible, but it was still a nod, and it gave Angela the courage to swallow the huge lump in her throat and brush the tears from her face. She wondered if she had always known that she would eventually come face to face with the child she had so obviously damaged. Chrissie had been saved by the intervention of Father John and his sister, but that in no way minimised what she had done to a helpless baby. It was right that she should shoulder the blame, but she was grateful to be given the opportunity to tell her daughter how it had happened. 'To explain it to you,' she said to Chrissie, 'I have to go back to the days of the Great War, after my husband Barry enlisted.'

'Connie told me that her father had died,' said Chrissie.

Angela nodded her head. 'He did,' she said. 'In the Great War, like a great many more. And so, I had to get a job. We were fortunate that we had Barry's mother living with us at the time, as she could look after Connie while I worked.' Angela wished for a moment that Chrissie had got to know Mary, who was a lovely and generous grandmother to Connie. 'War work was the best paid,' Angela continued, 'so I made shells. The hours were long and we were never allowed a day off, because the shells were so badly needed. There was a constant worry that there would be a shell shortage, which would be catastrophic for our loved ones fighting in France. It wasn't all bad, though. The thing I enjoyed most about that time was when they taught me to drive.'

'Drive?' Chrissie repeated in awe. 'You can drive a car?'

Angela shrugged. 'Don't know about a car, never tried driving one of those, but I can drive trucks well enough. I used to drive all over the city in trucks usually packed to the gunnels with shells.'

'Golly.'

Angela suddenly caught hold of Chrissie's hands, and Chrissie would have pulled away, but she was mesmerised by the story Angela was unfolding and felt sure it was a clue to why she had been abandoned all those years ago. 'I loved driving,' Angela continued. 'But sometimes now I think if I hadn't ever learnt to drive, none of this might ever have happened.'

'What do you mean?' Chrissie demanded angrily, tugging her hands away. 'You are seriously asking me to believe that if you hadn't learnt to drive, then you wouldn't have left me on the workhouse steps? Sorry, but I don't see any connection.'

'Let me tell you how it was, please?' Angela said, and then, without waiting for her response, went on to tell her about the day she had to drive a consignment of shells to the docks in the largest truck the factory owned, for there was no one else that could do it. 'It took a long time,' Angela said, 'so when I got back it was dark.'

She stopped and Chrissie urged, 'Go on.'

'I will, because you need to know,' Angela said with a sigh. 'Sorry I'm telling this so slowly, but this is extremely hard for me to tell.' She paused and then went on almost in a rush, 'I was nearly home when I was attacked by three drunken soldiers.'

Stan gave a start in his chair outside the room, and there was even a slight movement from Connie in the bed, but it went unnoticed, for all eyes were riveted on Angela, who gave a grim laugh and said, 'They said they thought I was a lady of the night. Do you know what that means, Chrissie?'

'Of course I know!' Chrissie snapped. 'I'm not a baby. But why did they think that of you?'

'First of all, it was late for normal factory workers to be coming home,' Angela said. 'And then I didn't wear a wedding ring. I wasn't allowed to wear any metal on the factory floor, so all metal had to be removed. I thought it was safer to leave it at home. I also had money in my pocket because, as the docks were a distance away, the boss gave me a ten-shilling note to get something to eat before I headed back. Thinking about it now, I don't think those soldiers really believed I was a lady of the night. I think that's what they told themselves to justify what happened next – because they raped me, Chrissie, all of them, and then beat me up so badly, I could barely reach home.'

Chrissie's mouth was agape. 'That's awful,' she said, aghast. 'What happened to them – the soldiers?'

'Nothing happened to them, for I never went near the police,' Angela said.

'Why not?'

'Because of Barry at the Front,' Angela said. 'We were told not to worry the men, especially as they couldn't help us at all.'

'But you wouldn't have to tell him.'

'And I wouldn't have,' Angela said steadfastly. 'But believe me, if I'd gone to the police, there would have been a fuss made. Maybe it would be in the paper and people would get to know, and it would only take one of those people to write and tell Barry. I couldn't risk that. All his life, he had tried to protect me.'

She shook her head from side to side and went on, 'If he knew I had been attacked and he wasn't here . . . well, I don't know what he might have done.'

Outside the door Stan shook with emotion. It was monstrous that such a terrible thing should happen to lovely Angela. It was unbelievable that brutes like that should get away with such an atrocious attack on an innocent young woman, but he knew she was right to keep such news away from Barry. The love between Barry and Angela was special. It was beautiful to see them together. And she was right, all the womenfolk were warned not to tell servicemen distressing news from home. If Barry had heard one hint of what had happened to his beloved, he might have decided his rightful place was with his wife back home. If he'd done that, Stan knew he would have been hunted down and shot as a deserter.

But Angela hadn't finished: 'All I wanted to do was to put this behind me, and Barry's mother Mary agreed with me. And then I found I had been made pregnant by one of those thugs.'

Stan could stand no more. He got up from his chair and opened the door to the side ward, to see Angela on the chair by the bed, hands clasped between her knees as she rocked backwards and forwards in deep distress. He crossed the room in seconds, put his arms around Angela and held her tight. 'Oh my darling! How you have suffered!' he said.

Angela nodded. 'I had help from an unexpected source,' she went on. 'No names, because even now she might get into trouble. She was a kind and sympathetic woman who helped me when I had no idea where to turn. She hid me away and after you were born, the plan was that she would take you to the Catholic orphanage where the nuns would find you a nice couple who would adopt you as their own little girl, and I'm sure they would have loved you very much.'

Chrissie thought that was a good sort of plan and she would have loved to have spent her first eleven years with people who loved her. But that hadn't happened, so she said to Angela, 'So what went wrong?'

'They wouldn't take you – well, couldn't take you, really,' Angela told her. 'They said since the war, the numbers of people willing to adopt had dropped off considerably, and they couldn't place the children who were in the orphanage already, and some had already been waiting some time, so they could take no more.'

'So what did you do?'

'You know the answer to that,' Angela said. 'In all this, I didn't expect to love you – you know, because of the attack and all – but from the moment I first held you in my arms, I found I did love you, with my whole heart.'

'You loved me?' Chrissie said incredulously. 'Are you sure?'

'Yes, my darling girl, I'm sure.'

'The people at the workhouse said you *couldn't* have loved me, or you wouldn't have given me away. And if my own mother didn't love me, then no one else would either. They said I must be unlovable.'

Angela was angered by the cruelty of the warders, taunting unprotected, innocent children. And yet what had she expected? Had she naively tried to convince herself that the people that ran the workhouse would be good and kind? She knew that was just a fraction of what her daughter had suffered. That was only one thing, but it was something she could put right straight away. She pulled Chrissie towards her and lifted her head, so she was looking into her eyes as she said, 'I loved you with all my heart, and just as much as I loved Connie. It was hard for me to sign you away to be adopted, but I had to do that to give you the chance of a better life. I believed it was the only option open to me, and I was filled with shame. I can promise you that the shame has never left me.'

There was silence in the room and then Chrissie said, 'But you left me on the steps.' Tears glistened in Chrissie's eyes as she went on in a shaky voice as she fought not to let the threatened tears fall, 'That was one of the hardest things to bear. I mean, you claim you loved me, but you just left me on the steps like a pile of rubbish. Funny kind of way to show love, if you ask me. I always wondered why you did that.'

'If I had taken you into the workhouse, they would have known who I was,' Angela explained. 'Then they'd have asked questions about who the father was, and I was petrified that someone might contact Barry, and then my subterfuge would have come to nothing. I might also have been forced to work someplace, and my wages would be given to them, to pay for your keep. I couldn't do that. I had already left Connie with her grandmother, Mary, for months.'

Chrissie had been watching Angela's face as she spoke and saw tear trails on her pain-ridden face. The hatred that had been burning bright in Chrissie's heart lessened a little, for she knew this woman – her mother, she thought disbelievingly – had spoken the absolute truth.

'Believe me, Chrissie,' Angela went on, 'if there had been any other road, I would have taken it. There hasn't been one day when I haven't regretted what I was forced to do, and I am still filled with guilt.'

She turned to Stan and said, 'That day I shuddered when you were admitting your feelings for me – I remember it all now. I didn't shudder because of the words you were saying – they were words I longed to hear – but because I didn't think I'd ever have the courage to tell you what had happened to me. Yet I knew I couldn't enter into a deeper relationship with you with such a secret on my soul. I am so disgusted with myself, and I couldn't bear to see disgust in your eyes too, because I care for you too much for that,' Angela said.

Stan replied, 'Angela, I can't think of any situation when you could do anything that I would feel disgust for.'

'Oh, you can say that,' Angela said with an impatient toss of her head, 'but how could you bear the thought that I am the kind of woman that sacrificed her baby – abandoned her to the workhouse! I can barely live with myself, I feel such self-loathing. How could I expect another to understand? You see how I've hurt and damaged Chrissie. Stan, I care for you and your good opinion too much to risk seeing revulsion in your eyes.'

'Why don't you try me?' Stan said. 'Let me make up my own mind and don't keep assuming how I would act and how I feel. You owe me that, at least.'

Angela swallowed the lump in her throat and gave a sigh and said, 'All right. Now that you know it all, what do you really think of me?'

'Well, not disgust, certainly,' Stan said determinedly. 'Personally, I think you were more sinned against than sinning.'

'How can you say that?' Angela cried.

'Easily,' Chrissie said, looking tentatively at Angela, her hatred having burnt itself out, 'for I think it too.'

'Chrissie, I am so sorry you had to suffer such things,' Angela said as tears trickled unchecked down her cheeks. 'If I could, I would wipe away all memories of that dreadful time.'

'I wish you could,' Chrissie said. 'They often come back to haunt me at night.'

'D-did you blame me?'

'Totally,' Chrissie said. 'And I hated you so much! But now you have told me how it was, and . . . well . . . sometimes things are taken out of our hands, and we are unable to change them. I think that's how it was with you. Circumstances dictated how you had to behave. Perhaps you had no real choice.'

Angela swallowed hard and her eyes were moist as she said, 'Chrissie, I really have no right to ask this question, but do you think you could ever find it in your heart to forgive me?'

Chrissie thought long and hard. She knew what Angela wanted was total forgiveness. She would have to work hard to cast from her mind all shreds of bitterness or antipathy, and write off the bleak years in the workhouse as if they'd never been. But she looked Angela full in the face and plainly saw the anguish there, and knew she was still suffering. Chrissie's heart softened, and she was suddenly touched with pity, not for herself, but for Angela and for the whole situation.

The silence had gone on so long, Angela was sure Chrissie was going to refuse to forgive her, and so she was surprised to feel a tap on her shoulder. She turned to find Chrissie's deep-brown eyes fastened on hers as she said, 'Yes, I will do my best to forgive you.'

Angela's relief was profound. She tentatively put her arms around Chrissie and tightened them as she felt the child sag against her, and from the bed came a deep and heartfelt sigh of relief. Angela was by Connie's side in seconds. Connie's eyes remained closed and she was as immobile as ever, but there was a fluttering beneath her eyelids that Angela couldn't remember seeing before. They had all heard the sigh, and Stan went off to find a doctor. He was delighted with the news, though he was quick to warn them that Connie was still a very sick girl, despite the signs that she was coming out of the coma.

'It's good news,' he said to Angela. 'You did the right thing, talking to her like you did. The nurses told me there was an almost constant hum of conversation from this room.'

Angela hoped it was just a hum the nurses heard, and not the actual words she had to say, but the doctor hadn't finished. 'Keep up the good work, and you are entitled to feel optimistic, but be patient and don't expect overnight miracles. She is not quite out of the woods yet.'

It was a very emotional group who tentatively celebrated Connie moving one step closer to coming back to the world. Angela wasn't quite sure where she stood with anyone, but she did know that Connie hadn't been taken from her, that Stan wasn't appalled by her story, and that she had faced the demons of her past. Whatever happened now between her and Chrissie, it was in her hands to finally make things right.

Angela was hopeful of Connie's eventual recovery, though she knew that she was still very ill. She had a number of injuries and as soon as the doctors thought she had recovered sufficiently, she faced several operations to repair damaged organs.

'I'm not a very patient person, that's the trouble,' Angela confided to Stan one day as they sat in the tea bar adjoining the hospital. One of the nurses had suggested that Stan should take Angela there to have a reviving cup of tea: 'She has been sitting by her daughter's bedside for hours, and now that Connie is asleep, she needs to get away, if only for a little while.'

'Come on,' Stan urged. 'They say Connie is now in a more natural sleep. It's good news.'

'What if she wakes?'

'Matron assures me we will be told. We will only be a step away,' Stan said. 'You don't look at all well to me.'

Angela went with Stan, knowing he was right, for she wasn't eating or sleeping properly at all and had begun to feel quite weak.

Stan waited till the cup of tea and buttered scones were in front of them before he said, 'Angela, none of this is your fault. You must start believing that. And despite all she has gone through in that hell-hole of a workhouse, Chrissie acknowledges it too. You're her mother and I'm sure she would like to get to know you better.'

'Do you really think so?'

'I'm certain,' Stan said. 'Eileen tells me she is a lovely young girl, and she doesn't appear to blame you – or at least, she is trying not to. And in time, please God, she will get to know Connie as a sister, too.'

'You think Connie will ever totally recover, Stan?'

'I've no doubt of it,' Stan said robustly.

Angela sighed. 'I know there have been signs of recovery,' she said. 'But they have been so slight. After a while, you wonder if you have imagined it. Sometimes it feels like she takes two steps forward, and then three back.'

'You mustn't think that way,' Stan said. 'Connie is young and until this terrible thing happened to her, she was fit and healthy. She needs you to be as positive and supportive as possible. So no more defeatist talk!'

'Maybe it's better to face it,' Angela said resignedly. 'I sit by Connie's bed, but I don't know if she's aware of me or not. I often wonder if that is going to be the pattern of my life from now on.'

Stan saw the life being sucked from Angela, enveloped in wretched sorrow. He said, 'Maybe the hospital would let Daniel visit. That might help bring her back to us.'

'What could Daniel do that we haven't already done?'

'Who knows?' Stan said. 'But like it or not, Angela, they are incredibly fond of one another. Daniel was the one almost buried with her in that shattered building for hours on end. From what my boy says, they told each other things they might not have done yet, if they hadn't been in such danger.'

'They admitted to feelings that weren't true?'

'To get the truth, you'd have to ask them,' Stan said. 'It's just that . . . Hell, Angela, they thought they were going to die in that wreckage. If you felt strongly about someone and you thought it was your last chance to tell them, wouldn't you take it?'

Stan sighed and continued, 'All I know is, Daniel just might be the key to unlock Connie's mind. Have we any right not to try, provided the hospital are willing?'

Angela nodded her head. 'All right,' she said. 'As you

say, it can do no harm and it might do a great deal of good. Let's go back in now?'

'Yes, come on,' Stan said, for he knew Angela was always loath to leave her daughter for long. Angela sighed with relief as she followed Stan into the hospital, but there was no change in Connie's condition and Angela took her place by the bed again.

Daniel asked for the lights to be dimmed so that if Connie opened her eyes again she wouldn't be dazzled by the light, and he had also asked if he could see little Bobby Gillespie. Another regular visitor at the hospital, Bobby was bemused at being sent for, and a bit shy, for the room was full of people and he only knew who some of them were. Daniel, seeing the child's discomfort, drew him towards Angela as he said, 'This boy is the real hero of the hour, and showed great bravery and resourcefulness.'

'You were incredibly brave,' Angela agreed fervently, remembering how he had come to her door to tell her about the accident in the disused shell factory, when she'd thought Connie would be at the library as usual.

'You don't know just how brave,' Stan said. 'Just as we lifted Bobby's brother out, the whole roof collapsed.'

Angela remembered Bobby's concern for his brother, and she said, 'Was he all right, your brother?'

'Sort of,' Bobby said. 'Or at least he will be, so the doctor said. He's hurt inside, so he faces some operations, and he busted his right arm and left leg, but they'll heal in time.'

'Yes, and from what I heard, Bobby was that intent on getting his brother out, he was nearly buried himself,' Stan said.

'I'm glad you're both okay,' Angela said sincerely. 'But it sounds as if it will be some time before your brother is fully fit and able to work. How will you manage?'

'Don't worry,' Stan said. 'We're all going to look after the family. Neither of the boys have to worry about going back to work before they are completely recovered.'

Bobby felt as if a huge weight had been lifted off his shoulders. And then he thought his mother might view this as charity, as if they couldn't manage on their own, and he shot an almost fearful look at Stan. Stan knew Bobby's mother well and he said to him in reassurance, 'I've squared it with your mother, Bobby, so you have nothing to worry about and you can get better in your own good time.'

Bobby let out a sigh of relief, but Angela was the only one close enough to hear it, and she smiled at him over Connie and he gave a cheeky grin back. 'I'm very grateful for what you did Bobby,' she said.

'She's your sweetheart, right?' Bobby asked Daniel.

Daniel gave a slight start, but Bobby had asked a direct question and he said to him, 'Yes, yes, I suppose she is.'

'Thought she was,' Bobby said, oblivious to the slight tension in the air, 'cos I saw you was holding her hand sometimes – when you were going home from the library, and when you said she was in a bad way when I lowered the water down.'

Daniel remembered how grateful he had been for that

water, that had tasted like nectar to his dust-caked throat. He had tried to get some water into Connie, but it had just dribbled out of the corners of her mouth. It was so dark, it was hard to see what he was doing. He had matches in his pocket but dared not light one. He knew gas pipes were probably fitted to the walls of the basement the factory had fallen into. If one of those pipes had been fractured in some way, a naked flame could easily cause an explosion. And so he soaked his hanky and wiped Connie's face, and he could have almost sworn that she licked her lips. He'd said nothing at the time because he hadn't wanted to raise false hopes.

Daniel's visit hadn't worked a miracle, but Angela had to admit that it was nice for Connie to have company beyond just her. So she asked Daniel if he would come back again, to which he immediately agreed.

He looked at Bobby and said, 'Connie appeared pretty bad, but I couldn't be sure because it was too dark to see anything much. I think she was drifting in and out of consciousness, but I wasn't even certain about that.' But now he looked at Angela and said, 'Bobby saved both our lives, I should say.'

'Yes, you and your sweetheart,' Angela replied sardonically.

Daniel was slightly annoyed by Angela's tone and replied firmly, 'This is not the time or the place, but if this accident hadn't happened, I would now be talking to you about how Connie and I feel about one another.'

'Are you aware of Connie's age?' Angela demanded. 'She is little more than a child.'

'You were not much older when you married Connie's father,' Daniel retorted. 'Mary told me that, and she said some people were scandalised because it was not long after two of Barry's brothers had been drowned on the *Titanic*. And you were very happily married to Barry, everyone says so, and Connie was the result.'

'There was a reason for that hasty marriage,' Angela said. 'Initially it was to give Mary something to plan, to try and distract her mind from the tragic death of her sons. And then it had to be moved even closer when my foster father became dangerously ill, and I wanted him to walk me down the aisle if possible.' And then she added, 'Barry was well aware of my age and behaved like a perfect gentleman.'

'That wasn't just the prerogative of Barry McClusky,' Daniel said. 'Do you think I will treat Connie with any less respect?'

Angela was prevented from answering by a noise from the bed. Connie had made no sound yet, but it was obvious she was trying to. Angela bent closer, 'What is it, darling?'

Connie fought to open her eyes, but they seemed to weigh a ton. But at last they were open, and she was looking at her mother's dear face, her expressive eyes full of concern. Connie croaked out in a voice just above a whisper, 'I love Daniel.'

Angela's heart was singing because she knew with sudden certainty that her daughter would eventually get better. Suddenly it didn't matter what she thought about Connie and Daniel. She knew it would probably take Connie a long time to get completely well, but it would be well worth it, because at the end of that road would be the daughter Angela thought she had lost. And if Connie wanted Daniel to share her life, Angela decided she would put no obstacle in their way. Instead she would give Connie all the support she might need.

SEVEN

'So, do you feel happier about the relationship between Daniel and Connie now?' Stan asked as they began the walk home that evening after visiting hours were over and Angela had been shooed out by the night-shift matron.

'Yes,' Angela said. 'It's funny, but when you come close to losing someone you love, your whole life takes on a new perspective. And why should I even think of Daniel as somehow unsuitable for Connie? He is older, but that in itself shouldn't be a barrier. Added to that, I am very fond of Daniel myself, and most important of all, he is Connie's choice.'

'Oh, Angela,' Stan said. 'You have made me a very happy man. Can I tell him?'

'Of course,' Angela said. 'It's not exactly a secret. You can tell the young couple they have my blessing to continue their relationship.'

'I think I can say without doubt that they will be

relieved,' Stan said. 'And now that we've got the young people sorted out, it's time for you and me.'

'Me and you,' Angela repeated. 'What about us?'

'Need you ask?' Stan said. 'We need to talk about us. Both of us need to admit how we feel about each other. I spoke words of love to you once and you shuddered, which hurt me a great deal. You said it was because of the secret of the abandoned child that you felt you couldn't tell me about. Now that is not between us any more, how do you feel about the words I said? You said once they were words you'd longed to hear. Was that true?'

'Of course it was true,' Angela said. 'I'm surprised you even had to ask.'

'I hoped,' Stan said. 'I didn't let myself think further than that.'

'Stan, you were speaking of feelings to me that I never thought I would hear,' Angela said. 'I longed for you to see me as more than just a friend. I felt the memory of Barry, who I dearly loved, was a barrier as far as you were concerned, and because of him you would not allow yourself to think of yourself as my lover. Am I right?'

Stan nodded.

'And then I shuddered, but you thought I was shuddering because of what you said?'

Again, Stan nodded and Angela stopped walking and turned him to face her. She looked into his deep-brown eyes and said, 'Listen to me, Stan. There are no words that you could say that would make me shudder, unless it was in anticipation of what was to come next.'

'You mean . . .?'

'I mean that those were words I yearned to hear, fantasised about, but I didn't think you felt that way about me.'

'And I was too cautious to say anything at all,' Stan said. 'It was Daniel who said I should speak out. I don't think we'll have any trouble with the kids being upset about us getting together,' he continued, chuckling.

'Nor do I,' Angela said. 'In fact, both of them have been far more sensible than we have. We have both been incredibly stupid and wasted a lot of time. And I want to waste no more. I love you, Stan Bishop, and I should have told you ages ago.'

She was surprised at the tears that glittered in Stan's eyes, and then he said huskily, 'You have made me the happiest man in the world, for I love you too.' And then Stan's arms enfolded Angela as he pulled her towards him, and his lips descended on hers. Stan's kiss was like nothing she'd ever felt before. She forgot all about her painful past, forgot she was standing in the middle of the street, and thought of nothing but the man she loved who was finally, finally holding her in his arms.

Bit by bit, Connie pulled herself from the morass that seemed to surround her brain. Her speech was slow at first, and hesitant, but it improved daily. She could sometimes be quiet with Angela, almost as if she didn't quite know how to talk to her mother. However, she was seldom quiet for long with Daniel, and the two chattered away ten to the dozen whenever they were together. Connie's spirits always seemed instantly lifted when he was by her side.

The holidays had long finished, and Chrissie had begun

at St Catherine's School and Daniel had returned to his classroom. He initially worked part time, and came to visit Connie after school and at weekends. She also welcomed a visit from the librarians, who brought her endless books to keep her entertained, as did some of her teachers. She was even enthusiastic when they offered to bring her work to do.

'Are you sure it won't be too much for you?' Angela asked anxiously.

'No,' Connie said. 'I'm so bored in hospital and I'd prefer to be doing something useful. I was worried that I would be too far behind to be allowed to take the librarianship exam when I'm out of here.'

'Librarianship exam?!' Angela exclaimed. 'Who's put you up to this?'

'No one,' Connie said emphatically. 'So don't think it. There's more to it than stamping books at the counter. I tried to talk about things I did at the library, but you never seemed that interested. I know you've had your heart set on me going to university, but I love working in the library. And Mammy, I think I'm good at it too.'

Angela knew herself she hadn't taken much interest in what Connie was doing at the library. It was small wonder she hadn't discussed this exam with her, but there was still the promise she had made to Barry. 'Your daddy . . .' she began, but Connie cut in.

'I know he was determined for me to get a good education. But from what you tell me of my daddy, he would have wanted me to have a good job, one I would be happy doing. If he was here now, don't you think he would support me, wanting me to continue my studies and take the librarianship course?' Connie paused. 'Shall we see if I pass the exams I need first, and then you can see how you feel about it?'

Angela nodded her head, 'That's fair enough.' This idea might stop Connie thinking and worrying about her recovery, so she supposed it could only be a good thing. 'All right,' said Angela. 'Your daddy wanted your happiness above all else, so you work as hard as you can for this exam, and I wish you the best of luck with it.'

'You mean it?'

'I mean it,' Angela said. 'I want only your happiness too. When I thought I had lost you, I knew my reason for living was gone, and I'm sure I'd have your daddy's approval when I say, "Go for it!"'

And then Angela put her arms around her trembling daughter's shoulders and held her tight as she wept.

'Connie darling, there's no need for so many tears,' soothed Angela. 'Maybe this is all a bit too much too soon, after all you've been through?'

Connie shook her head and tried a weak smile. 'It's just nice to be able to talk to you properly, Mammy,' she whispered. 'There were all those years when you wouldn't talk about the past, and now . . . now I know why you clammed up every time it was mentioned. It was because of what happened . . . because of Chrissie, wasn't it?'

Angela nodded. 'It was such a shameful thing to have done, Connie, and although I told myself I did it for the right reasons – for you, for Mary, for your daddy – I could never forget that tiny baby lying all alone. And now, while it's wonderful having her back in my life, I worry about how *you* are feeling as well, about having a brand-new sister?'

Connie didn't know what to say; she wasn't used to her mother being quite so open about her thoughts and feelings. But Connie was a truthful and kind girl and decided that honesty was the best policy. 'Mammy, to tell you the truth, I wasn't sure exactly what to think to start with. I love Chrissie, she's such a sweet girl, and I couldn't think of a better half-sister. But it does feel strange knowing that I'm not your only daughter any more.'

She paused, then gave Angela a much more convincing smile, and carried on: 'But I'm determined to think of it only as a positive thing. I've had you to myself for all these years, and what a great mammy you've been! And now I have the sister I've always longed for. We're going to be best friends, just see if we aren't. I've got someone to pass my favourite books on to, and someone else to really talk to. So aren't I the lucky one?'

Angela nodded, a lump in her throat, with her tears threatening to spill this time. She put her arm around her daughter and said, 'Connie, I'm so proud of you, and I always will be.'

'Right, enough of all this heart-to-heart stuff!' said Connie. 'I've got exams to revise for!'

'Go on then,' said Angela. 'I know you'll do me proud and become the best librarian Birmingham has ever seen!'

So throughout the spring of that year, though Connie worked on getting physically better, with her mother's help, she also did the studying the teachers had given her to prepare her for the librarianship exam. Eileen was able to help her there, and was more than glad to do it.

In the summer the hospital made special arrangements for Connie to take the first exam, the first step in becoming a chartered librarian. She also had the first of many operations she was scheduled for. It was a complete success, and she was also delighted to learn that she had passed her first exam with flying colours. Both of the librarians came to see her to extend their congratulations and talked to Angela for a long time about Connie's future. Everyone agreed that the distinguished pass was an amazing achievement, given all she had gone through. Connie, a little embarrassed by all the fuss, did appreciate their kindness to her.

Chrissie was visiting one day, when Connie noticed her looking troubled.

'What is it?' asked Connie. 'You know you can tell me if something's worrying you. That's what sisters are for, so we might as well make the most of us both now having one!'

'Connie, your mammy asked me if I wanted to move into your house with you both? And while that is so kind of her to ask, I know that in my heart of hearts I want to stay with Eileen and Father John. They are like family to me, the only family I've ever known. And while I want more than anything for you and your mammy to become my family too, I don't want to turn my back on two of the kindest people I know.'

'I think Mammy imagines you will move into our house

and play happy families, as if nothing had happened to separate us all for years. But I know she'll understand if you explain it to her just as you've explained it to me. Really Chrissie, she'll just want you to be happy. I know she will. It's all she's ever wanted for me.'

'Thank you, Connie. Although I have to admit, I'm still nervous about telling her.'

'The sooner you tell her the better,' said Connie. 'You'll feel much happier when it's all out in the open. Mind you still come to see me as much as possible, though. I enjoy your visits almost more than anyone else's.'

'I take it I'm second only to Daniel,' smiled Chrissie shyly.

'Some things are best kept private,' laughed Connie, 'even between sisters!'

Chrissie knew Connie was right, and as she believed in doing unpleasant things straight away, she asked to speak to Angela. She brought Eileen along for support, should she need it. When she said she wanted to continue to stay with Eileen and Father John when Connie was discharged from hospital, she saw not only disappointment and hurt flood Angela's face, but also a flicker of relief on Eileen's.

Eileen had been afraid Chrissie would go to live with Angela when Connie came home, and she dreaded that happening because she loved Chrissie dearly. She had been fretting about it for weeks. 'Angela is Chrissie's natural mother,' Eileen had said to her brother one evening a few days before. 'If it came to it, any court in the land would agree to her living with Angela.'

'Let's hope it won't come to any court action,' Father John said. 'That would hardly be helpful for Chrissie's mental state. And the Bishop also would more than likely take a very dim view of it. Anyway, pulling her between you like two dogs with a bone is not seemly. Surely the best thing to do would be to ask *Chrissie* where she wants to live.'

Stan also knew what Angela wanted and saw her frustration, but he couldn't blame Chrissie. He hoped Angela would soon come to terms with it, and he said to her, 'Angela, this is real life. You have watched too many soppy films.'

'How can you say that, when I seldom go to the cinema?'

'All right, you've read too many romantic books.'

'What are you on about?'

'Look, Angela, it's only in fiction that people run into the arms of some long-lost relative. Real people have feelings of their own. You told Chrissie what she had probably wondered about for years – who her mother was and why she was left on the steps of the workhouse. She has forgiven you, or is trying to forgive you, but she barely knows you, and you can't expect her to turn her back on the people she loves, just because you have revealed to her that you are her mother.'

'You are so aggravating,' Angela said. 'Why are you always so reasonable?'

'I'm not always reasonable, as you well know,' Stan said. 'But you can still see as much of her as you want. Give the girl time, and she may even change her mind when she gets to know you better.'

'You don't think, whatever she said, she resents me for abandoning her?' she asked Stan fearfully.

'I don't at all,' Stan said. 'But it must have been a hell of a shock, and really it's bound to take her some time to come to terms with it.'

Angela knew Stan was right and shock could do strange things. It had been a shock for her when she realised Connie had heard the whole story she had recounted to Chrissie. She still wasn't quite sure how her relationship with her eldest daughter had been impacted by the revelations.

In actual fact Connie had only heard snatches and even those were a bit hazy. It was Chrissie who filled in the bits Connie had not been sure about.

Later Connie said to Chrissie, 'Was Mammy upset when you told her you would be staying with Eileen and Father John when I leave hospital?'

'I think so,' Chrissie said. 'She tried to hide it, but her eyes looked really sad. I felt sorry for her, but know I made the right decision.'

'I can quite understand why you decided that way,' Connie said.

'Sorry Connie,' Chrissie said, 'but you haven't the least idea.' Then her voice became an awed whisper as she went on: 'I sometimes think Father John and Eileen, particularly Eileen, saved my life.'

Connie might have laughed at the expression on Chrissie's face, but she didn't, for she saw Chrissie was deadly serious, and so she said, 'Surely not, Chrissie?'

'I don't particularly mean physically,' Chrissie said and added, 'though I don't remember ever feeling full in the workhouse, and I was nearly always cold. It was other things, though, that hurt more and probably were more damaging.'

Chrissie seldom spoke of her life in the workhouse and Connie had never wanted to bring it up, in case it upset her, but curiosity got the better of her and she asked, 'Like what?'

'Like people saying my mother dumped me on the workhouse steps because she didn't want me, because I was unlovable, and that meant no one else would love me either.'

'What a cruel thing to say to anyone,' Connie cried, 'particularly to say it to a child!'

Chrissie shrugged. 'You get to believe it if people say it enough. Eileen was cross when I told her. She loved me and told me often, but Eileen is so kind that I'm sure, given half a chance, she'd love the devil incarnate.'

'I don't doubt that for a minute,' Connie said, for as she had come to know Eileen better and heard what she had done for this orphaned child from the workhouse who turned out to be her sister, she thought Eileen one of the kindest women she had ever met.

EIGHT

Now that Chrissie had elected to stay with them, Eileen decided to take her into the Bull Ring to buy her some lighter clothes for the summer. It was their second visit. The first had been when Chrissie was very much still in workhouse mood and not at all sure of Eileen, so she kept her head lowered most of the time. Thrilled though she had been with the clothes, she had found it difficult to say anything and was glad that Eileen seemed to understand. This second visit to the Bull Ring was very different, and as they descended the incline Chrissie said to Eileen, 'Who's he?' and pointed to a statue of Nelson, standing on a plinth with metal railings around him and the whole thing ringed by flower sellers.

'Nelson,' Eileen said. 'He was a very famous and very brave sea captain and so he is honoured with a statue.' And she added, 'When we pass by, sniff the air, and it will be fragrant with the aroma of the beautiful flowers.'

Chrissie did just as Eileen said and thought she was

right, the smell was just magnificent. But neither of them had money to waste on flowers, so they wandered down the cobbled incline. Barrows piled high with produce of every kind lined the road.

Opposite the barrows was a shop called Woolworths. Eileen had told her that everything in it was sixpence or less, and in front of it stood an old lady. Her strident voice rose above the clamorous chatter of the customers and the raucous calls of the costers shouting out their wares. It was a woman selling carrier bags, determined to let everyone know about it as she cried out incessantly, 'Carrier bags! Handy carrier bags!'

'Been there years,' Eileen said in explanation to Chrissie. 'She's blind and every day bar Sunday, her family bring her here and she sells the carrier bags.'

'D'you think she minds?'

Eileen shook her head, 'Doesn't appear to. I should imagine she is looked after by her family and this is her way of making a contribution. The alternative, if her family couldn't afford to keep her, would probably be the workhouse.'

'Oh, I'd sell the carrier bags and gladly,' Chrissie said so fervently that Eileen smiled.

But then Chrissie's attention was taken by the models and hobbies shop next door to Woolworths. Chrissie gazed at the wooden models of planes, cars and ships of all shapes and sizes. 'People can buy kits inside to make the models themselves,' Eileen told Chrissie. 'And lucky young boys might find one in their stocking at Christmas time.'

Chrissie was enchanted by the man selling mechanical

spinning tops from his barrow. Seeing Chrissie's interest, he wound one up and set it spinning. 'On the table, on the chairs, the little devils go everywhere,' he chanted. 'Only a tanner!'

Chrissie clapped her hands with pleasure at the sight of the brightly coloured tops weaving all over the table, but she had to shake her head. 'They are lovely, but I have no money.' And Eileen had no money to spare either. Yet Chrissie had been so taken with them, Eileen decided one of them would find its way into Chrissie's stocking at Christmas.

'Now we are crossing the market to the Rag Market at the side of the church,' Eileen said. Chrissie nodded, and Eileen went on, 'Watch out for the trams. Some of them come hurtling round in front of St Martin's like the very devil, and there might be a fair few dray horses pulling wagons as well.' Chrissie took care as they approached the church. It was beautiful, built of light-coloured bricks with stained-glass windows set in ornate frames and an enormous steeple pointing heavenwards. There were iron railings surrounding it, though these were mainly hidden behind trees, and there were more flower sellers there.

And then they reached the Rag Market. Eileen bought Chrissie some summer-weight dresses and lighter skirts as well as some pretty blouses and cardigans. Chrissie was again so overcome with gratitude, she could again barely speak. Eileen understood and she saw tears standing out in Chrissie's eyes. To give her time to compose herself and also distract her a little, she led the way to the Market Hall, a very imposing building built in the Gothic style, with large arched windows either side of the stone steps. But Chrissie barely noticed the grandeur of it once she saw the men on the steps. She thought all of them were shabbily and inadequately dressed. Some had long threadbare coats which Eileen explained were the greatcoats given to the demobbed soldiers. Their boots were well cobbled, and they had greasy caps rammed on their heads, hiding most of their grey faces. All of them had trays around their necks selling razor blades or shoelaces or boxes of matches. 'Black or brown, the best in town!' chanted the man selling the shoelaces in a thin, nasal tone.

Eileen watched Chrissie covertly, but she said nothing till they were inside the Hall itself, where the noise was tremendous. Eileen had thought she might have been impressed by the building, knowing she would have seen nothing like it, for the ceilings were lofty and criss-crossed with beams, and poles led down from the beams to hold up the roof. High-arched windows lined one side with smaller arched windows at the ends, spilling sunshine into the Market Hall and lighting up the stalls of every description that lay before them.

However, all this was lost on Chrissie, who turned to Eileen and asked her who the men were and why they had been on the steps. When she explained that they were old soldiers who had no work, for many hadn't had a job since they had been demobbed from the army, Chrissie felt sadness envelop her.

She couldn't tell Eileen why the sight of the soldiers upset her so much, for she didn't like her mentioning the workhouse, but she had seen men in there with despairing, deadened eyes in grey, pinched faces like the men on the steps. Eileen might not have understood why Chrissie had been so saddened by the sight of the old lags, but she looked really downhearted, so the first place Eileen led her to was Pimm's pet stall. When they reached it Chrissie's mood lifted immediately, and she stared at the animals, enthralled. She'd never even come near an animal of any description before. The canaries twittered around them in their cages and she knelt down to look into the large boxes on the floor. One held mewling kittens that she stroked gently, and in the other one boisterous puppies tumbled over one another in their eagerness to get to Chrissie's hand, and she laughed when they nipped her fingers playfully. She saw fish swimming serenely around in large tanks with small stones on the bottom, and cuddly baby rabbits and guinea pigs in cages. There were very colourful small birds that Eileen told her were budgerigars, or budgies. People said they could be taught to talk.

Chrissie looked unconvinced. 'I bet they were kidding,' she said. 'Have you seen one of them do that?'

'In all honesty, I haven't,' Eileen had to admit. 'But people who have them swear they can.'

Chrissie remained sceptical and Eileen laughed. 'It does seem unbelievable, but parrots do, of course.'

Chrissie wasn't even sure of that. There was a parrot tethered to a bar outside the shop and as they passed him as they left, he screeched out, 'Who's a pretty boy then?' Eileen's amused eyes met those of Chrissie, and they burst out laughing.

Outside the Market Hall the cacophony of noise had

decreased a little and there was an air of expectancy. Eileen said, 'They must be waiting for the clock to strike,' and indicated the wooden intricately carved clock on the wall edging towards ten o'clock. A tantalising tune played as three knights and a lady emerged to strike a bell ten times.

'Oh, isn't it just lovely?' said Chrissie.

'It is,' Eileen agreed. 'It's a pity the man who made it wasn't paid in full for it.'

'Surely that's wrong?'

'Of course it's wrong, but it happened,' Eileen said. 'The clock was placed in an arcade in Dale End then. They say the man put a curse on it. People say that's why the arcade failed to thrive, and now the clock is here.'

'I hope the curse has run out, if that's possible,' Chrissie said. 'And I hope the clock stays here for ages.'

'Not that we believe in curses,' Eileen said. 'Dale End failing to thrive had nothing to do with placing the clock there.'

'Of course not,' Chrissie agreed stoutly, but she had her fingers crossed behind her back as she said it.

Despite having seen people from all walks of life, Chrissie had had a truly magical day. She and Eileen went home from their day's shopping exhausted, but happy.

A couple of evenings later, as Angela and Stan sat together before the fire, Stan put his arm around Angela and held her close as he said, 'So have we stopped worrying about our respective children, who seem to be doing all right as they are anyway? Do we have time to concentrate on ourselves for a change?'

'Ourselves?'

'Yes, us – you and me,' Stan said. 'And now I have a present for you.'

'You don't have to give me presents, Stan.'

'This is special,' Stan said, withdrawing a small box from his pocket as he spoke.

Angela took it from Stan with hands that shook. As she took the lid off, she saw that nested on a bed of cotton wool was a silver locket on a silver chain that looked exactly the same as the original one.

Angela looked at Stan with eyes that shone. 'How?' she asked.

'Well, I had it in my mind for a while, and I have a mate in the Jewellery Quarter who said he could make a replica of anything if he could have a look at the original. I had to enlist Eileen's help, as the only time Chrissie takes off her locket is when she goes to bed. Eileen smuggled it out of her room as she slept, and my mate took some drawings and measurements, and this is the result.'

'It's magnificent!' Angela said, holding it in her hand.

'Look inside,' said Stan.

Angela pressed the clasp and the locket opened to reveal a miniature of the wedding of her grandparents, taken from the photograph that stood on her sideboard. The other side, however, was empty.

'This locket is about love,' she said. 'My mother gave me the locket to show me that though I loved Mary dearly, I also had a mother who loved me, though she couldn't look after me. And I gave Chrissie the locket for the same reason. This one will go to Connie on her wedding day with locks of my hair in it, to tell her how much I will always love her too. If you hand me my sewing box, there are scissors in there and I will cut off some of my ringlets, and I have some pieces of ribbon in there too.'

'Shall you mind cutting off your ringlets?'

'Of course not,' Angela said. 'It's just hair and will grow again, and it might matter to Connie to have the locket complete. But don't tell her, I will give it to her on her wedding day.'

'I'll not say a word, never fear,' Stan said, giving the sewing box to Angela. He watched as she hacked off three of her ringlets and tied them with a red ribbon. She held the closed locket in her hand and thought it was like a talisman. A guard against evil. It was a sign that all their troubles were behind them and they were all entering smoother waters.

Although more people now knew about the circumstances of Chrissie's birth and her incarceration in a workhouse, Angela still was reluctant to share it with all and sundry. She was a little astonished when Chrissie suggested telling Bobby, who had been another regular visitor to see Connie in the hospital.

'Why does he need to know?' Angela asked.

Chrissie shrugged. 'Oh, I don't know. I thought maybe it would help him to understand our complex relationships.'

'I still don't think that's a good enough reason to divulge family secrets.'

'Maybe not,' Chrissie said. 'But he helped save our lives

and I thought that sort of gave him the right to know. Anyway, surely the time for keeping secrets is past, especially as that's what caused so much trouble in the first place. I know it had to be secretive then, but I always think it is better to be open about things, as far as possible.'

Angela relented. 'Oh, tell him then if you must,' she said.

Chrissie did tell him, the whole story as she knew it. He listened intently, but was silent when she finished. He couldn't speak straight away, because he had heard the hurt and shame in Chrissie's voice as she recounted the degradation and cruelty she had experienced in the workhouse. He knew how the children growing up in such establishments were looked down on by ordinary people, and he had always thought it unfair, because it wasn't their fault they were there. He had always put the blame on their parents, primarily their mothers, but now he had to revise that, because it was not Angela's fault that she found herself having a baby at all. He wasn't totally sure of the mechanics of it, but he knew those drunken soldiers had attacked her in a way that resulted in her having a baby. Bobby also knew that while people looked down on children from the workhouse, their condemnation would be far worse for a woman having a baby with no husband, especially if the woman's husband was overseas in the Forces. Angela must have been desperate and very frightened when she found she was having a baby.

'Say something, Bobby, for goodness' sake. What are you thinking?'

Bobby sighed, 'What I am thinking,' he said at last, 'is

that it's a dreadful shame. You suffered in that awful place and Angela suffered because she had to put you there, yet both of you were completely blameless. The ones responsible were the drunken soldiers that attacked Angela, and they got away scot-free.'

'Oh yes,' Connie said. 'They were revolting and disgusting and yet . . . Oh, Bobby, one of them was my father.'

'Yes,' Bobby said. 'Just another thing you are not to blame for. No child can help who their parents are. Some fathers, in particular, often have a habit of not being around much. I think real fathers are the ones who care for you and look after you, whether they are your proper father or not.'

'Like Father John,' Chrissie said and added, 'he never will be a real father and yet he's been a first-rate one to me.'

'Good, and at the end of the day, that's all that matters,' said Bobby, and Chrissie nodded in agreement.

Angela sat by Connie's bed the following day, watching her chest rise and fall, and remembered Bobby describing Daniel and Connie as sweethearts, and Stan explaining them going out a few times, and she was a little surprised how little it mattered any more. She had come close to losing Connie, and she had still a long way to go until she was completely better again, but that was all that mattered. Everything else had to take a back seat.

She took Stan's words on board about getting to know the daughter she had given away, and once she was certain Connie was sleeping, she tried to talk to Chrissie. She found it hard going at first, for anything she asked her, she answered with brief, terse replies, so it was like an interrogation rather than a conversation. That also was a throwback to her days in the workhouse, where warders didn't encourage inmates to chat and she had swiftly learnt to answer anything she was asked as succinctly as possible.

She also thought it strange for her mother to ask questions she should know, things Eileen would most certainly be well aware of. 'Give her a chance,' Eileen said when Chrissie sought her out to complain. 'Through no fault of her own she wasn't able to know the child John and I grew to love so much. She will never be able to reclaim those years, and I am sad when I think of that. She wants to get to know you now, and that's not a bad thing, so why don't you help her out a bit?'

'How?'

'Tell her about yourself,' Eileen suggested. 'Tell her about what you like to do, the subjects you like at school and those you don't. About your teachers and your friends. Build a picture for her of your life so far.'

'About all the years in the workhouse?'

'That's entirely up to you and Angela,' Eileen said. 'If you want to tell her and she wants to hear, then that's fine, but you may prefer for her to hear about the girl you are today and your plans for the future.'

'All right,' Chrissie said, 'I'll try.'

She knew, however, she wouldn't share what she wanted to do in the future, for the only thing she wanted to do was train to be a teacher like Eileen. She also knew there wouldn't be money enough to keep her at school to do her highers and then to stay on to college for three more years, so she would keep her ambitions to herself, and certainly not share them with this woman trying to be a mother to her. But because Eileen wanted her to make more of an effort, to meet Angela halfway as it were, she started talking more to Angela. She started by describing the magical eleventh birthday that she had spent in Father John's house, where she'd had a present, and Eileen had made a cake, and the whole day felt special, as if it belonged to her somehow. She told Angela about her baptism, her First Communion, and school, which she thoroughly enjoyed.

'Eileen tells me you're a very clever girl,' said Angela.

'I'm not sure that's true,' Chrissie said. 'They always said I was stupid in the workhouse.'

'Seems to me they spouted a lot of nonsense in that place,' Angela said angrily. 'Tell me, Chrissie – who do you think is more likely to tell the truth, the workhouse warders or Eileen?'

'Why, Eileen of course.'

'Well, Eileen says you're a clever girl, so that must be the truth.'

'Maybe she's just a really good teacher,' Chrissie said.

Angela heard the wistfulness in Chrissie's voice and said, 'I'd have said she was a good teacher, all right, for she's done a first-rate job on you, but even a good teacher has to have good material to work with.' And then, remembering the wistfulness in Chrissie's eyes, she added, 'Is that what you want to be, a teacher like your Aunt Eileen?'

Chrissie looked at Angela, horrified. She'd intended never

to say that to anyone, and certainly not this woman she still didn't trust at all.

Angela smiled. 'It was the look in your eyes that gave it away when you were talking about Eileen teaching you.'

Chrissie sighed. She couldn't fight this, for she had no control over what her eyes were doing, and so she said, 'All right, so what if I do? This has got to be a secret.'

'A secret from who?'

'Aunt Eileen. Well, everybody really, in case she gets to hear.'

'But why?' Angela cried. 'I'm sure she'd be delighted.'

'No, she wouldn't,' Chrissie maintained. 'She'd be upset.'

'Why on earth would she be upset?'

'Because I know she can't afford for me to stay on for those extra years at school, let alone the college fees and books and things. I don't want her scrimping and scraping, trying to afford it and likely going without herself. So it's better she doesn't know what I want to do.'

Angela was silent when Chrissie finished, for she knew every word she said was true. Chrissie had a good grip of the situation at home. But Angela also knew she could get the money to fund Chrissie's education, by selling her jewellery in the bank. She had always earmarked it for Connie to go to university, but she wanted to go in for librarianship, a course that the librarians had explained would be funded by the library. She knew, though, she would have to break her word to Chrissie and discuss it all with Eileen first.

A few days later Angela called to see Eileen. This was unusual, but Angela didn't dislike the woman and anyway, she knew how much she owed her. Eileen made tea and as soon as the cups were before them Angela said, 'Pardon me just calling like this, but I thought . . . I wondered . . .'

'What is it, Angela? Why are you so agitated?'

'I think you may think me presumptuous. Plus, I'm just not good at talking about the past. I suppose I had to keep quiet about so much to protect others, as well as myself. I was afraid if I began raking up memories, I might let something slip. For example, Mary started to tell Connie things and one day she mentioned the locket.'

'The locket?'

'Yes, the one that hangs around Chrissie's neck.'

'She is very taken with that locket,' Eileen said.

'Maybe that was because that locket was the only thing she had from me,' Angela said, and at Eileen's quizzical look she went on: 'My real mother left that locket with Mary McClusky when Mary took me in to live with them to escape the TB my siblings were suffering from. When they all died, along with my parents, I stayed on living with the McCluskys, and Mary gave me that locket when I married Barry. I put it in Chrissie's hand when I left her on the workhouse steps. It should by rights have gone to Connie, but Chrissie was being deprived of so much, and it was all I had to give her.'

'Tell Chrissie that, just as you told me,' Eileen advised. 'She'd like that. She really wants to get to know you.'

'I will one day,' said Angela, 'but what I really came to ask you was, if you would tell me how you came to take Chrissie from the workhouse, and what sort of child she was then? Just as she wants to know me better, I need to know her story too.' Angela continued, 'So I would be interested in hearing anything you have to tell me.'

'John was in the workhouse that winter's night when you left the baby,' Eileen said. 'He was there when they uncurled her hand and saw that she was still holding the locket. Masters, the superintendent at the workhouse, told him families sell everything saleable to prevent them going into the workhouse, and that children seldom arrive with anything even remotely valuable.'

'I am surprised they let her keep the locket,' Angela said. 'Many times afterwards I thought I had been stupid to leave it with her.'

'Well, they didn't let her keep it as such,' Eileen said. 'Masters took charge of it because some of the trustees wanted to sell it and use the money for Chrissie's keep, but he opposed that. John said he is quite decent, for a workhouse superintendent.' Then she lowered her voice and said, 'Not even Chrissie knows this, but when she first came to live with us, the locket was missing. We were very upset about it and the only good thing was that Chrissie knew nothing about it.'

'Had someone taken it?'

Eileen nodded her head. 'A dishonest employee,' she said. 'He'd taken it and pawned it and pushed the pawn ticket into a hole he had bored in his mattress. Then when the convalescence ward at the hospital was set up in the aftermath of the Great War, they needed more beds and asked the workhouse if they had any spares. The bed belonging to the man who stole the locket was nearly thrown to one side because the mattress was torn and packed with paper. Closer examination revealed the pawn ticket!'

'I'm so glad you got it back.'

'Oh, so were we, for Chrissie's sake really,' Eileen said. 'When we gave it to Chrissie and told her that her mother had left it with her when she left her at the workhouse, she was speechless, overwhelmed that she had something that might have belonged to her mother.'

'I remember feeling that way when Mary gave it to me,' Angela said quite wistfully as she recalled the love Mary had freely given her as far back as she could remember. And she realised Eileen had done that for her daughter. 'Thank you for rescuing Chrissie from the workhouse. I don't think I have ever thanked you.'

'Don't worry about it,' Eileen said. 'You've had a lot on your mind. But back to the necklace, I think Chrissie hoped there would be some clue in that locket. She really wanted to know two things: Why, in her eyes, you didn't want her; and why you left her on the steps. "I often felt like a bag of washing from the laundry," she once said to me, "that comes every week and is left on the steps in a wicker basket, just as I was."'

'Oh, how unloved she must have felt,' Angela said as another pang of guilt smote her heart.

'The workhouse staff don't think love is necessary to be doled out along with the sparse, inadequate food they are given,' Eileen said. 'It's wrong, of course. Love was something we gave a lot of to Chrissie when she came to live with us. If you are loved as a child, you feel you are worth something, valued. Unless you know that, why would you try to make your life better? In fact, what would be the point of anything?'

Angela shook her head helplessly as she imagined her child growing up behind those grim walls – unwanted, unloved, totally uncared for. She realised Stan must have felt that anguish too, being forcibly separated from his son for years. She remembered how overjoyed he was when they were reunited and could make up for the years they had missed out on.

'We couldn't adopt Chrissie in the normal way,' Eileen said. 'As you said, that's never done, but people do sometimes have a girl brought out to help them in some way. It's seen as a good thing, a sort of training for going into service, which is all the workhouse children are deemed fit for – the girls, at any rate. The average age to take a girl out is usually twelve.'

'Chrissie wasn't twelve, though, was she?'

'No,' Eileen said, 'we couldn't wait until she was twelve because the workhouses were closing, with the children being sent to any orphanages that had space. That could have been anywhere in the city, or further. As I said, John kept a surreptitious eye on Chrissie and didn't want to lose touch altogether, so he suggested we take her into our house. Both of us wanted to give at least one of the children the chance of a better life. Of course, we couldn't get her out using that as a reason, for no one does that. People might have become suspicious, so John said that my arthritis was bothering me and we wanted a young girl to help me. Chrissie was then almost eleven. I don't know how John squared that with his conscience, because he is a stickler for the truth.'

'But you do have arthritis?'

'Yes, but it's not bad all the time. Anyway, Chrissie was nearly eleven and had three more years at school.'

'At least you gave her the chance of some proper schooling,' Angela said. 'I don't know for sure, but judging from the way the workhouses are in providing adequate food and clothes for the children, I wouldn't have said educating them was high on their list of priorities.'

Eileen smiled. 'And you are so right,' she said. 'However, I didn't send her to school initially. I taught her at home.'

'Oh,' Angela said, for she hadn't been aware of that.

'I am a qualified teacher,' Eileen said. 'And I didn't want to subject Chrissie to the rigours of school until she had more flesh on her bones and adequate clothes for the weather. Also, though your daughter is far from stupid, as you presumed, any education she got at the workhouse was very basic. I also didn't want her to be too far behind her peers. There was no need for her to be, because she is a very bright girl.'

'I know you encouraged her to go to the library, for Connie often saw her there,' Angela said. 'Is she still as keen?'

'Oh yes,' Eileen said. 'And she told us about your daughter too, though of course we didn't know whose daughter she was then, and Chrissie just called her the girl with the golden ringlets.'

'And the girl that she was so drawn to is her sister,' Angela said. 'That might take some getting used to, for both of them.'

'Yes,' Eileen agreed. 'But it's lovely, and I am sure that one day they'll be the best of friends.' And she went on to tell Angela of the places she had taken Chrissie in order for her to gain new experiences that she could maybe share with her peers when she did start attending school.

Angela listened to all the things Eileen had done for her daughter with tears in her eyes and eventually she said, 'Eileen, you have floored me, and I really don't know how to thank you.'

'There's no need,' Eileen said. 'I enjoyed it.'

'But . . . but I was even selfish enough to feel upset because you seemed to know more about my daughter than I did. I had no right to feel that at all.'

'I've never had a child of my own,' Eileen said musingly. 'I never felt the lack, for I was almost grown when John was born and I helped my mother rear him and loved him dearly. Then I met my husband and began to look forward to welcoming our own family, but before we could do that he was killed in the Great War. Then I heard John's cook and housekeeper had left to work in the more lucrative munitions factories, and I was glad then I had no children to see to, because I was able to come and look after my brother. But when John brought Chrissie into the house, I looked at that scrawny, undersized child – so nervous, terrified of putting a foot wrong and getting into trouble – and something twisted in my heart. Angela, Mrs McClusky, I love your daughter as if I'd given birth to her. But she is not my child and I do understand any bitterness you might have towards me. I have loved your child too much.'

Angela suddenly felt immensely sorry for Eileen, who had been robbed of her husband and children of her own, and yet she didn't appear to feel sorry for herself. Angela recognised that she was a selfless and compassionate woman, willing and able to open her heart and her home to a destitute, abandoned waif from the workhouse.

'Eileen, you are too gracious,' Angela said. 'You cannot love a child too much. Love is expandable. When you have your first child, you love that child with all your heart, and when you have a second child you love them too, but you don't love the first one any less. Chrissie has chosen to live with you now, which is perfectly understandable.' She hesitated and with a sigh went on: 'Eileen, I'm breaking a confidence telling you this, but I think you ought to know, for it concerns Chrissie. But I'd rather she didn't know I had shared it with you.'

'Mrs McClusky,' said Eileen, 'though it is John who hears confessions, I am often trusted with many secrets from women of the parish, and I never reveal these to anyone. So Chrissie will never know what we speak about this day.'

'Right,' Angela said. 'Do you know Chrissie would like to be a teacher like you when she grows up?'

'I did think that at one time,' Eileen said. 'But when I asked her, she said definitely not.'

'She said that because she didn't think you could afford it.'

'She's right,' Eileen said. 'It would be a real struggle to. I thought of maybe getting her into a secretarial college somewhere.'

'She wants to be a teacher like you,' Angela said to Eileen, 'and I could fund it, if . . . if you wouldn't mind.'

'Why should I mind something that helps Chrissie?' Eileen said, although secretly she did mind very much. She didn't begrudge all the years of providing for Chrissie, but she felt resentful that her natural mother could now pop up and give Chrissie her heart's desire, when Eileen couldn't. *What a daft attitude!* thought Eileen to herself. *Stop being silly and just think about Chrissie.*

Angela heard Eileen's words but watched her face as she fought to control her conflicting emotions. She said gently, 'You don't think I am doing this to buy Chrissie's affection?'

'Well, aren't you?'

'No,' Angela said. 'I couldn't do that if I wanted to, for it's you Chrissie loves like a mother, and that will never change.'

'If you don't mind my asking, how do you have the money to pay for Chrissie's education?'

Angela told Eileen about the jewellery her old employer, George Maitland, had gifted to her. He had put it in the bank for safe keeping. The bank manager had told Angela the jewellery had belonged to Mr Maitland's mother and he was leaving it to Angela as a personal gift, totally separate from his will.

'Such a kind man, he must have been,' Eileen said. 'And yet you have no idea of the value of the jewellery?'

'None at all,' Angela said. 'The bank manager said there were some nice pieces amongst it, but he admitted he was no jeweller. He has since offered to have them valued for me, and I am sure he will sell them for me if I wished him to.'

'And this money was to be for Connie?'

'Yes, for her education.'

'Have you told Connie of your change of plans for the money?'

'Connie doesn't need the money. She said as much.'

'But she knows about the jewellery?' Eileen asked.

'Yes, my mother told her.'

'They are, of course, your jewels, and you can give them to whoever you like. But I beseech you, please tell Connie of your change of plan. More than anything, I want Chrissie and Connie to continue building a strong, sisterly relationship. If Connie is left in the dark on this matter, it could disrupt that completely.'

'I shouldn't think Connie would object,' said Angela, who had been so excited about the opportunities she could provide for Chrissie, she hadn't given much thought to how Connie might feel about it all.

'You know your daughter much better than me, but she might feel a bit pushed out,' Eileen said. 'I know things between Connie and Chrissie are good just at the moment. Let's make sure we keep it that way.'

'You think I need to explain it to Connie in ways that she will understand, before I mention it to Chrissie?' Angela said. 'Yes, that's what I will do. Eileen, you are a very wise woman.

'And I still would like to get to know Chrissie a little better,' continued Angela, 'and I know you will help me do that, because you are that kind of person. We both love her, so with no jealousy or resentment between us, together we can watch over her as she leaves childhood behind and begins her journey as an adult, and both of us can take joy in it.'

Shortly after this, the doctors told Angela that Connie was able to come home. 'She'll have to come back often for physiotherapy, but we really think she will recover quicker at home, especially with all the support you seem to give her.'

Chrissie was visiting Connie when she received the news that she was to be allowed home, and she was thrilled for her sister. 'I'll still come and visit you, even when you're not in hospital, Connie, for you won't be properly back on your feet for a while, I wouldn't think.'

Feeling that she had cleared the way with Eileen, Angela wasted no time in asking Chrissie if she wanted to go for a walk one day.

'If Connie is coming home tomorrow, why don't you come over for tea on Friday afternoon?' she suggested. 'In fact, come a bit earlier, and we can go for a walk. It would be lovely to get some fresh air after spending so much time in this hospital. And then we three can all sit and have tea together.'

Angela was desperate to make up for lost time with the child she'd given away, but she was also aware that the best way to develop a relationship with Chrissie was to take it slowly. She had been so nervous the night before, fussing around Connie even more than usual in a bid to take her mind off it. Stan had noticed and tried to reassure her that it would all be okay, but Angela couldn't help the nerves. She had originally just thought of inviting Chrissie in for tea, but as Stan said, sometimes it was easier to talk when you were doing something else as well.

It was a bright day – cold, but sunny – and Angela and Chrissie set out at a leisurely pace. 'This seems a real treat, somehow,' Angela told Chrissie, 'walking just for the pleasure of it, not to deliver something, or buy anything.' *Chrissie is such a sweet-natured child,* thought Angela. Chrissie chatted away quite happily, answering Angela's questions and asking questions about the shops they passed.

Angela knew she should be thoroughly enjoying her company, and yet couldn't help but feel a sense of unease. It was the same guilt she'd carried for the last twelve years, she thought, that had churned her stomach every day and every night. Just because she had been reunited with Chrissie, didn't mean that all was forgiven and forgotten, but Angela didn't know how to even start making amends.

'Angela,' said Chrissie, after a while, 'is something bothering you? If you're not enjoying the walk, we can just go back?'

Angela stopped short. 'Oh no, Chrissie,' she said, 'it's nothing like that. It's just . . .' She broke off, not quite knowing how to carry on.

Taking a deep breath, she looked down into the wide, bright-blue eyes of her innocent young daughter and said, 'It's just that you've been through so much in your few short years, and everything – all the hardship, all the pain, all the sadness – is my fault, and I just wish I knew how I could make it up to you.'

Chrissie might be young, but she had a good head on her shoulders. Living with Father John and Eileen had shown her nothing if not the art of compassion. She and Angela started walking slowly again, both deep in thought. At last Chrissie spoke. 'Angela, what happened, happened. As I see it, we can continue on, always looking back and worrying about the past. But I know how guilty you feel, and you've told me time and time again how sorry you are. Yes, my life in the workhouse was appalling. But I'm not there now. Thanks to Father John and Eileen, I have the opportunity to have a much better future, and now, by coincidence, that future might also include you and Connie. Something that I'd like very much. Eileen always tells me that I can spend my life looking back at all that has happened, or I can make the most of what is still to come. So that's what I want to do. And . . .' she broke off and looked directly at Angela once more, 'I think maybe that's what *you* have to do too. I don't want every minute of time I spend with you or Connie to be shrouded in guilt and misery. That would be no fun for any of us.'

Chrissie stopped there, as if she wasn't quite sure if she'd said too much, and looked hopefully at Angela to make sure that her mother wasn't angry with her outburst.

Angela didn't know quite what to say. That so much sense could come from one so young made her marvel at this wise, sweet girl who had endured so much, but who seemed so determined to rise on top of it all. 'Chrissie, what you've just said is so brave and brilliant. I will try my hardest to stop harking on about the past. I suppose . . .' and here Angela had to choke down a sob, 'I know how proud I am to be able to call you my daughter, but what I'd like one day is for you to be just as proud to tell people that I'm your mother.'

Chrissie smiled and shyly held out her hand to take Angela's. 'From what I know about you, and all *you've* been through, and how you've raised Connie, who I adore, I think anyone would be proud to have you as their mammy.'

The tears that had been brimming in Angela's eyes threatened to spill over, so she said, 'Come on now, let's get away home and have a nice cup of tea. I want to show you some photographs of my family, and I know Connie will be waiting for us both, she so dearly loves to see you. I've been saving a pot of Maggie's homemade jam for a special occasion, and I think this could just be it.'

So Chrissie and Angela made their way home, their hands still linked. To Angela it felt like a corner had been turned. In no way did she want to replace Eileen in Chrissie's life, but if she could play another important role in giving the girl the support and love she needed to go far in life, then Angela was determined she would do it. She'd made enough mistakes in the past; this was one thing she was going to get right.

When they got home, Connie had laid out a real spread for them, and they all sat round the table talking and laughing. It felt, thought Angela, as natural as anything. Most heart-warming was sitting back and watching her two daughters, different as chalk and cheese, getting along like a house on fire. Their heads were bent together as Connie showed Chrissie how to play a simple card game she and Angela had always enjoyed when Connie was younger. The two were giggling away and Angela almost had to pinch herself. Never would she have been able to believe that she could feel so contented.

When Stan came in after work early that evening, he was delighted to see the three of them getting on so well. He had been worried for Angela when he'd headed out that morning, knowing how much store she'd set by this meeting going well. And it seemed it had been even better than he could have hoped.

When it was eventually time for Chrissie to head home, two of Connie's favourite books tucked under her arm, Stan said he'd see her back to Father John and Eileen's. Stan said to Chrissie, 'I hope you know that as far as I'm concerned, you're part of this family now, as much as you want to be.'

Chrissie linked her arm through his and gave it a squeeze. 'Thanks, Stan,' she said. 'I can't wait to get to know you and Daniel better. And thank you for walking me back, Eileen will really appreciate it. She always worries about me. Please say thank you to Angela again for such a lovely afternoon. Goodbye!'

Stan walked back to Angela's, thinking that this evening was the first time he'd seen the weight of the world, that had always been sitting heavy on the shoulders of the woman he loved, truly lift. He smiled. Maybe it was time he and Angela made things official . . .

NINE

Angela felt happier and more contented than she had been in years. Connie had begun her intensive physio, which left her feeling physically and emotionally drained on the two days per week when she was up at the hospital. But Angela was proud of how stoically Connie bore it, and she hoped to God nothing would happen to spoil the new life she could see unfolding in front of her . . .

One evening, as they sat together before the fire, Stan put his arm around Angela and held her close, and his voice grew husky with emotion as he said, 'Angela, I love you so much – more than I have words to tell you. Once I opened my heart to you and meant every word I said. And when all the confusion between us was over, you said those words of love were what you had longed to hear. Did you mean that, Angela?'

Angela took Stan's face between her hands, looked deep into his almost black eyes, alight with love, and said,

'Stan, I love you so much, it hurts. There are no words you could say in this world that would make me think less of you.'

'Angela,' Stan said, 'I confess, to my shame, that I began to love you when you were married to Barry. Obviously, I could not show my feelings or speak of them, especially as you gave me no indication that you felt anything more for me than friendship.'

'My, darling, darling Stan,' Angela said. 'We must tell the children how we feel about each other now.'

'Yes,' agreed Stan with a wry grin. 'But don't expect it to be news to them.'

'It hasn't been plain sailing for us,' Angela said and added with a rueful smile, 'it didn't start very well, did it? That day in the shop when I said we needed to talk, and you wouldn't let me speak . . .'

'I know,' Stan said. 'I was sorry about it afterwards, but I was frightened you were going to show even more of your disgust for the idea of me having feelings for you. Really, one of the reasons I took on the job clearing the bomb sites was to get away from you.'

That was news to Angela, and she said, 'Is that really true?'

'Oh, it's true all right. I know these people desperately need help, but there's plenty of unemployed men out there, and it hurts a man's pride not to be able to provide for his family. In fact, I felt guilty taking a job from one of them, but when you came in the shop that day, I wanted to show you how much I still loved you. But I thought the shudder showed your true feelings. If only we had spoken then, would you have told me about the abandoned baby, and so given a reason for that shudder?'

'Truly, I don't know,' Angela answered thoughtfully. 'Maggie asked me that and I couldn't really answer her either. What I do know is, if you hadn't felt driven to do something else to keep away from me, that ultimately involved our children, we might not be here, having this conversation now. In fact, we might never have met up at all. And though I would never wish any harm on my daughter or Daniel, I can't help but be pleased that we are together once more, and I think we should lose no time in telling them that.'

As Stan predicted, it was no surprise. 'Do you honestly think you're telling us something we didn't know already?' Connie said. 'I've known for ages how you really felt about one another, as has Daniel, though for some reason we didn't know, you refused to see that for yourselves.'

'Was it so obvious?' Angela asked them, laughing.

'I'm afraid it was,' Daniel said. 'It was worrying about you two that prompted me to get back into contact with Connie in the first place. We thought together we might think up some plan to get you two talking again, because the way you were acting was making everyone miserable.'

'Yes,' Connie agreed. 'That's how it began. And then we found we liked each other's company . . . Well, I liked being with Daniel.'

Daniel slipped his arm easily around Connie as he said, 'Do you imagine for one moment that I didn't feel the same?'

'I . . . I hoped you did,' Connie said hesitantly. 'We confessed a lot when we were buried together.'

Daniel drew Connie slightly away from where their parents were now chatting easily to one another. 'Do you feel differently now?' he asked quite anxiously.

'What do you think?' Connie said. 'I was afraid to tell Mammy, in case she forbade us to meet, as I knew how she felt about your dad. Doesn't that tell you how much I cared about you then and still care now? I told you how I felt when I didn't think we'd get out alive. But despite that, I meant every word then, and still do now.'

'Oh Connie,' said Daniel 'there's something I want to ask you, and I can't think of a better time than now, surrounded by the family we love. Will you do me the honour of becoming my wife?'

Connie's eyes opened as wide as they could. She couldn't believe that after all she'd been through, her heart would ever feel so full and so happy. 'Of course I'll marry you, Daniel!' she said. 'When we were buried in that shell factory, knowing you were lying by my side was the only thing that kept me going, that kept me fighting the darkness. You make me so happy, and I'd love nothing more than to be your wife.'

Daniel's smile was lost to her when he lowered his head to hers and placed the gentlest kiss on her lips. They broke apart, remembering where they were.

'My darling Connie,' Daniel said fervently, and snuggled Connie even closer.

Angela, catching sight of them, felt tears prickling behind her eyes. There was a lump in her throat as she saw the love light sparkling in their eyes. She knew that regardless of Connie's tender years and the age difference between them, Connie had met her soulmate. 'Have I heard that right?' she asked. 'Is there to be a wedding?'

Hearing the emotion in her mother's voice, Connie felt her voice wavering as she answered, 'Yes, Mammy. Daniel has just asked me to marry him.'

'Well, it sounds like congratulations are in order. Hey, no more tears!' Stan declared. 'I am here to care for all of us now.'

'Well, whatever it is you have planned to achieve that,' Connie commented wryly, 'you'd better put it into action straight away, because at the moment my mother is crying her eyes out.'

Connie was right. Angela faced them, and though tears trickled down her cheeks, her eyes were shining as she said, 'Happy tears, Connie.' And Connie hugged the mother she loved so much and sighed in happiness and relief. She hoped from now on, life would be smoother for them all.

Stan hoped so too, but there was one more thing he felt he had to get straight, so that night Stan sought Connie out as she tidied in the kitchen before going to bed and said, 'I know what you said in the room in front of your mother, but how do you really feel about the two of us getting together?'

'I thought you already knew that,' Connie said. 'Surprised you had to ask, really.'

'I hoped you felt all right about things, but really I had to hear it from you.'

Connie smiled, 'Well you've heard it from me. If you

want it spelt out, I think you and Mammy are made for each other.'

'Yes, but the thing is, I know what you thought of your father.'

Connie looked at Stan's face which was creased with anxiety, and she sighed as she assured him, 'Stan, I have never said this to Mammy, for I feel it might upset her, and don't you tell her I said this either, but I can't really remember my father.'

'You don't think I would try to take his place?'

'That's what I'm trying to tell you,' Connie insisted. 'He hasn't got a place, well not in my life, anyway. Mammy missed him sorely, I know, and Granny did too. Mammy would always consider my feelings before she agreed to marry you, because she's that kind of mother. If I had any doubts or misgivings, she'd talk it over with me, but she hasn't had to do that because I feel fine about the whole thing, and she knows I do.'

'I'm relieved about that, but I'd like to think your father would approve.'

'Well, we'll never know that for sure,' Connie said. 'So, let's look at what we *do* know. You were neighbours and work colleagues, and you thought enough of him to try and keep him out of the Great War. And when that failed, he died trying to save you. I think that says a lot about how the both of you thought of one another. I should say, if my father was not here to look after me and Mammy too, there is no one he would rather have doing it than you.'

'You don't resent me at all?'

'Not in the slightest,' Connie assured Stan. 'Never think that for a moment. Both you and Mammy have suffered loss and tragedy. Make Mammy happy, Stan – that's all I ask.'

'I will make it my life's work,' Stan promised. 'And your words have eased my heart.'

TEN

The following day the younger librarian, Miss McGowan, came to visit Connie at home. And though Connie was pleased to see her, she was surprised.

'Great result in your first exam,' she said as she placed a chair by the side of the bed and sat facing Connie.

'Yes, it was. I was very pleased.'

'You must have worked hard.'

'I find it easier to work when it's something I enjoy doing.'

'You still enjoy library work, then?'

'Yes, yes of course. Why do you ask? Am I doing something wrong?'

'No my dear, it's nothing like that, but you realise you have years of study ahead of you.'

Connie was confused. 'This was all explained to me at the beginning,' she said.

'You won't find it rather daunting?'

'No,' Connie said, 'I'm really rather looking forward to it.'

There was silence between them for a few minutes and then Miss McGowan said, 'I was talking to your mother yesterday.'

'Oh yes?'

'She wasn't too keen on you doing library work in the beginning, was she?'

'No,' Connie admitted. 'It was all tied up with a promise made to my father about educating me as much as I had the ability for. He died, you see, in the war, and I suppose she felt she had to fulfil that promise. It's very hard to fight, or even disagree with a dead hero.'

'What does your mother think of your career in librarianship now?'

'Oh, she's better about it, much better,' Connie said. 'I knew if I didn't make some sort of stand I might be pushed into something I didn't want to do. So I talked to her about Daddy and the promise she had made. I said it was a different world to when Daddy enlisted, and if he had survived the war he might well have supported me. She could see I was right, and she's fine about it now.'

'She also told me you were seriously courting, and I must say I was surprised,' Miss McGowan said. 'Are you seeing the young man you used to meet from the library sometimes?'

'That's right, Daniel Bishop,' Connie said, 'He's a teacher now at King Edward's High.'

'Only you seem rather young to be so serious about a boy?'

'Mammy was my age when she got *married*.'

'Yes,' Miss McGowan said. 'But you are not your mother. Your mother went to work at fourteen and gave her pay-packet unopened into your grandmother's hand. Her money helped pay for the rent, coal, oatmeal, candles, gas mantles and paraffin. She was lucky enough to work for George Maitland too, I believe. She told me that as well as her good wage he used to pack her a boxful of groceries every week. She said that without that food they would have been in dire straits.'

'She felt beholden, I suppose,' said Connie, 'because my granny wasn't even my mammy's real mammy. She was her friend's child that my granny took in when the whole family died of TB.'

'That's right,' Miss McGowan said and she paused, looking serious. 'Have you known this boy a long time?'

'Not that long really,' Connie said, 'though Mammy has known his father Stan for years before the war. Then the war came and Daddy and Stan joined up. After the war Stan sort of disappeared and Mammy thought he'd been killed too. Daniel was brought up by his aunt in Sutton Coldfield because his mother died just after he was born. Then Mammy found out Stan was not dead, and reunited him with his son, and I became friends with Daniel. We seemed to be just friends for ages, but when we were trapped in the shell factory, we found our feelings had changed to something more.'

Miss McGowan leant closer to Connie and her voice was low and gentle as she said, 'And what would you say if I was to tell you that if you were thinking about marrying Daniel, your career as a librarian would be over before it's even begun? That all the work you've done for those exams, the plans you may have for the future, would come to nothing?'

Miss McGowan could see by Connie's reaction that she hadn't considered that possibility.

Eventually, Connie said hesitantly, 'Is that really true?'

Miss McGowan nodded her head sagely and said, 'Only too true, I'm afraid. Do you think I'd come here to tell you a lie?'

'No, of course I don't think that, not really,' Connie said as she felt her dreams crash around her ears. 'It's just . . . well, I can't really believe it.'

'It's the law, I'm afraid,' Miss McGowan said. 'Why d'you think I'm still *Miss* McGowan?'

'Did you . . .? Were you . . .?'

'Yes,' Miss McGowan said, 'there was someone I was very fond of once, but then I realised that once we married, his life would go on as before but I wouldn't have the future I'd planned. He couldn't quite believe it when I turned him down.'

'Have you ever regretted it?'

'Sometimes,' Miss McGowan admitted. 'But if I'm honest, my real regret is not having a family. I'd have liked children. But I made my decision and now you must make yours.'

'Yes,' Connie said.

Connie thought about Miss McGowan's words over and over as she lay in her bed. She ate her tea without really tasting it and realised she needed to discuss this unexpected dilemma with Angela.

Angela saw her daughter's agitation straight away when she got back from work. She pulled a chair out, sat down at the kitchen table and took one of Connie's hands in hers and said, 'What's happened?'

Connie looked her full in the face and saw her eyes looking at her in concern. 'I can do one of two things,' said Connie. 'Now I have passed the initial exam, I can join the librarianship course, or I can carry on seeing Daniel and eventually get married, I hope. I just can't do both.'

'What are you talking about?' Angela cried.

'Just that,' Connie said. 'Libraries won't employ married women, or even have them on the course.'

'Who told you this?'

'Miss McGowan,' Connie said. 'She's the younger librarian. When you told her I was seeing Daniel seriously, hoping to get married, she came to tell me about the course restrictions, knowing I wouldn't have a clue. I just don't understand why.'

'Nor do I,' Stan said, who had been listening in from the doorway. 'When you think what the women did in the war, running the country, doing jobs and doing them well – and it was things few men thought they were capable of. Many people are saying now that if it wasn't for the women who made all the weapons, we might not have won the war, because no one can fight a war without the means to do so. And yet they still have an archaic rule like this! I'll check it out, but it's probably right if the librarian said so. I have a feeling there's a similar restriction on married teachers.'

'You must talk to Daniel,' Angela said. 'But what do you want to do?'

Connie shook her head helplessly. 'I don't know, Mammy,' she said. 'I love Daniel, and of course I'd like to marry him someday soon. But I also love my work in the library. I never thought I'd have to choose one or the other. But Miss McGowan said it's the law.'

'Ah well, that's it,' Stan said. 'I think it isn't fair and you shouldn't have to choose, but if it's the law of the land you have to obey it. Your mother's right, have a talk with Daniel. Are you seeing him this evening?'

Connie nodded her head, for Daniel visited every night, but that night she looked forward to seeing him with little enthusiasm, for she couldn't see any sort of solution and doubted Daniel could come up with one. Connie couldn't shake off her despondency.

Angela felt very sorry for Connie and the decision she had to make. Because of all she had gone through, Angela had decided to do all in her power to smooth the way for them, removing any objection she might have had to Connie seeing Daniel, and even having no outward objection to them marrying, despite any misgivings about Connie's tender age. She had come close to losing her daughter and so she intended to do everything she could to ensure she had a good and stress-free life.

When Connie told them what Miss McGowan had said, Angela was stunned. But she decided she would have no part in Connie's decision as to which road she should take. It had to be Connie's choice alone.

Later Daniel could feel anxiety running all through Connie when he took her in his arms. However, she didn't mention the most recent dilemma straight away, because Stan had also told her Daniel had no idea who Chrissie was, and Connie was surprised. 'But Daniel was at the hospital when Mammy told us everything.'

'Daniel was in a different part of the hospital,' Stan explained. 'I got him settled on a ward before I came to see how you were. Of course, you were ill yourself, so you might not remember much.'

'I remember it only in snatches,' Connie said, 'and even those are a bit hazy. But Chrissie filled in the bits I had not been sure about.' However, because Chrissie told her the bare facts without any of the emotion Angela had shown in the telling of it, Connie didn't fully understand the predicament her mother had been in, and was still slightly shocked by her behaviour.

She'd said to Stan, 'My mother abandoned Chrissie on the steps of the workhouse. Whatever the circumstances, she was a new-born baby and she just left her there! I was shocked, to tell you the truth.'

'When she heard the whole story, Chrissie forgave Angela,' Stan reminded her.

'I know,' Connie said. 'I didn't understand that either and when I asked her why later, Chrissie said, "It wasn't her fault, and she couldn't help it." But if you heard all that, why didn't you tell Daniel?'

'I don't really know,' Stan said. 'Initially I was concerned for Daniel. He seemed to have got away unscathed but he might easily have something wrong internally. When he was pronounced fit and healthy, you were not, and I was worried about you and how Angela was coping with it.

And then after that there didn't seem to be a right time. It was only this morning that I realised he knows nothing about it, and he's the only one in the family who doesn't know.'

'So you'd like me to tell him tonight?'

'Well, I think he ought to be told by someone. If anything is to come up in the future, he might feel it if he's the only person who's in the dark.'

'All right,' Connie said. 'Don't fret. I'll tell him.'

So when Daniel held Connie in his arms that evening, he could feel that something was wrong, and he held her a little way away from him and said, 'Connie, is anything the matter?'

Connie sighed. 'There is something I want to discuss with you, but first I'd like to tell you how Chrissie came to be my sister.'

Daniel had been curious about Chrissie because when he'd first made contact with the family, there had not even been any mention of Connie having a sister. He'd often wanted to ask Connie about it, but it never seemed the right time, so he was keen to hear what Connie had to say.

What he wasn't prepared for was hearing about Angela being attacked and raped one evening as she returned home late after delivering a consignment of shells to the docks, using a large truck to do it.

In the middle-class area of Sutton Coldfield where Daniel had been brought up, there had been a few babies born out of wedlock. He remembered one girl he had been very fond of. Her name was Rose, and she'd been small and pretty with black curls that framed her face and often bounced on her shoulders. She had big brown eyes that often sparkled in amusement, for she was nearly always happy and vivacious and fun to be with. Aged eleven, they went to different schools, but he would see her at Mass, and despite his aunt's disapproval he always considered this girl his friend. But then she suddenly changed and would barely bid him the time of day and scurried home from Mass, flanked by her parents. He couldn't imagine what was wrong, although he did note that his aunt and uncle never mentioned her name, and if he tried they changed the subject.

Nothing was discussed openly, but children are experts at surreptitiously listening in to conversations considered definitely not for their ears, and eventually the rumour reached Daniel that she was having a baby. He was stunned. He didn't know much but he did know that for an unmarried girl to have a baby was just about the worst thing she could do, and he wondered what she was going to do.

Rose was moved down South to her auntie's 'for a holiday', her parents said, and some months later she returned, though there was no sign of any baby. People said it had been put up for adoption, which was deemed the sensible thing to do, but she was not the same girl at all. Her face was sombre and her manner serious, without any sparkle in her eyes. Her friends fell away and Daniel imagined that, like him, they had been told Rose wasn't a nice girl at all, and it was not suitable for him to be friends with her or even to speak to her any more.

Two months after she returned home, she travelled to the coast and threw herself off a cliff into the sea.

Remembering all this, he asked Connie gently, 'You said your mother was raped. Was there a child resulting from this rape?'

Connie nodded. 'Chrissie was the result,' she said. 'So, she is my sister, though I didn't know this until fairly recently.'

'Is this your terrible secret?'

'Only part of it,' Connie said. 'Chrissie was due to go to a children's home and be adopted from there, but the home couldn't take her because they were full, and Mammy had nowhere else to turn and so she left Chrissie, who was just a wee baby, on the steps of the workhouse and ran away.'

Daniel was quiet for a moment, remembering Rose and how she had been treated by people she'd once known well. He also knew that while society condemned those who had a child out of wedlock, that condemnation would probably be increased tenfold if the child was born to a woman whose husband was a serving soldier who had been overseas for years.

Eventually, Daniel said, 'Your mother must have been very frightened and desperate to do that, but if she hadn't done it, what would have been the alternative?'

Connie was silent and Daniel went on, 'There was no alternative, darling. Angela did this to save all of you, and not just herself, for you would have all been tainted by a child born to a woman whose soldier husband was overseas fighting. Don't condemn your mother without thinking on that.'

'You know,' Connie said after a minute or two, 'I've never thought about what Mammy did in that way before.'

'Knowing your mother as I do,' Daniel said, 'I imagine she would have considered every possibility before deciding her best and only option was to abandon her new-born baby to the workhouse.'

Connie felt a little ashamed. Surely, she knew her mother better than Daniel did, and yet she hadn't really considered her mother's dilemma sufficiently. She had told Chrissie, the one person who needed to know, the explanations surrounding her conception, which led to her being left on the workhouse steps. But instead of feeling slightly ashamed of her mother, she should be proud of her bravery and resourcefulness in trying to keep everyone safe from the contempt of their neighbours.

ELEVEN

'So is that all you wanted to talk about?' Daniel said. 'Or is there something else bothering you?'

'There's just one thing. A big thing! Miss McGowan – you know, the young librarian?' Daniel nodded and Connie went on, 'Well, she came to tell me that if I ever get married, then I won't get on the library course or be employed by the library.'

'Hey, what's she got against me?' Daniel cried. 'I've barely spoken to the woman.'

'Oh, it's not you, Daniel,' Connie said. 'It's any man.'

'What are you on about?'

'Marriage, Daniel,' Connie said, and Daniel saw tears lurking behind the words that Connie flung at him. 'Doesn't matter that I passed their flipping exam, and with a good grade. There will be no place for me on the course, and no job at the library. Stan seems to think that applies to teachers as well.'

Daniel was stunned. He remembered back to his primary

school days. During his time there were a couple of teachers who married and never came back to the school. He'd been a child and so thought nothing of it. His secondary school was for boys only, and no female staff were employed, so the policy of employing married women or not hadn't arisen, but he could make a guess that the rules would be the same as those in the library.

Despite Daniel detecting tears lurking behind Connie's earlier words, he didn't realise how truly distraught she was and he said with a grim smile, 'So it's me versus the library, is it, and you have to choose which you love the most?'

Connie swung her head round and the eyes she fastened on him were flashing fire, and too late Daniel realised he had made a mistake. 'I don't see any cause for levity, when I have heard such bad news!' she snapped.

Connie remembered Miss McGowan saying she had refused a young man whose life would not change much on marriage, while she would have to give up the job she loved. Connie didn't know whether she wanted to go that far, for she loved Daniel very much, but it wouldn't hurt to let him think she might throw him over, and so she said, 'What would happen if our positions had been reversed and you had to leave your teaching job in the future, something you'd trained hard for, and loved – not because you're not good at it, but just because you got married?'

Daniel could see how unfair it was. 'I'm sorry, Connie,' he said. 'I know how hard you have worked to get where you are.'

'I'm glad you understand how upset I am and why,' Connie said. 'But a decision still has to be made, and the only logical one that I can see is cancelling our wedding.'

'Don't bite my head off,' Daniel said, 'but I think that's the only solution. You've worked so hard for what you have achieved and I think you have been very brave to decide on this course of action. But let's not talk of cancellation, it's mothers with children that may not be allowed to stay on in their jobs. We could postpone having a family. As soon as you're ready to, we'll go out and choose an engagement ring.'

Connie hadn't thought that far ahead. 'Can we afford a ring?'

'Of course,' Daniel said. 'We have been saving for our wedding. But we're too young to have children. I think we should wait.'

'How long?'

'About five years.'

Connie made a face, knowing it was true, although five years when you are not quite sixteen seems like a lifetime.

'You will need that much time to qualify,' Daniel said. 'You have two years at St Paul's doing highers, and then three further years doing a librarianship course, and then you will be a fully qualified librarian. All we can hope is that the marriage rule will be relaxed before you finish, or we could choose to make a stand and fight against it. I will support you all the way, I promise.'

'Eileen told me once the rules were relaxed a bit in the Great War.'

'We can hardly wish for another world war so you can work in the library,' Daniel remarked drily.

'Hardly,' Connie agreed. 'So many were killed. My daddy wasn't the only one who didn't come home. But at least there won't be any more wars, because they say that was the war to end all wars – I read it in the paper.'

Daniel didn't say anything to that, because he had heard some rumours of unrest and worse in Germany of all places, but he wasn't going to share that with Connie and maybe worry her unnecessarily. Instead he said, 'Best be off before they throw me out. Can I tell Angela and Dad about the news, or do you want to tell them?'

'Oh, you may as well,' Connie said, and added, 'and Daniel, I know Mammy and I were planning a double wedding. But since they have already been kept apart, for one reason or another, for some time, I think it's unfair to make them wait.'

'I thought that too,' Daniel admitted. 'Everyone will ask,' Daniel pointed out. 'They'll see the ring on your finger.'

'I intended, for now, to wear it around my neck, as I don't want everyone to be talking about it just yet.'

'All right, if that's what you want,' Daniel said. 'I'm glad we've got a plan we're both happy with. And you *are* happy, aren't you, my darling Connie?'

'Oh yes!' replied Connie.

'Right, I'm glad we've sorted that out. But before I go,' Daniel continued, 'tell me how you really are getting on with Chrissie. Must be very strange to suddenly have a new sister?'

'It is odd,' mused Connie, 'but it isn't Chrissie's fault. Many times as I was growing up I wanted a sister. I envied my friend Sarah. Though she'd moan about her two big sisters, I could tell she loved them and missed them sorely when they left home when they went to work in the hotel. But Sarah had grown up with her sisters and that had to be different. The part I find the hardest is how Mammy is – how much she listens to Chrissie. She's always asking her questions, and takes an interest in every aspect of her life. I used to tell her things once about the library and stuff like that, but I stopped because she just wasn't interested. You asked me once where my mother thought I was, especially all those Sundays when we were out all day. Well, I never had to lie because she never asked, not even once.'

'You haven't told your mother how you feel, have you, Connie?' Daniel asked. 'It would really upset her to think you were this jealous, for that's all this is.'

'Tell Mammy – are you mad?!' Connie cried. 'I want the head left on my shoulders a little longer. And anyway, I am actually ashamed of how I feel, and I know I will have to put up with the situation anyway, like everyone else.'

Daniel was right – Angela had no idea Connie felt such mixed emotions towards Chrissie. But Chrissie had spent her young life watching people, so that she could almost anticipate what the warders might want before they made a request, which had helped her over the years to avoid a kick from them for being too slow. So she knew exactly what Connie was thinking and it saddened her. She tried to think up ways to make things better, for that would please Eileen as well as Angela.

Connie had finished a particularly gruelling physiotherapy session, and that evening Daniel had said he'd pick her up from the hospital in a taxi. He met her, and directed the taxi to the Jewellery Quarter, which wasn't far from the hospital, so that Connie could choose her engagement ring.

There were so many beautiful rings to choose from, Connie found it hard to decide, but eventually she chose a ring of rose gold with a central ruby surrounded by cut diamonds.

Daniel added a gold chain to thread the ring onto. As he fastened the chain around Connie's neck, he said in a low voice, 'This is my promise to you, that we will marry as soon as possible, and that this ring will grace the third finger of your left hand, where it will be joined by a wedding band.'

'Can't come soon enough for me,' Connie said, 'and just at the moment I can't wait to show the ring to Father John and Eileen.'

Father John and Eileen thought the ring exquisite and both said it was sensible to hide it from view for now, as they couldn't get married for years.

When they got home, Connie loved showing the ring to Angela, who thought it was simply marvellous. Angela thought she would tell Connie about the jewellery now, while the conversation with Eileen was fresh in her head. 'Granny told you about some jewellery that had been left to me, didn't she?'

'Yes,' Connie said. 'It was ages ago, and they opened the bank 'specially for you, so that you could see it, as you were working in shell production and your time off was almost non-existent.'

'And if I had sold the jewellery, what was I going to do with the money?'

'Fund my education,' said Connie, 'so my time in college or university would not be curtailed through lack of money. You said it was what Daddy wanted, so after he died you were even more determined.'

'But,' continued Angela nervously, 'now your librarianship course is fully paid for, I wondered what you'd think of my using some of that money to help pay for Chrissie to train to be a teacher. It's her deepest heart's desire, and I think you'll agree, she'd be very good at it.'

Connie was silent for a while; she honestly did not know what to say. But the more she thought about it, the more she realised that any reaction other than whole-hearted agreement would seem churlish. 'Mammy, I can't say the idea won't take a little bit of getting used to,' said Connie slowly. 'But I have had a loving childhood, I have the career I have always dreamed of, and I am in love with the man I was destined to be with. I am happy – and I think that's what I'd want for my sister too. She deserves a real chance in life, and between us all as a family, including Eileen and Father John, we have the opportunity to give her that.'

Angela's heart swelled with pride. This was the kind-hearted and generous daughter she had raised. With no words left to speak, she simply reached for Connie and held her tightly in a warm embrace.

TWELVE

Connie hurried as she got off the tram from the hospital early one evening, for sleety rain was falling. She was looking forward to reaching home, for home was such a pleasant place to come back to, now that Stan and Daniel were part of the family. Connie's love for Daniel got stronger every day and she felt happier than ever. Added to that, the physiotherapist had been delighted with the improvements she had seen. She had said that after two more sessions, Connie might be able to be signed off from the hospital altogether and could return to work.

Connie had been relieved to hear that. The library and college had been remarkably patient so far, but she didn't want to push her luck, and anyway, she felt time heavy on her hands now and wanted to be doing something useful. And so, Connie was in a buoyant mood as she returned from the hospital that night. She was surprised to see Maggie waiting in Bell Barn Road. 'Hello,' she said, turning her collar up with a shiver. 'Have you been to see Mammy?'

'No, no, I haven't seen her.'

Connie was puzzled. 'Then are you going to see her now?' she asked. 'Shall I tell her you're here?'

Maggie shook her head. 'No, it's you I really came to see.'

Connie was a little alarmed by that, especially as she noted how agitated Maggie was. 'Why? What is it?' she cried. 'Come inside, for we're both getting soaked here.'

Maggie shook her head but, seeing the sense of what Connie said, drew her into a nearby entry. She ran her tongue over her dry lips. She would have given anything not be here, delivering such news to Connie – such a young girl, who had already been through so much. Yet she knew it was better coming from her than anyone else, and so she said, 'I am sorry to have to tell you this, Connie, but Eddie McIntyre is back.'

Connie gave a gasp. She felt as if she had been kicked in the stomach by a mule. Her mind flew back to the time when her mother seemed to be so in thrall to McIntyre that she had almost forgotten she was a mother. McIntyre would urge her to drink, a thing she had never done before, so she would arrive home drunk and with her clothes in total disarray. Connie had been ashamed of her for the very first time, and even Maggie had spoken to her about it. Together they had tried to make Angela see sense before her reputation was ruined altogether, for people were beginning to talk. But Connie's words of warning to her mother fell on deaf ears.

Connie felt sick at the thought of all that carry-on starting again. But just maybe, Maggie was mistaken. After all, the man had been away years now. Why should he suddenly reappear now, after all this time? 'How d'you know he's back?' she asked.

'He came in the pub, large as you like,' Maggie said. 'I didn't see him at first because I was in the snug with Muriel, arranging . . . er, making plans . . .'

'If you are talking about arranging a party for me that's supposed to be top secret, don't bother,' Connie laughed. 'You can't keep secrets in this place – I'm afraid to say I know all about it.'

'Oh, what a shame! Sorry about that.'

'I'm not,' Connie said. 'I'm not that keen on surprise parties, to be honest. Anyway, I still think it's a lovely idea.'

'Initially it was to welcome you home, but your mother didn't think you were strong enough then.'

'I think she was right,' Connie said. 'Though I was fed up with hospital and wanted to come home when I arrived, I found I was as weak as a kitten and quite tearful at times, too. I'm much stronger now and well enough to really enjoy a party.'

'Good,' Maggie said. 'Anyway, Muriel and I were discussing this party, and I suddenly heard Eddie McIntyre's drawl on the other side of the door. He made my blood run cold. Muriel thought I had gone mad, as I was on my feet in seconds and threw open the door. Eddie was as surprised as me, but before he had time to recover, I yelled at him, "What are you doing here? Whatever it is, you're not welcome, so why don't you just sling your hook!"

'Course, Muriel had no idea what was going on and said, "Maggie, what's got into you? It is up to Noel and myself to decide who's welcome and who isn't, and as Mr McIntyre has done no harm to me or mine, he is as welcome as the next man."'

'You can't blame her,' Connie said. 'She wouldn't know anything about what happened.'

'And I couldn't tell her – not the whole of it – without casting your mother in a bad light,' Maggie said. 'So, what I came up with to explain why I had acted that way sounded very tame – certainly not behaviour extreme enough to bar someone! I felt such a fool.'

'What's he doing here anyway?'

'Well, I wasn't going to put myself out to speak to him,' Maggie said, 'but he had been drinking with some of the regulars, who are also unaware of his reputation. Seems he'd told them his uncle's business had been badly affected by the Wall Street Crash. You remember that some of the aftershocks were felt over here?'

Connie gave a brief nod and Maggie continued, 'Apparently when he was over here before he made a good impression on many factories and businesses, and his uncle wants him to regenerate the trade with those businesses, to get them out of the mire in the States.'

'Did he give any indication of how long he'll be here?'

Maggie shrugged. 'As long as it takes, I suppose.'

'I suppose so,' Connie agreed miserably.

'And you must warn your mother,' Maggie said. 'It'll

come better from you than anyone else – soften the blow a bit.'

Connie had no desire to share that news with her mother. After all, maybe if they kept their heads down he would do what he had to do and go away again, like he had before.

'Why say anything to Mammy at all?' she asked Maggie. 'She's not likely to see him.'

'Connie, she could meet him in the street. I don't know where he's living but he could have taken lodgings in any of the boarding houses not that far from here, just like he did last time he was over here . . . From what the men were saying, he has been here nearly three weeks already. We've got to do something before Angela bumps into him in front of an audience. You remember how much talk there was about her back then. The last thing she needs, now that she's finally found happiness with Stan, is for Eddie McIntyre to mess everything up for her once again.'

Maggie was right – Eddie had been in England three weeks. When he had first arrived, he'd kept well away from Bell Barn Road and Angela McClusky. Mindful of his uncle's threats, he'd concentrated on getting orders so that he would not be thrown out of his uncle's house and business.

He was pleasantly surprised by the reaction in many of the places he had revisited. He wasn't remembered personally but order books showed how lucrative the trade had been for both sides of the Atlantic, and a fair few were more than willing to re-establish trade links between

Britain and America, and keen to discuss further negotiations. So he was in a buoyant mood when he sent a telegram to his uncle telling him this. His uncle's reply gave him cautious hope that he might be taken back into the firm again on his return to New York:

WELL DONE STOP KEEP UP THE GOOD WORK STOP EARLY DAYS YET STOP

However, Eddie had no intention of keeping up *all* his good work. After a promising start in the UK, he decided to award himself a little treat. A working man needs some distraction now and again, he told himself, and Angela McClusky, when she was in the mood, was the best distraction he knew. Eddie knew better than to go at it like a bull at a gate, though, so first he loitered about the area for a few days, seeing if he remembered anyone who might also recognise him, but he could see very few familiar faces.

He approached the pub with greater caution. Before entering, he first made certain, by listening to overheard conversations in other pubs, that the previous publicans – the Larkins, who knew and despised him – had retired. The new landlord and landlady who had taken over from the Larkins made him welcome, and a surreptitious glimpse across the bar reassured him that there was no one in the pub that he knew well. He thought it a nuisance that he eventually ran into Maggie, but on the other hand, it was interesting to learn that she clearly hadn't shared their past dealings with the new landlords. He was able to glean from Muriel that there had been an accident involving Angela's daughter, and that they were having a party for her on Saturday in thanks for her recovery – all welcome! He couldn't believe his luck. He could legitimately see Angela and find out if she was as crazy about him as ever.

That evening when Maggie told Connie about the unexpected and unwanted arrival of Eddie McIntyre, she said to Connie, 'If he has arrived here now in these streets, there is only one reason, as far as I can see.'

'What?'

'I think he still has a hankering after your mother.'

Maggie wasn't far off the mark, but Connie didn't want to believe it. 'Surely not. Not after all this time.'

'Are you prepared to risk it?' Maggie asked. 'What if he was to knock at the door?'

'He wouldn't dare.'

'I wouldn't like to say what that man is capable of, would you?'

Connie thought for a moment and then said resignedly, 'No. Not really.'

'Tell your mother.'

'What about Stan?'

'Stan isn't your concern,' Maggie said. 'It's up to your mother to tell Stan.'

'Just when everything was going right for them at last,' Connie said. 'What if whatever Mammy tells Stan puts a barrier between them?'

'If they allow that to happen,' Maggie said grimly,

'neither of them deserves happiness, for they will have learnt nothing.'

Connie enticed her mother up to her bedroom as soon as she got in that evening, for she was afraid of McIntyre coming directly to the door, as Maggie had intimated he might. She pretended she wanted Angela's opinion on something she'd bought. 'What is it you want me to look at?' Angela asked, rubbing her hands together. 'We can't linger long, for these bedrooms are like iceboxes.'

'Mammy, I don't want your opinion on anything,' Connie confessed. 'I needed to get you away to tell you something.'

'What was it that you couldn't say in front of everyone?'

Connie didn't answer. Instead, she said, 'Maggie was waiting for me on the road when I came home from the hospital earlier today.'

'Maggie was?' Angela said. 'Why didn't she come to the house?'

'She said she wanted to see me, tell me something, so that I could break it to you gently,' Connie said. 'The only thing is, I don't know that there is a way to say this gently.'

'Tell me, Connie!' Angela cried frantically, worried by the look on Connie's face. 'For Christ's sake tell me.'

Connie sighed and said, 'Eddie McIntyre is back here.'

Angela felt as if all the breath had been sucked out of her body, and she felt for Connie's bed and sat on it, because she didn't think her legs could support her any longer. In her mind she saw the glorious future she was hoping to have with Stan crumble away like dust.

Connie held her shaking hand, but it didn't help Angela,

for the advent of Eddie McIntyre brought back a shameful period she would have liked to draw a veil over. She wanted to pretend it never happened.

However, it *had* happened. She had been shameless, and a terrible mother to her precious child, Connie, whom she had pushed from her mind. All she had cared about then was Eddie and pleasing him. She had been even more willing to do that when she had drunk plenty, as Eddie encouraged her to do. She was like a different person then, and one that Connie didn't like very much. And now Connie looked her full in the face and said, 'You must tell Stan.'

'No, I can't do that!' Angela cried, her whole mind recoiling from it. Not in any way did she want Stan involved in that smutty period in her life. She said, 'Stan doesn't need to know any of that. Anyway, how does Maggie know McIntyre's here?'

'She saw him in the pub.'

'Maggie doesn't go into pubs.'

'She was seeing Muriel about something, and McIntyre came in.' Connie remembered Maggie's words and said determinedly, 'Maggie said he has been here nearly three weeks already, and she thinks he has come to seek you out.'

'Surely not? Maggie must be wrong.'

'If she's wrong, there's no harm done, but if she's right . . . I mean, what if he came to the house?'

Angela shook her head. 'He wouldn't do that.'

'How can you be so sure?' Connie demanded. 'He meant you harm before, and don't deny it, because I saw his handiwork. Why would he make it easier for you now? What if he saw Stan in the pub and told him about the nights you both indulged in?'

'Connie, Stan is the man I love. I can't confess all that to him.'

'You can't *not* tell him,' Connie said emphatically. 'Not telling him, not confessing all, is the very worst thing you can do.'

'This could be my last crack at happiness,' Angela cried. 'How can I risk losing Stan by telling him about a period in my life that I wish had never happened?'

'You know Stan better than me,' Connie said. 'You'll know how to handle him, but I'd say you have a far greater chance of losing Stan if you allow Eddie McIntyre to get to him first. Immediately you'll be on the defensive then. Once before you didn't trust Stan. You must have trust in the man you intend to marry. Please Mammy, tell him.'

Angela saw her daughter's pleading eyes and knew every word she had spoken was correct. She inclined her head. 'I will tell Stan straight after the meal, never fear.'

'Promise?'

'I promise.'

In a sigh of relief Connie let out the breath she hadn't been aware she'd been holding. She knew now her mother would tell Stan, for Angela had never broken a promise. Connie felt strongly that honesty was the only way to cope with a slimy, lying creep like McIntyre.

However, for all the robust words she'd said to her mother, she too was nervous of Stan's reaction, for her future was linked with her mother's. Connie herself had no idea if she should tell Daniel, or how he would react either. But she felt she could hardly marry him without saying anything, because he might not wish to join such a disreputable family. Connie had no doubt that McIntyre would lose no time in spreading rumours about them all, and unfortunately there was absolutely nothing she could do about that.

THIRTEEN

Talk around the table once Stan had arrived home didn't touch on anything that Connie and her mother had spoken about earlier, but instead focused on the good news Connie had had earlier that day from the hospital. 'Soon have your nose to the grindstone, like every other body,' Daniel said with a grin. 'Not a lady of leisure much longer.'

'Yes, thank goodness,' Connie said. 'I am bored rigid at home, and anyway, I can't expect the library and college to wait for ever.'

'No,' Stan agreed. 'They have been very good, but remember, there's no point going back before the hospital's say-so, or you might end up having to take time off again.'

'Heaven forbid!' Connie said vehemently.

'I heard of a house just today,' Daniel said. 'It's in Edgbaston, not far from King Edward's High. It would be great for us, if we weren't delaying our wedding.'

'Shame, that is,' Stan said. 'I believe good houses aren't that easy to find.'

'I know,' Daniel said. 'In fact, rather than lose it completely, providing Connie is agreeable, I'm going to see if the owner would be willing for me to rent it, for now.'

'Mmm, the rent might be high,' Angela said. 'Could you manage that on your own?'

'Just about,' Daniel said, 'but it would be fairly easy to find a flatmate, or I'll take a lodger. Young teachers are always looking for places and don't usually earn enough to pay much rent.'

'Has it been so dreadful living with me?' Stan asked Daniel, but he was smiling as he said it.

'You know it hasn't,' Daniel said. 'And it's been a great way to really get to know you, but when you and Angela marry, Connie and I think you deserve a place of you own.'

'That's very considerate of you, Daniel,' said Angela.

'Yeah, I can be when I set my mind to it,' Daniel answered with a smirky grin.

'Come on,' Connie said, getting to her feet. 'If everyone's finished, we'll clear away. Give me a hand, Daniel, and if we're quick enough, we might go out and look at this house you heard of.'

'We'd need to make an appointment.'

'I don't mean inside yet,' Connie said. 'I just want to look at the house and the area.'

Angela guessed Connie was trying to give her and Stan time alone. Angela sighed, knowing she had to bite the bullet now, before her nerve failed her altogether.

Stan gave a rueful grin and said, 'Is it my fertile

imagination or was Connie a bit too anxious to leave the house tonight?'

Angela was going to laugh it off, saying Stan was imagining things, but she stopped herself. This was no time for flippancy or lies. To do this properly, she had to be straight with Stan from the beginning, so she said, 'She wasn't just anxious to leave the house. She really wanted to give us time alone.'

'Well, I'm not going to argue with that,' Stan said with a broad smile at Angela, 'but was there any special reason for leaving us alone?'

'Yes,' Angela said. 'It's because I must talk to you about something very serious – so serious that you might decide not to marry me when you hear it all.'

'I doubt that very much,' Stan said determinedly. He caught up one of Angela's trembling hands and held it tight. Angela swallowed the hard lump in her throat and began to tell her story. She would have liked to have glossed over what happened, but that wouldn't really have been fair to Stan. Nor would she make excuses for her behaviour, though she did say truthfully that she had been incredibly lonely, for she hadn't allowed herself to make many friends at the time when Connie had been busy with her schoolwork. 'I thought I knew this Eddie McIntyre,' she said. 'I mean, I had served him in the bar for months. He was funny and charming and very popular, but when he asked me out the first time, I refused him.'

'Why?'

'I don't know really,' Angela said. 'I suppose it was all mixed up with sort of betraying Barry. I mean, Eddie wasn't the only one to ask me out. Many did initially, but I refused them without a thought, because the majority were married men. I mean, I know a lot of their wives, but apart from that, married men are not available, in my book. Oh, I don't know . . . It was the Larkins – you know, they used to run the pub. Do you remember them? They urged me to go out with Eddie in the end. They said I was a young woman, and I should have a little fun in my life. They were sure Barry wouldn't begrudge me doing that. All of a sudden, I knew he wouldn't. He wasn't that kind of husband.'

'No, he wasn't,' Stan said. 'Barry truly loved you, Angela.'

'I know he did,' Angela said sadly. 'And I loved him too, with all my heart and soul. So why, feeling this way, did I fall hook, line and sinker for Eddie McIntyre?'

'Did you?'

Angela nodded her head. 'I did. I would like to say he forced me, because maybe I would look better in your eyes, but certainly he didn't. When I started drinking alcohol what he was trying to do didn't appear as outrageous as it had seemed when I'd been sober.'

'You mean you got drunk?' Stan said, for he had never seen Angela drink anything but lemonade. And at Angela's nod he cried, 'That man took advantage of you! It's obvious. Tell you the truth, I despise men like that. They go out of their way, plying girls with drink till they don't know whether they are coming or going, and then take advantage, and afterwards claim it's all the girl's fault. And perhaps they even threaten to tell others about it.'

Angela gasped. 'That's exactly what he did.'

'It would be,' Stan said. 'That's how they work. They are despicable, and you are not to blame.'

'But I didn't have to drink the alcohol. That's what Connie said.'

'Connie's young yet, and the world is black and white to the young,' Stan said. 'I know how easily these things can happen. I just want to ask you one question: Do you love me now?'

'Do you have to ask?'

'Humour me.'

'Stan, I love you with everything in me,' Angela said earnestly. 'If we had been friends, the episode with Eddie would never have happened. I want no other man while I have you. You are everything to me.'

It was enough. Stan's arms went round her, and she snuggled into him and sighed in contentment. Stan dared a kiss, and Angela kissed him back with a passion so deep and sensuous, he was taken by surprise but also filled with delight. The kiss told him clearly that Angela loved him as he loved her, and he bitterly regretted the barren years they had spent apart.

Angela was surprised that Stan seemed able to forgive her for drinking too much and allowing Eddie McIntyre such liberties and assaults on her body. She was very glad, though, that she had confessed all to Stan, for if Eddie did try to drip poison in his ear, nothing would come as a shock, because she had told him everything and found he still loved her in spite of it.

Stan wondered what Angela would say if he told her

that he too used to drink too much, to numb the pain of thinking he had lost her. Daniel had felt the rough edge of his tongue more than once and he hadn't exactly lived like a monk either. One day he would confess all this to Angela. He thought it odd that if people had been aware of his behaviour at the time, most would have shrugged their shoulders and not thought him any the worse because of it. It was monstrously unfair that many of those same people wouldn't feel the same if they found out a woman did these things.

Eddie McIntyre could have destroyed Angela, ruined not only her reputation, but also that of those connected to her, like Connie. The worst of it was, he couldn't seek this man out and trounce him for his behaviour towards the woman he loved, because if the police became involved, it could open a whole can of worms that could impinge on Angela. So if he was to meet this excuse for a man, he had to keep his hands off him, and while that stuck in his craw, he knew that's how it had to be.

'Connie, what's the matter with you?' Daniel asked as they found a seat on the tram as they returned from looking at the house.

'What you on about?'

'You. Don't bother saying "nothing's wrong", because you have been peculiar ever since you came home.'

'You're imagining things.'

'No, I'm not,' Daniel said. 'And then you asked your mother to go and look at something in the bedroom. What was all that about?'

'Is that really any of your business?'

'I don't know. I mean, we are getting married.'

'Yes, just that – married, but not yet joined at the hip,' Connie retorted, though she knew in her heart of hearts she had no justification for snapping at Daniel. Really, she was just worried about what he'd say if she plucked up the courage to tell him the truth about her mother.

Daniel suddenly looked very downhearted, and Connie felt ashamed of biting his head off. He turned to her with confused eyes and said, 'Connie, what are we fighting about?'

'Nothing,' Connie said. 'Or at least, nothing we need to concern ourselves with.'

'But . . .'

'I can't tell you any more at the moment without betraying a confidence, but as soon as I can, I will – I promise. I'm sorry I have been so distracted.'

They alighted from the tram on Bristol Street and went up Bristol Passage to Bell Barn Road. Sometimes, after a major row, there is still tension lingering in the air, but stepping into the house, Connie noted that there was none. And while there was no sign of Stan, Angela was in the kitchen, as she usually was, and she smiled when she saw Connie and Daniel. 'Oh, there you are,' she said. 'I'll make a cup of tea and you can tell me what you thought of the house.'

And that is exactly what happened, and Angela talked and asked questions about the house they had viewed and listened to the answers. Connie allowed herself to relax a little, but she couldn't be totally sure her mother and Stan were still as together as they had been until she spoke alone to her mother. Angela knew this too and when Daniel finished his tea she said, 'Daniel, I gave your father a shopping list to get some things in the shops on Bristol Street, but he's been away hours. Would you go and look for him, and maybe give him a hand getting the stuff home?'

Daniel nodded, though he knew it was a ploy to get him away and give Angela time alone with Connie, but he made no protest because he thought that Connie's strange mood might in some way be linked to something Angela had to say to her daughter. Connie was well aware of what her mother was up to, and watched Daniel leave with slight relief, knowing now she would find out how it went between her mother and Stan. Barely had the door closed behind Daniel when Connie faced her mother and said, 'Did you speak to Stan?'

Angela inclined her head. 'Of course. I promised, didn't I?'

'Yes, but did you tell him *everything*?'

'Everything,' Angela said. 'There is nothing McIntyre can tell Stan that he doesn't know about already. And if he tried,' Angela added with a smile, 'he might find himself spreading his length on the ground.'

'Why?'

'Because Stan thinks McIntyre took advantage of me when I was alone and lonely and vulnerable. He said he's known men like him before – men who prey on women in my position. He despises men like that and called McIntyre a predator. He has, however, promised not to beat him to pulp, as he would actually want to do. In fact, he promised not to lay a hand on him, because of the implications falling on us too, if the police became involved and started looking through past files and talking to people. Well, let's just say I'd rather not take any chances, and I'd like it better if they never got to meet at all.'

And then, seeing Connie's brow puckering in concern, she said, 'None of this is anything to do with you, and I will do all in my power to keep it that way. All you have to worry about is what to wear to your party on Saturday.'

'And whether to tell Daniel about McIntyre, or not?'

'He knows nothing?'

'No. How could I tell him anything when I didn't know how it had gone between you and Stan?'

'Fair enough,' Angela conceded. 'But now you know how it went, Daniel must be told without delay.'

'You think so?'

'I know so.'

'But . . .'

'Connie, you were the one who said I had to trust the man I was marrying,' Angela said. 'Do you trust Daniel?'

'Of course I do,' Connie replied and went on, 'and I do see what you're saying. It's not fair not to tell Daniel, and I will tell him as soon as I can, and certainly before the party, when he might actually meet the loathsome McIntyre in person.'

FOURTEEN

Connie met Daniel from the tram that night and, as she'd never done it before, he was surprised – pleased but surprised. 'More family secrets?' he asked with a smile.

'There's just one thing, and it concerns Mammy and a man called Eddie McIntyre . . .'

'Go on.'

'Well, it was after Mammy and your father fell out.'

'Because your mother shuddered, because she felt she couldn't tell my father about the baby she'd left outside the workhouse,' Daniel said.

'Yes, but neither of us knew that then,' Connie said. 'All I remember is being friends one minute, and then a great silence. It was like a hole in my life, and because no one explained anything, I suppose I blamed my mother. Anyway, she said she was lonely, and she probably was. I know I was.'

'So where did she meet this man? What did you say his name was?'

'Eddie McIntyre,' Connie said through gritted teeth. 'He was an American over here on business, he said. And the thing is, she didn't meet him – not really. She knew him, or thought she knew him, because she worked behind the bar at The Swan. He was a regular and he asked her out, and the second time he asked her, she went.'

'Connie, I know that probably upset you,' Daniel said, 'but your mother was doing nothing wrong. It wasn't as if she was hurting anyone.'

'She was!' Connie cried. 'She was hurting me because it was as if I didn't exist. All she seemed to care about was Eddie and pleasing him. It wasn't just that they went out together. I mean, this Eddie encouraged her to go into pubs and to drink, and she came home unsteady on her feet, with her clothes all messed up. She didn't seem to care. She'd say it was none of my business, and then do the same again the next night. He hurt her too, sometimes, but she didn't seem to care even about that.'

Daniel hid a smile, because his father had reacted in a similar way. He had never seen his father drunk before the great silence between him and Angela, but he saw it a good few times after. Daniel thought he was hurting because of what had gone wrong between him and Angela, and this was his way of dealing with it.

'Never mind. All that will stop now, and Angela will settle down to married bliss with my father.'

'And Eddie McIntyre?'

'If this McIntyre needs dealing with, my father and I can deal with him, but you said he's here on business.'

'Yes, Maggie told me that.'

'Well then, when his business is concluded, he will, I'm sure, go back to America, and hopefully stay there, and neither you nor your mother need worry your pretty little heads about him any more.'

'Oh Daniel, I do love you!'

'And I love you too, my darling girl,' Daniel said, and there in the middle of the street, he put his arms around Connie and held her tight.

FIFTEEN

Connie's party was planned for the following Saturday, and Angela and Stan said it was a good way to also celebrate her sixteenth birthday, which was only ten days away. They'd given her a beautiful watch, and then her mother said, 'I have something extra,' and gave Connie an envelope. Inside the envelope was her father's medal and the letter from his commanding officer.

Connie was speechless for a moment with pleasure and amazement. 'You kept it all this time?'

'I didn't,' Angela admitted. 'I should have done, but it was your granny who kept it safe. I was so upset, I said to her, I didn't want a letter or a medal – I wanted a live husband. And Granny put it away in case you wanted it. I knew she'd done it – she told me and asked me to give it to you on your sixteenth birthday. But she never told me where she'd put it. I was going through her personal effects a few days ago, and there it was amongst them.'

Connie read the letter for the first time. She read of a

brave and dedicated soldier who was a credit to his unit. The officer went on to say that the loss of such a man, who was a husband and father, must have been a heavy one to endure. Tears were in Connie's eyes as she folded the letter up and put it back in the envelope. Overcome with emotion, she put her head in her hands and, for the first time, wept for the father she had never really known.

Angela was so nervous of meeting Eddie that she told Stan she didn't think she could face the party.

'Not go to Connie's party?' Stan said incredulously. 'Connie will be heartbroken if you don't go. You are the most important person in her life.'

'Eddie McIntyre will almost certainly be there,' Angela said. 'Muriel and Noel see no harm in him.'

'You can't blame them for that. So if we take it for read that he will be there, why are you so nervous?'

'You can ask that?'

'Yes, I can, because this time I will be by your side,' Stan said. 'And I will not leave you for one minute. We will both face your demons together.'

'Do you really think that's best?'

'I do,' Stan said firmly. 'It will be good for your self-esteem. And don't worry – though I have a great desire to send the man's teeth down his throat, I will not lay a finger on him.'

'Thank you, Stan.'

'This may help you stand up to the bully,' Stan said, producing a ring box from his pocket. Angela gasped with pleasure when she saw the sparkling ring inside. It wasn't too ostentatious – he knew Angela well enough to know she would have hated that. But it was very beautiful, with a central diamond and five smaller diamonds clustered around it.

'It's lovely,' she said. 'Truly lovely.'

'You've already agreed to be my wife,' Stan said. 'This is to show everyone, including this Eddie McIntyre, that we belong together, that there is no room for anyone else.' He slipped the ring on as he spoke, and as Angela turned her hand this way and that, Stan said, 'It looks good on your hand, and it will look even better joined by another ring the day we get married, which I hope is not too long away.'

'Not if I can help it,' Angela said, delighted with the ring. 'This is the first I've ever had, for Barry and I never bothered with an engagement ring. It was a lot of money for us at the time, and I thought it a bit unseemly. I mean, planning a wedding was bad enough, with his two brothers only dead a few months. But there was a reason for that, but sporting a very beautiful and expensive engagement ring didn't seem the right thing to do.'

'Maybe it wasn't then,' said Stan, remembering back to those sorrow-filled days when the story broke about the big ship's impact with an iceberg that sent it to the bed of the Atlantic Ocean, and the few passengers who had escaped a watery grave. 'For those who drowned on the *Titanic* and their families, it was a tragic and very sad affair,' Stan agreed. 'But we cannot change history, though we can perhaps learn lessons from it. Now it is absolutely the right time to wear this ring, which I bought to show my love for you.'

'And I will wear it with pride,' Angela said, and she felt such contentment as Stan's arms went around her.

Noel Lampeter had decorated the pub beautifully and the back room of The Swan looked better than Angela had ever seen it. Streamers festooned the room and lanterns spun in the heat from the candles that graced every table. Angela knew the tables grouped around the room were old and probably scratched to high heaven, but all had been transformed with white tablecloths, candles and small bunches of flowers. And if that wasn't enough, the long table at the back of the room was piled high. Angela's eyes opened wide in delight and Maggie, who had come to greet them, said, 'The food's not all from the pub. So many wanted to contribute, they worked it out with the Lampeters.'

'Oh, how kind of them!' Angela cried, and thought even though their houses and the area generally might have looked a bit run down, the neighbours were exceptionally kind. With her arm linked in Stan's, she felt surrounded by love. She looked back to the door to see that Connie hadn't even got right into the room yet, as so many people wanted to shake her by the hand or give her a hug. Stan followed Angela's gaze and said, 'Popular girl, your Connie.'

Angela nodded. 'So many were upset by what had happened to her. They all wanted to do something.'

'Contributing to this party is one way, I suppose,' Stan said. 'Now we have to do our level best to make sure she has the time of her life.'

Angela agreed happily and she swung around with a smile on her face. But suddenly she didn't see the splendour of the room or hear the good wishes from friends and neighbours, because she'd spotted Eddie McIntyre at the other side of the room. Stan felt her stiffen and followed her gaze, and knew by the expression on Angela's face that he was looking at the infamous Eddie McIntyre. Angela felt sick; this was the moment she'd been dreading.

But then their view of Eddie was restricted by the crowds of people surrounding both her and her daughter with cries of welcome, and when the ring was spotted glistening on Angela's finger there was further excitement and many 'Ooh!'s and 'Aah!'s. Angela wondered whether she should just ignore Eddie altogether, but that might be noticed, and as few knew what Eddie had done to Angela, they'd just think her very ill mannered. Anyway, she would not give him the satisfaction of thinking he had disturbed her in some way. No, she decided the best thing was to greet him as just a casual acquaintance, a person of little or no account. And that was what she did when she saw Eddie weaving his way between the crowds to reach her. 'Oh hello, Eddie,' she said as if she had just noticed him. 'Come and meet my fiancé, Stan Bishop.'

The news shook Eddie, as did the offhand way Angela had greeted him. But in a moment the scowl vanished from his face and he was the charming Eddie again, as he shook hands with Stan and offered him hearty congratulations.

Watching him, Angela felt as if the scales had fallen

from her eyes, and she saw Eddie for the person he was. She realised he was a fake who could don a cloak of respectability or charm as a lover, but beneath that cloak was a vicious, cruel, self-centred bully. She didn't understand why she had been so besotted by him. She stole a look at Stan's dear, familiar face and felt her heart swell with love for him, and she smiled.

Stan was holding himself back with difficulty. When Eddie leant forward to shake his hand, he said to Stan quietly, 'Got a real goer there, buddy. Proper little goer, is our Angela McClusky.'

For two pins Stan could have hauled Eddie outside and given him the hiding of his life for making such a comment about Angela. He sorely wanted to, and his fists balled in readiness. However, he had promised Angela he would not harm the man, so he let his hands hang by his sides.

Muriel, though, had also heard the remark and was surprised Stan hadn't gone for Eddie, though she was pleased he hadn't. She didn't think Eddie should be able to say things like that unchecked, and so she said sharply to him, 'Less of that sort of talk!'

'What?' Eddie said, throwing his hands wide in mock innocence. Then with a leering smirk he added, 'T'isn't as if I'm saying anything that's not true. And I know that from experience.'

One man gave a grim laugh, and though he spoke to Stan, he also addressed the other men grouped around as he said, 'If anyone disrespected my missus like that, I'd take the head from his bloody shoulders!' There was a murmur of agreement to this, and Muriel realised it could get very ugly if she didn't put a stop to it. So she said, 'Eddie, I think you've outstayed your welcome.'

'You're not putting me out because of one innocent remark?'

'Yes, I am,' Muriel said. 'I didn't find it that innocent, to be honest. And let me remind you that today we are celebrating Connie's recovery after being trapped in a collapsed building for a long time. Nothing shall get in the way of that, including any snide innuendos from you, Eddie. Now, are you going to go quietly, or shall I ask a few of the boys to help you on your way?'

Eddie knew when he was beaten, but as he slunk out, he said to Angela, 'See you, Ange.'

Angela replied coolly, 'I very much doubt it. There would be no point.'

Eddie's eyes narrowed and Angela knew he was cross, but she still had hold of Stan, and with him she felt safe. 'We will both face your demons together,' he had said, and that was what she intended to do.

Eddie wondered what had got into Angela, to talk to him in that offhand way. Maybe she spoke that way in front of her fiancé, but he knew she would sing a different tune if he got her on her own. But he said nothing further, for Muriel was looking at him quite savagely, and he thought she might easily hit him on the head with something heavy.

Angela didn't breathe easy till the door closed behind him.

After that the party was wonderful. The drink flowed and vast inroads were made in the food, and the band on the stage made sure that everyone was up dancing, and neither Angela nor Connie sat down much that night. Dancing in Daniel's arms for the first time, Connie felt a little stiff initially. Holding her close, he murmured, 'Relax, darling.'

'Oh, Daniel . . .'

'Darling, you aren't putting on a performance,' Daniel said. 'Move to the music how you want to, and enjoy the feeling of my arms around you, holding you safe, as I longed to do in that hell-hole we were buried in, but I couldn't get close enough.'

'I wanted that too,' Connie said, 'but I couldn't get any nearer because I had a roof beam pinning me down.'

Daniel gave a brief nod. 'I saw that,' he said, 'when they brought down the torches. It was over your legs too, as I remember.'

'Yes, the doctors were surprised my legs weren't broken,' Connie said. 'It ripped sinews and muscles and almost crushed my kneecaps, though.'

'It's surprising that you were eventually able to walk again.'

Connie nodded, 'I know. Even the doctors didn't know whether I would or not. I would say that was down to the physiotherapists, who refused to give up on me. I did exercise after exercise and spent many hours using a walking frame. Sometimes it hurt like the very devil, but it worked, and here I am.'

'And very lovely you look too,' Daniel said and added, 'I suppose they advised you to keep exercising?'

Connie nodded vigorously. 'They kept on and on about that.'

'And I know the best exercise to do.'

'What's that?'

'Dancing to good music in the arms of your beloved,' Daniel said with an impish grin as he took Connie's hands and swung her onto the dance floor as the music started up again.

Angela looked at Connie's glowing face and knew she was happy. She realised that it was Daniel who brought that glow to her whole face, and she accepted the fact that he might become the most important person in Connie's life before she was much older. Angela thanked God that the unfortunate incident at the beginning of that evening hadn't marred the rest of it. Though it was Connie's night, many folk wanted to talk to Angela and Stan too, and all seemed more than pleased to see them together. Those who hadn't had a good look at the ring to start with, because of the crush of people, had a better look at it now. Angela was hugged by so many men and women, and Stan's hand seemed to be shaken continuously.

'Sorry,' Angela said to Connie.

'For what?'

'Stealing your thunder. Do you mind?'

'Not at all,' Connie said. 'I am delighted, as most of the street are, that you and Stan have seen sense at last. I'm happy for you, Mammy, really!'

Many hours later, Stan walked Angela and Connie home. 'Don't let them go in by the entry door,' Maggie had warned Stan. 'It will be pitch black. Tell them to go in the front door.'

Angela seldom used the front door, for another door opened from the entry, which was seldom locked. But that night, when Stan suggested she go in the front door, to please him she got her front-door key out of her handbag.

'What a good night,' she said to Connie as she turned the key. She wanted to relive it. She'd talked to many old friends that night, some of whom she hadn't seen in years. She'd danced to the foot-tapping music from the band on the stage. They'd all belted out the old Music Hall songs in the sing-song at the end, and the whole thing had been made even more enjoyable by the sumptuous food on offer. 'What say we have a cup of tea before bed?'

Connie felt the same about the evening. 'Oh, yes please,' she said. 'I'm tired, but I'm not ready to sleep just yet.'

Angela opened her mouth to reply to this, but the words froze in her throat, because Eddie McIntyre was sitting in the chair before the fire, as if he had a right to be there, with a supercilious smile on his face. She was surprised and unnerved, but overriding all that was total outrage and anger, such as she had seldom felt before. 'What are you doing here?!' she almost barked.

'Waiting for you?' Eddie replied mildly. 'We didn't have much time together earlier tonight, before I was thrown out.'

'You were thrown out because of your bad behaviour,' Angela snapped. 'And I had no desire to talk to you then anyway, and I have even less desire to do that now. You had no right at all to enter my home uninvited, and I would like you to leave now.'

Connie heard her mother's voice and saw her face with some relief, for it seemed to her that her mother felt very differently towards Eddie McIntyre than she had in the past.

Then Eddie said, 'Oh yes, Angela, we never did that much talking, as I recall. We did things you much preferred – things you're probably missing now.'

Angela bounced on the floor in rage and shouted, 'That will do! You disgust me, do you hear?! I am engaged to a man I love dearly, so I want no truck with you, or what you have to say. Just go now, before I lose patience altogether.'

'I presume your intended knows what a sex-crazed harlot you are?'

Connie gasped and put her hands over her eyes, but Angela was made of sterner stuff. She was glad she'd heeded her daughter's advice to tell Stan everything, and she was able to face Eddie squarely and say in a determined voice: 'Those are the filthy words you choose to use, Eddie, but I have told Stan everything. There are no secrets between us, and he loves me in spite of it. So, nothing you say is of any importance.'

Angela's words shook Eddie, for he didn't think for a minute she would have confessed her past to anyone, and certainly not to a man she hoped to marry. But he didn't doubt what she'd said, and Angela saw the slight hesitation and said angrily, 'So you have no business here, and you can get out right now.'

'You're asking me to go without a farewell kiss?' Eddie asked in mock incredulity.

Connie had had enough, and she leapt to her feet. 'You heard my mother. Just go, why don't you, and don't ever come back!'

'Isn't it your bedtime?' Eddie asked Connie witheringly.

'Don't you dare try and order my daughter about!' Angela snapped. 'Connie, stay right where you are.' And she faced Eddie and said, 'Are you going to go under your own steam, or will Connie and I have to push you out and go for a policeman?'

In the entry, Stan straightened up. Maggie had advised him to wait on for a while after he delivered Angela and Connie home. 'Just in case,' she said. 'Eddie has waylaid Angela in the entry before – she told me that.'

'I'll suggest she goes in the front door,' Stan said, 'as you advised.'

'Yeah, but the lavvies are down the yard,' Maggie said. 'Angela is bound to go there before she goes to bed, and if I know that, so will Eddie.'

Stan realised Maggie had a point, and ducked into the entry when he saw Angela and Connie go through the front door. He was even more glad he'd agreed to do that when he tried the entry door and found it unlocked, and he realised anyone could have got into the house unseen. And so he heard the entire argument that took place when Angela found Eddie already ensconced in her house. He was totally astounded by the way McIntyre was verbally abusing the woman he loved, and by the suggestive and downright insolent remarks he was directing her way. He could listen no longer. He remembered the promise he had made to Angela, but a man could only stand so much.

He moved to the head of the entry, intending to go into the house and hurl Eddie McIntyre from it, but he saw that the combined efforts of Angela and Connie had managed to eject the objectionable man from the house with such force that he fell in a heap on the cobblestoned pavement outside. Stan watched him get to his feet and then followed behind the lurching creature, vowing that that night Eddie McIntyre was going to get what he had been asking for this long while.

SIXTEEN

Angela was tired the next day but she got up as usual and got ready for Mass. She hoped she would see Stan there and would then probably find out what happened between him and Eddie after he left the house. Through her attic window Connie had spied Stan following after Eddie in the light from the streetlight outside their house, but they were soon swallowed by the darkness. She told her mother and the two of them had sat into the early hours, drinking cup after cup of tea, waiting for Stan's return. But he didn't come back, and though worry for what might have happened to Stan pounded in Angela's brain, sheer weariness eventually caused her to get to her feet and say, 'Well, I'm afraid I must seek my bed.'

Connie's mouth dropped open in astonishment. 'But . . . but . . .' she stammered.

'Connie, it's no good stopping up any longer. If Stan

intended to come back this way, he would have done so by now.'

'So, what do you think has happened?'

'How would I know?'

'Well, don't you even care?' Connie cried.

'Of course I care.'

'Maybe Stan was prevented from coming,' Connie said in a panicky voice. 'Stan followed McIntyre, so maybe he did something to Stan, injured him. He's evil enough to do anything.'

Angela knew that full well and was agitated herself, but she knew Connie needed calming down. 'Speculation like this does no good,' she said, 'and really there's nothing we can do tonight. So let's go to bed now, and if Stan isn't at Mass tomorrow and we have had no word from him, we will rethink, maybe enquire at the hospitals.'

'D'you think he might be in hospital, then?'

'Connie, I have no idea where he is,' Angela said with a sigh. 'But we have no way of finding out tonight.'

'Mammy, I couldn't sleep.'

'Well then, you must at least rest,' Angela said. 'Otherwise you will be no good in the morning, when I might need you. As for myself, if I don't lie down soon, I will fall down.'

Before Angela made her own way to bed a little later, she climbed the stairs to the attic where Connie slept, to find that despite her claim that she couldn't sleep if she went to bed, she was in fact dead to the world.

Angela was dead tired, but once she was in bed her mind

kept jumping about from one scenario to another, and she prayed over and over that nothing had happened to Stan, until she eventually fell into a troubled sleep, punctuated by nightmares.

Angela didn't wake Connie that morning and was glad she still slept on, for she knew she would find it hard to cope with Connie's agitated state when her own nerves were jangling, and she knew they wouldn't settle till she saw Stan and he told her what had happened.

Angela surreptitiously looked all around the church when she arrived but there was no sign of Sam. Normally the Latin Mass soothed Angela, but that morning she stayed on high alert, scrutinsing the other parishioners, especially as they left their pews to go to the rails to take Communion. Still there was no sign of Stan. A knot of worry squeezed in Angela's heart and a pulse was beating in her brain, and she could scarcely wait for the Mass to be over, when she intended looking for Stan and not stopping until she found him.

As the Mass finished and the congregation stood up to leave, she spotted Stan at the back of the church, and her relief was immense. She'd never known him go to the back like that, but no matter where Stan had stood, he was there and whole, and that was the main thing. Once outside church, she understood why he had skulked at the back and possibly snuck in when Mass had already begun, for he had obviously been in a fight.

Angela opened her mouth, but Stan put his fingers to his lips and drew her to the back of the church, away from the main congregation, before stopping and facing her. She gasped, for Stan's right eye was nearly closed up, with a black ring already forming around it. His lower lip was split, his nose was bloody and squashed, and there was a gigantic bruise forming beneath the graze on his left cheek.

'Oh, Stan!'

Stan attempted a wry smile, which was a bit lopsided due to his split lip, and said, 'S'all right. You should take a look at the other fellow.'

'What happened?' Angela said. 'Though really, I don't need to ask . . . Connie saw you go after McIntyre. I suppose you fought?'

Stan nodded. 'I know what I promised, and I intended to keep that promise, but I was in the entry and heard everything, and I just couldn't listen to him abusing you so a minute longer. I followed him well away from here, though, before laying into him. One of my punches laid McIntyre out, so I pulled him into a nearby entry and hightailed it home.'

'I thought you'd come and tell us,' Angela said. 'We waited for ages, Connie and I.'

'You wouldn't have wanted to see me, the state I was in,' Stan said. 'I cleaned myself up for Mass.'

'I would have cleaned you up, Stan.'

'It was better I kept away, because I don't want you implicated in any way,' Stan said. 'I beat Eddie up, and if he comes around and is able to say who attacked him, then it is between him and me alone.'

'Was he badly beaten?'

'Bad enough,' Stan said. 'Do you care?'

'Not for him, I don't,' Angela said. 'He likely deserved that and more. I care only for you – any trouble you may get into because of it.'

'Angela, he and I had a fight and I beat him. I used only my fists and when he passed out, I pulled him into a nearby entry. And that's the end of the story as far as I am concerned. If he wants to make something more of it, then I will admit it, but will not mention your name.'

'But I am involved, surely?' Angela cried. 'You fought because of me.'

'And I shouldn't have,' Stan said. 'I promised you I wouldn't, but when I heard that filth spilling from his mouth, and directed at you, the woman I love who has agreed to become my wife . . . I'm afraid I just forgot that promise.'

'Hush,' Angela said, putting her finger gently on Stan's damaged lips. 'This is my fault more than anyone else's, getting mixed up with that creep in the first place.'

Angela did feel guilty about the potential danger she had put Stan in, especially as Stan thought it was best to stay away from her, in case there were any repercussions from the fight.

Another week passed and Stan said, 'I am going back to the entry where I left Eddie. I pulled him in there so he wouldn't be found too quickly, but I did think he would have been discovered by now.'

'Don't go,' Angela said. 'I don't see what good it will do. And what if the police are waiting? They might be expecting you to visit the scene of the crime.'

'A fair fight between two evenly matched men hardly

merits the term "crime",' Stan said. 'The police have more to do than bother too much with the victims of such incidents. Anyway, I must go to satisfy myself.'

Angela said nothing further because she could see that Stan's mind was made up. So he went under cover of darkness, armed with a powerful torch, but when he searched the entry, he found it completely empty. Stan wasn't that surprised, but he did look all around the entry, just in case, but he found no trace of McIntyre or anyone else either.

This news unnerved Angela. 'Where could he have gone?' she asked.

'Well, he could have got to his feet and made his own way to where he's staying, but even the police won't know where that is, so we can't check,' Stan said. 'Or maybe someone else found him and called an ambulance, and that would probably involve the police.'

'So, he could still talk, say who it was who attacked him?' Angela said.

'I suppose,' Stan said. 'If he was conscious enough, he could. We'll just have to wait and see.'

The news did nothing to stop Angela's nerves jangling. 'What are you worried about?' Maggie asked when Angela went to tell her friend what had happened after she had gone into the house on the night of the party.

'The police coming to lift Stan, of course.'

'Why would they?' Maggie asked. 'There is nothing to link Eddie McIntyre to either you or Stan.'

'Maggie, he had a fight with him.'

'And not before time,' Maggie said. 'A lot of people in

the pub were surprised when he didn't react to what McIntyre was saying about you then.'

'He'd made a promise not to, but when I went home and found Eddie sitting there, as if he had a right . . . well, Stan heard the argument when I told Eddie to leave, because he was in the entry. I didn't know he was there, but I suppose it was a good job he was.'

'I advised him to bide there for a while after he walked you and Connie home,' Maggie said.

'Why?' Angela asked. 'Did you know Eddie was in the house?'

'Course I didn't,' Maggie said. 'But I knew he could probably get in easy enough if he wanted to, because you often leave the entry door on the latch. I thought he might waylay you on your way to the lavvy or something.'

'He could easily have thought of that,' Angela said. 'Anyway, because Stan was there, he heard all the accusations Eddie levelled at me and was coming in then to chuck him out, but Connie and I between us managed to manhandle him out of the door, and he fell onto the pavement. Connie watched through the attic window and saw him get to his feet and shamble off, and she saw Stan go after him. He admitted they fought.'

'What did you expect him to do – shake him by the hand?'

'Well, no, but . . .'

'But nothing,' Maggie said. 'It's Eddie McIntyre we're talking about, Angela, and he is a crafty, cruel devil of a man, and whatever you say, he still has a hankering after you, and you have to be on your guard.'

Angela nodded her head. 'I know,' she said. 'And I can't seem to ever be rid of him. He tried to spoil Connie's party, and when I should be happily planning her and Daniel's wedding, I'm worried that Eddie might come and make a scene. Even if he goes back to the States . . . I mean, he went there before and I thought I could draw a line under the whole episode, but then up he pops again and tries to ruin things between me and Stan. And I don't want him involved in any way with Connie and Daniel's wedding. Connie despises him.'

Maggie knew Connie despised Eddie McIntyre, and with good reason, so she couldn't reassure Angela, but she hoped and prayed the man was gone from their lives for good.

'Look Maggie, I know all you said is right,' Angela said at last. 'And I know Eddie deserved whatever Stan did to him. Stan's face is a bit battered, and though he claimed he only used his fists, he knocked Eddie unconscious, and the police might think the force he used was excessive, and we might have to deal with the consequences of that before we are much older.'

However, one uneasy day followed another, and nothing happened. Then, just over a week later, a man's body was found in the canal, pulled out by two boys fishing. Stan read the article in the *Despatch* and laughed. 'Fishing! Bet they didn't catch much. I can imagine few self-respecting fish will be residing in our oil-slicked canals.'

'Well, these lads caught more than fish,' Angela commented, looking at the picture of the boys over Stan's shoulder.

'They did indeed,' Stan said. 'The hook on their home-made line got stuck in the man's shirt, and they dragged it in, and it was the body of a man. He'd been in the water some time, the police say,' Stan said.

'Maybe it's Eddie,' Angela said, and her voice had a hopeful note to it.

'Why on earth should a body pulled out of the canal have anything to do with Eddie McIntyre? That canal is nowhere near where I caught up with him.'

Angela shrugged. 'I dunno,' she admitted and added, 'Don't suppose you dumped him in the canal at the end of the fight?'

Stan was appalled. 'Angela, what do you take me for?' he said. 'I told you what I did with the man. I pulled him into the entry and left him there. Eddie McIntyre is probably back in New York now, and the poor individual in the canal is someone else entirely.'

However, no one knew who the man was, for he had nothing on him to identify him. In fact his pockets were empty, and the police were thinking it might have been a robbery gone wrong, or maybe the man had fallen into the canal accidently. But who he was remained a mystery, for there had been no reports of any missing person, and the police were baffled.

SEVENTEEN

A few days later Stan said, 'I've something to tell you. It concerns McIntyre and an incident in New York. It was probably the reason he came to England in the first place. Do you want to know?'

'Of course I want to know.'

'I thought the man's name might upset you.'

'Not unduly,' Angela said. 'I did wonder why he suddenly just appeared in Birmingham that time. He was an affluent man and so was his uncle. I often wondered why a man of his standing, here on legitimate business, hadn't booked into a hotel somewhere, instead of the seedy lodgings he had.'

'Did you ask him?'

'Well, yes, but he never liked discussing business,' Angela said. 'He made that very plain. But how would anyone know what happened all those years ago? Who told you this, anyway?'

'A man called Archie Gilmore – he's a friend of Len's.'

As soon as Len was well enough and had left hospital, Stan, with Angela's full approval, took he and Bobby into the shop. Len was taken on as his assistant, and Stan said he was shaping up very well. After their wedding Angela was going to teach him to drive the new van Stan had bought. Bobby helped generally in the shop, as well as delivering papers and groceries in the large basket at the front of the bone-shaker of a bike. Their mother was pleased and somewhat relieved that both her boys were in safer employment, and their respectable wages were supplemented by a big box of groceries every Friday night. That reminded Angela of having a similar perk when she had worked in the same shop when old George Maitland owned it.

'So out with it,' Angela said to Stan. 'If this man is a mate of Len's, I'm sure he must be an all-right fellow.'

'He seems to be,' Stan said. 'Len doesn't see as much of him as he once did, because Archie joined the Royal Navy. He was decorated in the Great War for continuing to lift sailors out of the sea when their boat was struck by a German U-boat. He carried on through heavy bombardment and saved a lot of men, who would have died but for his intervention. Anyway, he was given a medal but had been injured himself, and it was touch and go for quite a while. While his life was hanging in the balance, he unburdened himself to Len, telling him something that he said had lain heavy on his conscience for years.'

'Oh, I'm so intrigued Stan,' Angela said. 'Do tell all.'

'Right,' Stan said. 'It was like this. Archie had finished

his tour of duty and had decided to head for New York to see if he could make a fresh start, earn some money – you know. Meanwhile his family had fallen on hard times, his father was out of a job and they had been evicted and were living on the streets. He had not known things were so bad, for they hadn't breathed a word in their letters, knowing he could do nothing about it – a bit like you were told not to tell depressing news to Barry at the Front in the Great War.

'He was making his way home in New York along the dockside late one evening, when he saw McIntyre approaching, and he decided to make himself scarce because everyone knew about McIntyre's temper. He was the sort of person, Archie said, who would beat up a man just because he didn't like the look of him. Anyway, Archie was taking no chances and he crept onto one of the smaller boats bobbing in the water on the dockside, and he hid under a tarpaulin he found on board.

'From his hiding place he watched a man he knew called Tom Goldsmith also approach, and he knew him to be a decent enough fellow, by all accounts. Anyway, seems McIntyre had been with Goldsmith's daughter and she was pregnant, and he wanted to know what McIntyre was going to do about it. Course, he said awful things about his daughter, saying it was all her fault, for she had chased him, not the other way round. He said the child might not be his at all, because she'd spread her favours widely. He made her sound really cheap, and Archie maintains she wasn't like that at all. McIntyre said Goldsmith had to watch his daughter, for she was sex-crazed, and he'd have more than the one bastard to look after before he was much older.

'Tom sprang at him. Archie said he wasn't surprised – any father would have done the same. He raised this bar he'd got from somewhere. But McIntyre wrested it from him and beat him about the head with it, and put his boot in over and over when he fell to the ground.'

'What did Archie do?'

'Well, he said he couldn't go to the police, for likely they wouldn't take his word against McIntyre's, because he was rich and powerful, and so was his uncle. And Archie might have got into trouble himself for breaking into someone's yacht to hide. If it ever came to court, McIntyre could and would hire big-shot lawyers who would get the case dismissed. And then he'd know what Archie had said, and would have hunted him down, because he's that kind of man. But he knew that Goldsmith needed medical attention. After McIntyre left, Archie went over and could see Goldsmith was in a bad way, but he did manage to croak out McIntyre's name.

'So, Archie scribbled a note on a piece of paper, saying a man had been beaten up on the dockside and needed urgent medical attention. He gave an urchin a tanner, or whatever the equivalent is over there, to take it to the police station, following him to make sure he did.

'Tom Goldsmith died and Archie felt bad that he hadn't done more to bring his killer to justice, but then McIntyre disappeared off the face of the earth anyway. People said he'd gone to England, but no one knew for sure.' Stan added, 'We know he came to England, don't we, and continued to wreak havoc here.'

'Oh yes,' Angela said. 'He did indeed, but no blame can be attached to this Archie.'

'I agree,' Stan said. 'He's back in the Royal Navy now, on active duty, but he still feels guilty that he didn't do more for Goldsmith.'

'I know about guilt like that,' Angela said, 'and he won't rest until he confesses. Get Len to urge him to go to the police as soon as he can.'

'That's what I told them,' Stan said. 'Archie wasn't keen on Len telling me at first, but of course Archie doesn't know me. Len said I should be told and that I would never betray them, but I would know what to do. I said the first course open to them was the police. Len assured me they'd go straight to the police station, but they didn't do that. I work beside Len every day and every time I ask him about it, he makes excuses. I don't know what they intend doing about it.'

'Well, we can do nothing other than advise,' Angela said. 'It's not our tale to tell.'

'No, we could never betray them,' Stan said. 'But like you said, if he doesn't tell someone in authority who can do something about it, the guilt will stay and probably fester inside him.'

'Yes,' Angela said. 'T'isn't as if he's done anything wrong.'

'You didn't do anything wrong,' Stan pointed out. 'But you carried guilt and shame for years.'

'That's because what I did caused hurt and misery to another, and that person was the very one I should have protected. It didn't really matter whose fault it was in the end. As for Archie, I don't see what else you can do that hasn't already been done.'

Just a few days after this conversation, Len and Archie appeared at Angela's door. 'Come in,' Stan said. 'And tell me why you haven't been to the police. You said you were going to go straight there.'

'It was me,' Archie said. 'I got cold feet. And I had to tell Suzy first.'

Suzy was Archie's wife and neither Angela nor Stan knew her, so Stan said, 'Didn't she want you to tell? Did she try to stop you?'

'No,' Archie said. 'On the contrary, I got it in the neck from her for not telling what I saw back then. She said if I had, McIntyre would probably have been caught, but there was little point of spouting about it now when McIntyre has seemingly disappeared off the face of the earth again.'

'Yes,' Stan said, 'probably high-tailed it back to America now.'

'No one seems to know where he is.'

'Well, wherever he is, you need to tell what you saw,' Angela said. 'There might be more urgency to the search for McIntyre if they know he is wanted for murder.'

'If he knows that, then he definitely won't want to be found,' Len said. 'It's the death sentence for murder over in America.'

A shudder ran through Angela, but then she remembered all that he had done to her, and more importantly, what he had done to Tom Goldsmith. Killed a man without a thought as he tried to get justice for his pregnant daughter, and the condemnation and prejudice that daughter would face, all through her pregnancy. Knowing that she would give birth to a child who would be stigmatised and taunted all the days of its life. Eddie McIntyre deserved all that was coming to him, and if the court found him guilty, well so be it.

'Will you come with us?' Len said to Stan and Angela.

'Come with you?' Stan scoffed. 'What's up with the pair of you?'

'Neither of us are used to going to a police station,' Len said. 'Not willingly, anyway. Whenever I was taken there as a nipper for playing it up, it usually ended up in a walloping from the old man.'

'You're a bit big for that now,' Stan said. 'Even if your dad was still around to try. And I can't believe you're scared to go to the coppers and tell them summat they should have been told years ago.'

Angela had seen the panicky look on Archie's face and knew he was scared stiff of confessing what he had done. She knew first-hand how hard that was, and she scolded Stan, 'Stop being a bully.' Then she turned to Len and Archie and said, 'We'll both come with you as far as the station, but I'm afraid the rest you must do on your own. Deal?'

'Deal,' Len and Archie agreed happily, and both shook Angela's hand warmly, and nodded in acknowledgement to Stan.

Len and Archie felt very nervous when they got to the door of the police station. Stan said, 'You've nothing to worry about. Just tell them the total truth of what happened.'

Archie nodded and forced his feet to move forward, and then he was in front of the duty sergeant and telling him what it was all about. He was led into an interview room, where the sergeant told Archie and Len to sit on one side of a polished wooden desk, while he sat on the other side. Archie sat facing the sergeant, his limbs trembling. When the sergeant had established the facts of the case, he said he wanted to speak to Archie alone, but told Len he might also want to speak to him later.

After Len had left the room, the sergeant said, 'You have information. Tell me what happened,' and Archie, remembering Stan's words, recounted the whole tale he had told Len in the hospital, and the policeman believed him. He even understood his reticence to say anything at the time, as Eddie McIntyre then lived a privileged life under the patronage of his uncle, Sam Winters. Even across the Atlantic Ocean, he knew who they both were, influential and powerful men. The sergeant agreed that it was very unlikely that the American police officers would have believed the word of a young sailor against such a rich and powerful man.

But before him now was a polite and courteous young man who had served his country in the Great War and had been commended and given a medal for his bravery. This man, Archie Gilmore, was a man to be reckoned with, while Eddie McIntyre, like so many other greedy Americans, had lost almost all his money, and therefore influence, in the Wall Street Crash. But the sergeant, who considered himself a good judge of character, believed Archie Gilmore had told him the whole truth.

He had a word with Len, and then both were allowed to go home, and then he asked to speak to Stan and Angela. 'It's just routine,' he said. 'Not really to verify Archie Gilmore's story, for I'm certain it's a very truthful account, and he assures me you knew nothing about any of this, and were only made aware of this a few days ago yourselves.'

'That's true, Sir,' Stan said. 'As soon as we knew, we advised him to come and tell you.'

'So,' asked Angela, 'can you find out where McIntyre is now?'

'The only thing we are sure of is that he did arrive in this country, because we checked the passenger lists,' the sergeant said. 'But we have checked the hotels and lodging houses he used last time he was here, pubs he frequented. We've talked to friends and acquaintances and followed up dozens of leads, all to no avail. He has not travelled back, unless he's done so under a false name. But we have had a watch put on all ferry ports, so it's unlikely he could have left this country without us being aware of it. Even his mother and uncle don't know where he is, for though he writes very occasionally, he never gives an address that they can write back to.'

'Doesn't that strike you as odd, Sergeant?'

The sergeant nodded his head. 'Very odd, I don't mind telling you. It suggests to me that he knows we are tracking him down. He's a wily character, by all accounts, and if he knows we have something on him, I imagine he will be harder to find than ever.'

'I suppose you don't like to leave any stone unturned in a case like this,' Angela said.

'No, no, of course not. What are you getting at?'

'Well, seems to me that you have a suspect's name but no body, and a body pulled out of the canal that has no name.'

Stan was exasperated. 'Angela, I have told you, it's highly unlikely one has anything to do with the other.' He raised his eyes to the sergeant's and said, 'Sorry, she has a bee in her bonnet about this man in the canal.'

'No, I haven't,' Angela retorted. 'And don't talk as if I'm not here. I just think it must be awful to be buried in a plot with no name. All I'm saying is, if this body turns out to be Eddie McIntyre, not many people would recognise him now, but I probably could.'

'Mrs McClusky, it's not a pretty sight,' the sergeant said. 'Most of the flesh has rotted away. There is no way of recognising him.'

'Are most of the bones intact?'

'I believe so, at the moment,' the sergeant said, puzzled.

'Then I will recognise him,' Angela said. 'For Eddie McIntyre had six toes instead of five on his left foot.'

Angela's words caused a deep silence to descend on the room. The policemen in the room were in shock. Angela, on the other hand, seemed completely calm, but in fact she felt as if her nerve endings were exposed, and her mouth was unaccountably dry. However, she knew it was imperative she viewed the body, and to have the opportunity to do that, she had to give the impression that she was in control. So when the sergeant rapped out sharply,

'Are you sure?' she held his eyes as she answered confidently and without the merest hint of a tremor:

'Eddie McIntyre had six toes instead of five on his left foot, as I told you before. If the dead man you pulled out of the canal is similarly afflicted, then he is in all probability Eddie McIntyre.'

The sergeant looked into Angela's eyes and saw that she spoke the absolute truth. Not given to snap decisions, usually wanting all the information beforehand, he arranged for Mrs McClusky to visit the mortuary without delay.

A younger policeman took the sergeant's place at the other side of the desk and said, 'How did you know that about the toes?'

'He told me himself,' Angela said. 'I met him the last time he was in England. I worked at the pub then because my husband died in the Great War, so I had to work, as I had a daughter to provide for. Eddie was from New York, where two of my foster brothers lived, so at first, I was anxious to know all about it. He was very embarrassed by this extra toe and I could hardly believe him when he told me, so in the end he showed me.'

It was one of the hardest things Angela had ever done, to walk into that room and see the mound on the marble slab covered with a white sheet. Stan had insisted on coming with her, and they both travelled to the mortuary in the sergeant's car, but Angela knew she had to go into the room alone.

The sergeant had warned her it wasn't a pretty sight,

and it certainly wasn't. 'They've tried to clean him up a bit,' he'd said in the car, and she'd wondered how much cleaning up they could do to a skeleton, for that was what she was looking at. She gave a gasp of shock and said to the attendant, 'I thought the police explained it to you. It's his feet I need to look at.'

The attendant looked at her notes and said, 'I'm sorry, Mrs McClusky. It's an unusual request and I didn't check.'

She drew the cover over Eddie's face and Angela sighed in relief, glad that the sight of Eddie's skull – deep caverns where his eyes had once been – was hidden from her, as another attendant began uncovering his feet. And there on the left foot was the extra bone with some skin attached to it, and she knew without a shadow of a doubt that the skeleton was Eddie McIntyre's. Her overriding emotion was not sadness, but relief that he could not hurt her or her loved ones ever again. She felt quite guilty that she felt so relieved that McIntyre was dead.

She wondered out loud what would happen now that she had formally identified McIntyre. 'He is still a murderer,' the sergeant said, as he drove Angela and Stan back to the police station.

'Yes, but a dead murderer,' Angela pointed out. 'That can't be a usual circumstance, so it must make a difference.'

'And what if someone put him in the canal?' the sergeant asked.

'Is that a possibility?'

'Well, it isn't certain,' the sergeant admitted. 'The body was too decomposed to see if there was evidence of a struggle. Cuts and bruises and the like could have been caused by his falling into the canal when he'd imbibed too freely. His friends said he was a heavy drinker, or maybe he had been in some sort of skirmish and stumbled into the canal that way. Either way, his death would probably have been considered accidental.'

'Well then, unlike Tom Goldsmith, there is no true indication that anyone had anything to do with McIntyre's death,' said Angela.

'Well, no. I suppose not,' the sergeant had to admit.

'So why not inform his family in New York, and see if they want to arrange some sort of burial, and file this case under "No further action"?' Angela said.

The sergeant was definitely nonplussed but eventually said, 'I will have to inform my superiors, take their advice.'

'Of course,' Angela said, 'I would say that's your first course of action, wouldn't you?'

It was a little later, as they were walking home, that Angela realised Stan was chuckling to himself. 'What's up with you?'

'You,' Stan said, 'and the way you dealt with that sergeant. I have a feeling that if he ever sees you go in there again, he will hide under the table.'

Angela smiled. 'Good job I don't frequent police stations on a more regular basis, then.'

'I'm sure they're glad about that,' Stan said. 'But talking of police stations, would you mind if we call at the Gillespies', for that's where Len and Archie were making for. We need to tell them about McIntyre's left foot.'

'If you like,' Angela said. 'Archie needs to know. Might ease his mind a bit. Although the police didn't say so, I think it's better to keep a bit quiet and not share that information with all and sundry.'

'Agreed.'

'And let's not be all day at the Gillespies',' Angela said. 'Connie will be very interested in what happened to McIntyre as well. And after she has digested that news, we can move on from all this unpleasantness. After all, we have a wedding to plan!'

EIGHTEEN

So before going home they called at the Gillespies' house to let Len and Archie know what had transpired since they'd left the police station. They weren't the only ones to be relieved, either, for Mrs Gillespie (who insisted Angela call her Grainne) was equally relieved. She confessed to Angela, 'It's a load off my mind, right enough. But I can't help thinking it seems wrong to be glad when you hear of a person's death, even if that person is not known to you, and likely deserved everything he had coming his way. Do you feel that?'

'I did,' Angela confessed. 'Like you, I have never felt that way about anyone dying before, but I did know Eddie McIntyre, or at least, I got to know him last time he was in England, because I was serving at The Swan at the time, and McIntyre was a frequent visitor.'

'Stan told Len your husband was killed in the war.'

Angela nodded, 'Yes he was,' she said. 'I needed a job and the Larkins, who ran The Swan back then, offered me a job there, and it was handy being so local. We had my Barry's widowed mother living with us at the time, so she was able to mind my Connie.'

'My dear, us women had to do what we had to do back in those awful days, in order to survive,' Grainne said. 'So you got to know McIntyre well?'

'That's it,' Angela said. 'I thought I knew him, because he was familiar, coming in so often, but really I didn't know the man at all. Initially he appeared courteous and charming, and he was popular, confident and beguiling, especially with the ladies, for he was a proper ladies' man.' Angela was glad Connie wasn't there when she admitted to Grainne, 'Even I was brought under his spell for a time. But then I found his real character was totally different to the one he had displayed to begin with.'

'That is often the way.'

'Yes,' Angela said. 'Then I found McIntyre to be cruel and manipulative – a real bully. He killed Tom Goldsmith because he had no intention of helping the girl he'd made pregnant. I imagine Tom wanted McIntyre to take some responsibility for the child, but Tom would have been well advised not to waste his time. McIntyre was the sort of man who had his fun and then moved on to the next victim, when the first one proved difficult in one way or another.'

'Archie said this McIntyre seemed to blame it all on the girl,' Grainne said.

'Oh, that was his stock-in-trade,' Angela said. 'Another was, once a girl submitted to him, whether she was forced to or not, he would threaten to tell everyone what a slut she was, whisper in the right people's ears, destroying that girl's standing and character, and that of her family. So the terrified girl had to give in to whatever McIntyre wanted. Eventually the inevitable would happen. That scene between McIntyre and Goldsmith could be played out by fathers with daughters all over Birmingham, for men like McIntyre are insatiable, and they think women and girls are good for just one thing. Grainne, I have to be straight with you: McIntyre was a thoroughly bad lot.'

'Hmm, I've met fellows like him before,' Grainne said grimly. 'All told, I think he did the world a favour. I suppose he did do himself in?'

'The police haven't much of an idea how he came to be in the canal in the first place,' Angela said, 'and a fast-decomposing body isn't great at revealing clues. It might well have to remain a mystery.'

'So, we probably will never know if someone pushed him in, or if he jumped.'

'He wouldn't have jumped,' Angela said. 'I know him well enough to say he was altogether too cocky to do such a thing. But it could easily have been accidental, because he was a very heavy drinker. He could have just missed his footing and fallen in. Either way, the police are taking no action. And no matter, for however he died, the end result is the same.'

'Yes, and that lovely lad Archie won't have to go to court and explain himself,' Grainne said with some satisfaction. 'And however guilty I feel, I truly believe a world without McIntyre in it is going to be a safer world for a lot of people, and it's just a pity it came too late for poor Tom Goldsmith.'

'And his daughter too,' Angela said, 'who had to bear and raise an illegitimate child.'

'It must have been a hard road she had to follow, right enough,' Grainne said. 'But hopefully, she had the love and support of her family around her. As for McIntyre's soul, I hope it's firmly turned away from the pearly gates, and when he arrives in hell, I hope old Nick is around to give him a good, hard poke.'

Angela chuckled at the picture Grainne's words conjured up. Angela was anxious to get home and give Connie the good news, so they left the Gillespies' soon after handing an invitation to Connie's wedding to Grainne and her two sons, plus Archie.

As Angela told Connie the story, she listened to every word and didn't interrupt once. When Angela had finished, Connie said, 'Are you absolutely sure that the man that drowned in the canal was Eddie McIntyre?'

'Absolutely certain, Connie. Honestly, you have nothing to worry about now, as far as McIntyre is concerned.'

Connie sighed in relief and then said, 'It's just that you never said anything before about McIntyre's *extra toe*.'

'Connie, it was years ago I found out about it, the last time he was in England – so long ago, I had almost forgotten all about it myself. At that time, I recall you were not at all interested in knowing anything about McIntyre.'

'Mammy, that's because . . .'

Angela held up her hand. 'I know you had reason to dislike the man, but because you felt that way, you wouldn't have been the slightest bit interested if I had said one day, "Oh, by the way, did you know Eddie McIntyre has got an extra toe on his left foot?"'

Connie grinned as she said, 'You're right, I wouldn't have cared a bit.'

'Added to that,' Angela said, 'I would hardly want it known to everyone I had that information, as surely people would've wondered how I knew it. I let myself forget about it. It was only when that man was pulled out of the canal and the police had no idea who he was, that I thought about that extra toe again, so I offered to check whether it was him or not. You know Stan fought with him on the night of the party?'

'I thought he would have when I saw Stan following McIntyre,' Connie said. 'Did you think he had something to do with McIntyre's death?'

'I did wonder,' Angela admitted. 'You once said to me that I had to trust the man I intended to marry, and I do trust Stan, for I have never known him tell me a lie. He is always as straight as a die. He told me he fought with McIntyre using only his fists, and he knocked McIntyre out and pulled him into an entry and left him there.'

'If Stan said that's what happened, then that's what happened,' Connie declared and added, 'though I wouldn't have minded if he had dumped McIntyre in the canal. But I feel awful, really, because I've never before been glad about someone dying.'

'Yes, I feel the same, and it's an odd feeling. Thinking about Stan, while I know he was telling me the truth about the fight, if the police knew about it, they might try and make a case against Stan, despite the fact that they are treating McIntyre's death as accidental at the moment.'

'We'd better not tell them then,' Connie said. 'Just think – we can now go ahead with plans for our wedding, confident in the knowledge that McIntyre won't be making an appearance. Oh, Mammy, you don't know how happy that thought makes me!'

'I have a good idea how it feels,' Angela said, 'for I feel the same. And McIntyre might not have lived much longer anyway, if he hadn't drowned in the canal. The police were waiting to arrest him on a charge of murdering Tom Goldsmith in New York, before he fled to England the first time. Archie was willing to be a witness, as he saw the whole thing. So McIntyre would almost certainly have been found guilty, and murder carries the death penalty.'

NINETEEN

Connie reminded her mother about her plan to have a double wedding, and Angela now felt Connie was just being kind and might regret her decision later.

'Why would I?' Connie asked.

'Well, many brides wouldn't like to share their special day with another,' Angela said.

Connie laughed. 'It's not another, though, is it?' she said. 'I want a double wedding with my mother who I love so very much, and with whom I have already shared so much, both good and not so good. That's extra special for me.'

'Anyway,' Daniel put in, 'I want to make sure my father makes an honest woman of you at long last. You both have waited long enough.'

'Are you absolutely sure?'

'Absolutely!' Connie and Daniel said in unison, and Stan caught Angela around the waist. 'We've been over-ruled, darling,' he said. 'Let's give the children what they want.'

'Oh yes, my darling Stan,' Angela said, laughing. 'And we have to get busy, for we have two weddings to organise now.'

As it was to be Angela's wedding too, there were more people to invite, and many of them were old friends and neighbours that used to live in and around Bell Barn Road. She knew some might have died and others might be ill or just too frail to make the journey, but she felt she had to invite all those she could remember.

Angela was particularly glad to hear that Breda and Paddy Larkin were coming, for Breda had been a stalwart friend and confidante to Angela when she had needed one so much. Angela had told her things she didn't feel she could share with anyone else, knowing Breda would never betray her. For many years the Larkins had been the licensees at The Swan, where Angela had been employed, and they were generally well liked. The Lampeters, the new licensees, were pleased when they heard the Larkins had been invited to the wedding. 'I am so glad they felt they could it make it,' Angela said to Muriel. 'Breda said she wouldn't miss it for the world, but you know her arthritis is very bad at times.

'I owe the Larkins a great deal,' continued Angela. 'They are very fond of Connie, of course – they have seen her grow up. But when I wrote and told them I was getting married too, on the same day, Breda said they were beside themselves with joy for me. I hope Paddy will walk me down the aisle. I am a bit short of male relatives, and Paddy was almost a father to me, especially when I lost Barry.'

'They must be getting on a bit,' Muriel said.

'Oh yes, they are,' Angela said.

'And they are travelling from the south coast?'

Angela nodded. 'Yes, it's a bit of a trek for them.'

'It's a lot of a trek, if Breda has arthritis, and going out in the cold night air makes it worse,' Muriel said. 'I know, for I have a touch of it myself now and again.'

'I know,' Angela said. 'But there's no way around it.'

'There is though,' Muriel said. 'They can stay here overnight.'

'That's incredibly kind of you,' Angela said. 'Won't you mind?'

'Not a bit of it,' said Muriel airily. 'Tell you the truth, I have heard so much about them, I'd really like to get to know them myself. Broach it to them in your next letter.'

'I will,' Angela said. 'And thank you!'

The build-up to the wedding sped by in a happy whirl of planning and excitement. Breda and Paddy said it was very kind of the Lampeters to offer them overnight accommodation, and Paddy was tickled pink when Angela asked him to walk her down the aisle. But Breda knew her husband well and saw there was something bothering him. And because she was the sort of woman who got to the point straight away, she looked him full in the face and said, 'All right. What is it?'

Because Angela held a special place in Paddy's heart, he had a few misgivings about the man she was planning to marry. Breda, though, was irritated when he voiced these doubts.

'Who would you have her marry – Eddie McIntyre?' Breda demanded.

'No, I wouldn't, as you know full well,' Paddy said. 'Stan's a hundred times better than that ne'er-do-well. If Angela wanted to marry McIntyre, it would be a huge mistake. He's the love-them-and-leave-them type of man.'

'Well, Stan isn't like that.'

Paddy shook his head from side to side and said, 'I wouldn't have said so either. But I can't get it out of my head – the shabby way he treated her before. Look what she did for him – welcoming him into her home, connecting him with his long-lost son, even cleaning out the flat to give Stan and his son a place to live. They seemed good together, I will say that – and then suddenly Stan wasn't in her life any more, making her ripe for a predator like Eddie McIntyre.'

'Mmm, that was puzzling, all right,' Breda said.

'Well, what if he does it again?'

'He wouldn't.'

'How can you say that so definitely, when he did it once before and neither of us knew why.'

'No, it was odd, that,' Breda admitted. 'Angela never did discuss what went wrong. I mean, she'd always been so open with me before that, but she fair bit my head off when I asked her about it one day.'

'Well, let's hope Stan Bishop does the decent thing and marries Angela this time,' Paddy said. 'Nothing we can do about it now but turn up and support her.'

'That's all,' Breda said with a sigh. 'And don't you go

round saying anything like that and upset her on her wedding day.'

'You might credit me with a bit of common sense now and again, Breda.'

'I might, if you showed any, a time or two,' Breda retorted, and before Paddy was able to reply to that, she went on: 'And I'll tell you something for nothing. If that slime-ball Eddie McIntyre should come back from America and pop his head up anywhere, I shall hit him with something heavy.'

Paddy chuckled and said to his wife, 'You might have to join a queue for that.'

There was another dilemma facing Breda that she wasn't going to share with Paddy yet, and that was the identity of the second bridesmaid. It was fair lovely meeting up with Angela again, Breda thought, and both women had tears in their eyes as they embraced. Noel and Muriel Lampeter were more than welcoming when the Larkins arrived the day before the wedding. Breda could see Angela had a lot already organised, but still asked if there was anything she wanted her to do. 'You could see to the bridesmaids, if you would?' Angela asked.

'Course I would,' Breda said. 'You know what I think of Connie, and she has made a remarkable turnaround after such a nasty experience in that disused factory. I was sorry to have missed the party in thanks for her recovery, but the old arthritis flared up and put paid to all that.'

'How's the arthritis now?'

'Not so bad,' Breda said. 'It's always better in the warmer, drier weather. But tell me how the party went.'

'I was sorry you had to miss it, but she had a lovely time,' Angela said. 'And you'll never guess who turned up!'

'No, who?'

'Eddie McIntyre!'

Breda's lips drew back in almost a snarl as she hissed, 'McIntyre! That slime-ball! He has a nerve to even show his face here. What's he doing this side of the Atlantic?'

'Oh, that's the best bit yet,' Angela said. 'He lost all his money in the Wall Street Crash. You must have read about it in the paper.'

'I did, but when I realised it was in America, I didn't take much notice, for it's a country I have never had a yen to even visit. So he's lost all his money, has he?'

'Apparently,' Angela said. 'He was here to drum up new business and revive contacts he made the last time he was in England. Probably his uncle insisted on him coming here, because some say it wasn't his money he lost, but his uncle's.'

'Uh huh, bet that didn't go down well when McIntyre's uncle found out.'

'Shouldn't say it did.'

'Mind you, it's made my day to think he's lost all that. And if his uncle takes him to court, I hope they throw the book at him. He deserves all he gets! Bad news that he's back over here, though. He'd better not be out to cause trouble.'

'He tried to cause enough at Connie's party,' Angela said, 'making rude and suggestive remarks about me.'

'And Stan was there? Didn't he trounce him?'

'No, he promised not to, in case the police got involved and McIntyre started spreading vile rumours about me. Not that I'm worried about Stan hearing them, because I have told him everything.'

'Everything?'

'Everything,' Angela repeated. 'Connie convinced me that I had to do it as soon as we knew McIntyre was back, and I'm so glad I did!

'Anyway, McIntyre's appearance didn't spoil the party at all,' Angela continued, 'because Muriel put McIntyre out before there was any trouble, and with him gone, we all had a great time. Stan did fight McIntyre later, because when Stan walked us home after the party, we found that McIntyre had got in the entry door and was sitting in my house – can you believe it?! He was waiting for me, and when he started shouting filthy abuse at me, Stan, who was in the entry, heard everything. He followed McIntyre after Connie and I had pushed him out of the house.'

'That man is like a bad smell.'

'I agree,' said Angela. 'You can just imagine how pleased I am that there isn't the remotest chance he will try to scupper Connie's wedding or my own.'

'You sound very sure of that.'

Angela gave a brief nod, 'As sure as anyone can be about anything,' she said. 'Eddie McIntyre is dead, Breda.'

Breda's mouth dropped open in astonishment and then she said with a rueful grin, 'That's wishful thinking, I'd say,' and added, 'you are joking?'

'Am I likely to joke about that man's death?'

'No, I suppose not,' Breda conceded. 'But are you absolutely sure?'

'Sure as I'll ever be about anything,' Angela said. 'I identified the body.'

Breda's eyes were wide and bulging out of her face as she blurted out, 'You did what?!'

'Identified his body,' Angela repeated. 'D'you remember the dead body that was pulled out of the canal a while ago? It was in all the papers.'

'Yes, and the police didn't know who he was.'

'And if the police and coroner and anyone else who dealt with that body hadn't been half asleep, they may have noticed something that might have identified the man sooner.'

'What?'

'McIntyre had an extra toe on his left foot.'

'Never!'

'It's true,' Angela said. 'He showed me when he was last in England, and on his skeleton that extra bone was still there. All I felt, looking at that corpse, was relief that he could hurt no one any more.'

'Well, that's true,' Breda said. 'I could dance a jig on his grave. Has he any relatives?'

'Only an uncle and a mother, I believe,' Angela said. 'They're both getting on and the uncle is quite frail, I believe, but it's up to them what they do with the body. There's something else, and it's not been in the papers. Before he came to England that first time, he had killed a man. A reliable witness saw it all and was willing to testify. If they had found McIntyre, he was going to be arrested for murder.'

'So, did someone push him in the canal?'

There was no hesitation in Angela's voice as she said, 'The police think it was an accident, that he stumbled in after drinking heavily.'

'Well, he surely did know how to sink those pints,' Breda said. 'So your Stan had nothing to do with it?'

'Nothing at all,' Angela said firmly.

'Fair enough,' Breda said, 'though none would blame him.'

'The police would blame him if they thought he had anything to do with it.'

'But he didn't, so we don't have to bother the police,' Breda said. 'It isn't as if we have anything new to tell them, is it?'

'No, we don't,' Angela said, and in an effort to change the subject she said, 'Before you go, let me show you the girls' dresses for tomorrow. Mine is more or less the same, except mine is cream satin and the girls' are peach.'

The satin dresses were overshot with lace caught up at intervals and fastened with blue and pink rosebuds. Clusters of lace also decorated the sleeves and the necklines, and they all had silver satin slippers to wear on their feet.

'Ooh, they are beautiful!' Breda said, slightly awed by them. 'Truly, truly beautiful.'

'Aren't they just?' Angela said in satisfaction. 'It was a friend of Maggie's made them, and I think they will look magnificent.'

'They will indeed,' Breda said, 'but why did she make two?'

Angela hesitated before answering, but realised she had to tell Breda the truth about Chrissie. Her daughter was fed up with all the subterfuge about her origins, and had told Angela that the time for keeping secrets was passed. So she looked Breda full in the face and said, 'They are for my two daughters – Connie and Chrissie.'

To say that Breda was shocked would be putting it mildly.

To her knowledge, Angela had one child, and that was Connie. There had been that unsettling business with McIntyre, but she had thankfully miscarried his child, and never in all the letters she'd written did she mention any other relationship – and Breda knew this was not another immaculate conception!

It was as Maggie came into the room that Breda thought she had solved the riddle, for Michael and Maggie had brought their three adopted children with them: baby Harry, astride Michael's broad shoulders, and three-year-old Jenny and two-year-old Grace holding Maggie's hands.

They had adopted all three when their parents had been killed in a traffic accident. Angela had been worried that Maggie might be worn to a frazzle, but she had flourished and the children were delightful. The two girls were going to be bridesmaids at Connie's wedding. So Breda was convinced that was what Angela had done – she'd adopted a young girl, probably as a companion to Connie.

TWENTY

The night before the wedding, Stan went with some friends to the pub for his stag night. Angela asked Breda, Eileen and Maggie to her house for the evening, and when she came in with the first pot of tea of the evening, Breda took up a cup gratefully and said, 'Nothing beats a cuppa. You can keep all your wine and whisky and beer, you just can't beat a cuppa at the end of the night.'

'And that advice is from a publican's wife!' Angela said, and the women burst out laughing. And then Breda said to Angela in a stage whisper that everyone heard, 'Is she adopted, your younger daughter?'

Angela gave a start and paused, and then said, 'Chrissie is not adopted – she's my natural daughter, conceived as a result of a brutal assault and rape against me one night as I came home from the shell factory during the war. Actually, that day I hadn't been in the factory, I had driven to the docks with the largest truck we owned, because there was a ship leaving on the afternoon tide with space on it. I was scared stiff, because I had never driven the big truck before nor driven so far, but the man who used to do it had been taken ill and there was no one else.'

'Took some courage, that,' Breda said. 'It's one hell of a way to the docks in any case – and in a truck you had never driven before, packed with shells!' Breda shook her head. 'Even if I had learnt to drive, I don't think I could have done that.'

'When we were frightened of something or didn't want to do something, we would remember our loved ones at the Front,' Angela said. 'I'm sure Barry was sometimes frightened or told to do things he didn't want to do, but he had to cope with any fear and obey the orders he'd been given. Before any major battle the Allies would pound the enemy with thousands of shells. To run out of shells would be unthinkable and disastrous for our loved ones, and I owed it to them to get that consignment to the docks so it could be taken over to France as soon as possible.'

'Mary was worried about you that day,' Breda said. 'I met her at the shops, and she said they were expecting too much of young women these days.'

'But she didn't know what I was doing that day.'

'Yes, she did,' Maggie said. 'You didn't know you were going to be asked to do that until we went in that morning, and you knew you would likely be very late home and didn't want Mary worried, so I popped in on my way home from the factory and told her where you'd gone, and said you'd likely be much later home than usual.'

'That's right,' Breda said. 'I met Mary after Maggie had

called. She said you were working incredibly hard and she was looking for something tasty for your tea.'

'Well, I was late,' Angela said, 'but Mary was more worried about the state I was in than the time I came home, because by the time the soldiers had finished with me, I was beaten up so badly, I could barely make it to the house, for all it was no distance away.'

To say that Breda was shocked would be putting it mildly, and as Angela seemed incapable of speech too, Maggie put in, 'Angela didn't go to the police, even when she found she was pregnant, in case news of it got to Barry at the Front. And she was right – even Michael said she was right to keep quiet. He said, even though it must have been heart-breaking for Angela, if Barry had got to hear about it, he might have come home to see for himself what had happened to her.'

'Could he just do that?' asked Breda.

'Course he couldn't,' Maggie said. 'We were at war, it wasn't some game. For some lads, even most of them, it was their first taste of battle. Do you think they could just decide to go home and say they'd changed their minds? They would have hunted Barry down and shot him as a deserter, and he would have been branded thereafter as a craven coward.'

'That would have destroyed me,' Angela said. 'Barry was no coward.'

'I know that, and probably with the thought of what might happen to Barry in your mind, you made the brave decision to not inform the police or make waves of any sort. Remember the people who snubbed Barry when he claimed exemption, the sender of the four feathers, and many others who might have written to Barry and told him what had happened to his beloved Angela.'

'It was the only way,' Angela said. 'But for me, it led to heartbreak and sorrow. Help came from an unexpected source – a woman offered to hide me away till the baby was born, and put it up for adoption. I thought it would be easy, that I would feel nothing for this child because of the way it was conceived, but in actual fact I loved Chrissie almost as soon as I had given birth to her. I signed away all rights to her, thereby ensuring she was available for adoption, thinking it would be the best thing for her. But then the orphanage couldn't take her because, since the war, the number of people willing to adopt had dropped off dramatically.'

'You could understand how that could be,' Breda said. 'Many of the women who were once willing to adopt could have been widowed, or left with a husband so damaged or maimed, they were unable to work. And the war was still going on, and they couldn't take any more children or babies, for they hadn't room.'

'I know, it's understandable,' Angela cried. Her voice had a shrill, panicky edge to it and her eyes shone with lurking tears as she went on, 'But that was catastrophic for me and my baby.'

Angela threw off Breda's hands as she tried to comfort her, and everyone in that room knew she was not merely telling her tale any more, but reliving it. They listened, spellbound yet heartbroken, as Angela recalled walking to the city centre, holding the basket with her arms breaking, for she didn't dare take a tram where she might be recognised later, for she was going to do a heinous thing. She was going to take her new-born, vulnerable baby and leave her on the steps of the workhouse. Her baby was going to be sacrificed for the good of everyone else.

She knew it was wrong but didn't know if it was a crime or not. If it was, and the police became involved, it wouldn't do for fellow passengers to remember the crying of a new-born baby out in a black winter's night, and many could give a good description of Angela, for her golden ringlets were very striking.

Tears were running unchecked down Angela's face and her body was shaking all over. Although Breda was shocked to the core, her body ached to put her arms around Angela, but she couldn't accept comfort from anyone. In her mind, Angela was in the little alleyway that led from Whittal Street to the back of the workhouse, hesitating to do what she had come to do. She couldn't do it – no one would expect her to do such a thing to her new-born baby. But in the end she knew there was no alternative, and with a sob she placed the locket in the baby's hand and watched her fingers close over it. Then she crept along the yard, placed the basket on the steps, rang the bell and ran like the very devil, as she had been advised to.

'She ran to St Chad's, as it was just yards away at the end of Whittal Street,' Eileen said, for Angela could say no more. She had her head in her hands and was sobbing.

'So, you saw Angela then?' Maggie asked.

Eileen shook her head. 'I was at home, trying to keep

John's supper warm, and John was over at the workhouse when they discovered a baby on their doorstep.'

'But how come you have the care of Chrissie?' Breda asked Eileen. 'She does live with you, doesn't she?'

'She does,' Eileen said. 'And she is the light of my life. And that was because of John. Angela confessed to him what she had done, and as a priest he goes to the workhouse more than me, to attend to any Catholic inmates. So he sees the conditions they live under and the meagre food they are fed. One day he asked if they had ever traced the girl who had abandoned her child on the steps, and the superintendent told him they had not, and explained about the locket the baby had in her hand when she was found.'

'So that's why the locket is so important?' Eileen said. 'I often wondered. If John knew more, it would probably have been said to him in Confession, and so he could never tell me, of course. I think he felt somehow responsible for the child, and as far as he could, he kept an eye on her surreptitiously. So then, when he heard the workhouse was being closed to extend the hospital and provide convalescence facilities for soldiers, he suggested we take Chrissie into our care and give her a chance of a better life. We did, and we have never regretted it.'

'I'll take a bet Chrissie feels the same way,' Maggie said with a smile. 'The child has a constant smile on her face.'

'Why did you leave the locket with Chrissie?' Breda asked Angela.

'The locket was given to Mary by my mother, who took me to the McCluskys when TB was running rife at the school. I was too young to be at school and my mother sought to protect me.'

'She was right to do that, for they all died but you,' Breda said. 'Mary McClusky told me herself.'

Angela nodded. 'Yes, none survived, not one sibling, nor my parents either,' she said sadly. 'I stayed living with the McCluskys, and Mary said the locket, which has locks of my mother's hair in it, would always remind me that I had a mother other than her, and she loved me very much, but wasn't able to look after me. I felt the same about Chrissie, so I put the locket in her hand, although I felt bad that I couldn't do what Mary asked and give that locket to Connie. But did you know that Stan knew how I felt and had a replica made for Connie?'

'I know about that,' Eileen said, 'because I had to sneak the original out of Chrissie's room as she slept, so the jeweller could take a look at it. Does Connie know about it?'

'Not yet,' Angela said. 'I'll give it to her tomorrow and fulfil the promise I made to Mary. I want both girls to wear the matching lockets as they walk behind me down the aisle.'

'If that's what you want, then it will be done,' Breda said. 'If at all possible, every bride should have her heart's desire on her wedding day, and your wants are so modest and so do-able.'

Angela wasn't aware when she had begun to cry, and she struggled on to say, 'I was bitterly ashamed of what I'd been forced to do to my baby daughter, and I felt guilty about her life in the workhouse – and those emotions never leave me. Sometimes shame almost consumes me.'

'I am appalled by what you have suffered,' Breda said brokenly. 'But you have nothing to blame yourself for.'

'Oh, I have,' Angela said. 'Chrissie is a lovely girl, and now that she knows it all, she has forgiven me for what I have put her through.'

'There you are,' Breda said. 'Despite it all, look at the fine turn-out the child has made after all.'

'Oh no,' Angela said. 'I can claim no credit for the way Chrissie is today. It's all due to Father John from St Chad's and Eileen, who took her from the workhouse just before her eleventh birthday. I owe them an immense debt of gratitude.'

'Not at all,' Eileen said. 'Chrissie has been a joy and a pleasure to rear. She would like to be a teacher, like me, but there is not the money for that. But at least we can find her something better than service work, which are the only positions open to girls leaving the workhouse.'

'You're right there,' Breda said and then turned to Angela and said, 'Angela, you can say it's none of my business, if you like . . .'

'I wouldn't dare,' said Angela. 'Not that you'd take any notice if I did, so what is it that's puzzling you?'

Breda remembered telling Paddy to say nothing about anything on Angela's wedding day, but her curiosity had got the better of her. 'Well . . . it's just . . . I mean, I know you're marrying Stan tomorrow, but you were very close to him once before, years ago. We remember when you cleaned out the flat for Stan and Daniel to live in, and then suddenly Stan wasn't there any more. Tell you the truth, Paddy thought he had treated you in a shabby way. He even said to me that he hoped Stan wasn't going to do a similar thing again.'

'That wasn't Stan's fault,' Angela said. 'It was mine. I rejected him because I couldn't bring myself to tell him I had abandoned my new-born baby. I could hardly believe myself that I had done such a thing. I couldn't bear to see the disgust for me in his eyes.'

'I told her to tell him the whole story,' Maggie said.

'You should have listened to your friend,' Breda said. 'I have heard what happened to you and feel no disgust – just heartfelt sorrow and sadness – but certainly no disgust. Does Stan know all now?'

Angela nodded. 'I told Chrissie and he overheard.'

'And what was his reaction?'

'He said, in his opinion, I was more sinned against than a sinner.'

'I agree with that,' Breda said. 'Now put away your cups, for I am going to open the bottle of bubbly I have chilling in the fridge. We will drink to the health of the two couples getting married tomorrow, who will be beginning a new chapter in their lives.'

Paddy was nearly asleep when Breda reached their bedroom, but Breda made no apologies about disturbing him, for she had learnt things that night she had to share with him, or risk him making a fool of himself on the wedding day. However, sleep was driven from Paddy's mind when Breda described the ordeal that Angela had suffered – the brutal attack and rape that resulted in a child being conceived. Angela had known she had to keep all knowledge of the attack and its consequence from Barry at all costs, but that meant she had to make a heart-breaking decision to abandon her child. Angela could barely live with the shame of it, nor share it with anyone. And it was Angela who had sent Stan packing, and not the other way around. In fact, the only cheering news was that McIntyre was dead and gone, and would never again be a threat to anyone.

TWENTY-ONE

The morning of the wedding, Angela gave Connie the locket Stan had made for her. She was speechless and then said hesitantly, 'Is this Chrissie's?'

'Oh no,' Angela said. 'I could never take Chrissie's away from her. She thinks so much of it.'

'Yes, she does,' Connie said. 'And I know why you gave it to her, and you were right. I was ashamed that I was resentful that she should have it and not me.'

'You never showed that.'

'I shouldn't have felt even the tiniest bit of envy,' Connie said. 'I was quite disgusted with myself, especially when I realised Chrissie knew how I felt.'

'Did she say so?'

'No,' Connie said. 'She offered me her locket.'

'Did she?' Angela said in surprise. 'I never knew that.'

'No, we decided not to tell you in case you were upset, and you thought maybe Chrissie didn't like the locket.'

'I'd never think that,' Angela said. 'But why did she offer it to you? Did she say why?'

'Yes, she said it was mine by right,' Connie said. 'It was after you explained everything. She said you were given that locket on your wedding day, and I was supposed to be given the locket on mine. I couldn't take it, of course. But what a selfless thing for Chrissie to do! Tell you, that taught me a lesson better than any words of censure would have done, and any frustration or jealousy towards Chrissie disappeared into thin air, and I haven't had the slightest bit of it since. In fact, I love her more than I ever thought I would, and I love the fact that she is my sister.'

'I'm glad,' Angela said. 'This is a special locket – your own locket, which is a replica of the one Chrissie has.'

Connie turned it over in her hand. She said, 'It's . . . it's amazing!'

'Thank Stan and his mate in the Jewellery Quarter,' Angela said. 'Open it!'

Connie opened it and saw the same miniature that Chrissie had in hers, but she was puzzled by the ringlets. 'Mammy, are those ringlets yours?'

'Of course.'

'You cut your hair to put it in a locket?'

'You're as bad as Stan,' Angela said. 'He didn't like the thought of me cutting off my hair either, but it will grow again, and it was important for you to have the locket complete.'

'Oh Mammy, I do love you.'

'And I you, my darling girl,' Angela said. 'And now we

must away and get ready, or the Larkins will arrive when I am only half dressed.'

At last, everyone was ready, and the sun shone in a Wedgewood-blue sky as the wedding party walked to St Catherine's Church that mid-June day. Those not going to Nuptial Mass stood at the threshold of their houses and cheered and waved them on their way.

Father John had also invited Mr Masters, formerly the superintendent of the workhouse, although when Eileen found out about it, she wasn't best pleased. 'Why did you invite him?' she asked.

'I wanted him to see Chrissie,' Father John said. 'To see what can be achieved with these children when they are better clothed, fed and educated.'

Eileen nodded. 'All those things would help,' she said. 'Though love is the most important thing these children need. But how can he change things in any significant way now? Didn't you tell me he once tried to get the allowance for food for the children increased, and they refused to raise it by one farthing?'

'Yes, he told me that. He was appalled.'

Eileen nodded her head. 'I'm sure he was. Any decent person would be, when they see the half-starved children in the workhouse. He was the superintendent back then, but despite his outrage, they ignored him. What chance would he have to effect any change at all, now that he's just a normal man in the street?'

'None, I suppose,' Father John had to admit.

'And,' Eileen went on, 'have you considered the effect

on Chrissie? Oh, you can say he's not at the workhouse now, but he was at the workhouse when she was, and dreadful things happened to her on his watch. I don't know, and nor do you, whether Mr Masters was aware of them or not, but Chrissie might well hold him at least partly responsible. John,' she said, putting a hand on his arm, 'she has come so far. Don't risk destroying all we have done – for seeing Masters might well remind her of those harsh, bleak days. And not today, of all days, when her beloved half-sister Connie is getting married, as well as her mother, whom Chrissie has come to adore!'

'I am ashamed,' Father John said. 'I didn't think. I must see him, explain.'

'I think that would be wise,' Eileen said. 'Go quickly and be as discreet as you can. Chrissie hasn't seen him yet.'

So, thankfully Chrissie never saw Masters, and Angela, arranging Connie's gown in the porch, was unaware of all that was happening. Then the Wedding March began, the congregation stood, and Connie and Stan began to walk down the aisle to join Daniel and his best man as they left their pew and stood in front of the altar.

TWENTY-TWO

Outside the church, as well as the official wedding photographer, there were cameramen and journalists from the *Evening Mail* and the *Despatch*. Both papers had covered the story after the explosion, and someone had told them that two of the young people – one of them the young woman who had been in a coma for so long – had fallen in love. And not only that, but their parents were getting married too. So, they came along to get some pics and to have a word with the young couple.

'Our readers will love the fact that you recovered from that horrific explosion and have just got married,' a reporter explained to Connie with a beaming smile. 'A proper love story. They love happy endings.'

'If you want a real romance, you should talk to my mother,' Connie said. 'She's also getting married today.'

'I will talk to your mother,' the journalist said, 'never fear. And I will ask the editor to hold the front page. Newspapers are full of gloom and doom now, and that is understandable with unemployment so high, but a story like this – triumph over adversity sort of thing – cheers people up no end, and that will sell papers. Thanks to you both! Now I am away to see your mother.'

'Hope we've done the right thing, telling him all that,' Daniel said when the journalist had gone.

'Too late to worry about that now,' Connie said. 'But don't worry – Mammy will send him away with a flea in his ear if she doesn't want to talk to him!'

Unaware of all this, Angela was thinking of the future she could see ahead of her with Stan. Running a shop held many happy memories for her, and she was delighted to be going back into it. Talking about their finances, Angela had discovered that Stan had bought the shop, helped by a cash injection from Daniel. She wanted to return Daniel's money and for her and Stan to buy the shop as joint owners in both their names. Daniel used to do all the ordering, stock control, bookkeeping and accounts to help his father, but now Angela was confident she could take that on board too, if Daniel could run through it with her a couple of times. She intended telling no one at home about her plans yet. She wouldn't even tell them about the existence of the jewellery till life was back on a more even keel, so she had told the bank manager she was leaving the jewellery where it was for a little longer, for safe keeping.

Breda gave Angela the nod to join Paddy in the porch, who she knew would be waiting for her. As Angela joined him, Paddy was misty eyed as he told her she looked beautiful. And she knew she did, because Maggie's dress-maker friend had done wonders with the dresses. Around the necks of both of Angela's daughters were the lockets that sparkled in the lights in the church porch.

A man who was vaguely familiar approached the group assembled in the porch. For a moment or two Angela couldn't place him, and then she remembered he had been one of the journalists looking for human-interest stories after the explosions. She remembered that for a journalist, he had been quite sensitive and seemed genuinely concerned about those still trapped after the roof caved in, but she had no idea what he was doing there today. She was about to ask, but the young altar boy arrived to ask if they were ready for the organist, who was just about to start the Wedding March.

She turned to the journalist and said, 'I don't mind photos after the Mass is over, but stories will have to wait for another day, for now I have a wedding to attend.' And she said to the altar boy, 'Tell him I'm ready.'

Angela took Paddy's arm as the strains of the organ could be heard. She thought she would have to be careful what she told the journalist. Chrissie might say the time for secrets was over, but Angela didn't know if that extended to all and sundry reading about her in the pages of a newspaper. She decided not to worry about it now, but to concentrate on her wedding day. And as they entered the church, she gave a gasp as she saw how full it was. It was packed so tightly that there were a fair few without a seat standing at the back.

Angela had the urge to fly down the aisle of the church and be enfolded in Stan's arms, but, on Paddy's arm, she began the slow walk to the altar, where Stan stood with his best man Daniel.

Angela took a surreptitious glance around the packed church. Maggie was sitting at the side of the church with her children, and Angela guessed she had chosen to sit there because it would be easier to take the children out through the side door if they misbehaved. Many women were crying, and Angela wanted to tell them not to shed tears. 'I am marrying the man I love!' she wanted to say. 'We were kept apart for so long, I began to think this day would never come. Now that it has, it's a time for celebration, not tears.'

Of course, she could say none of this. She still thought it, though.

When she threw back her veil and Stan saw her radiant face, he felt his stomach lurch, and he realised he loved Angela much more than he thought humanly possible.

They both gave their responses without hesitation, and when the priest eventually said, 'I now pronounce you man and wife,' Angela heard Stan give a deep, heartfelt sigh. The priest heard it too and he smiled as he added, 'You may kiss the bride.'

Stan took Angela in his arms and she suddenly felt so loved and cherished. She would be alone no more. No more secrets, no more guilt. Only joy, happiness and love. And it was true, she loved Stan with everything in her, more than she thought possible, and she knew that whatever else life threw at them, they would face it together. Man and Wife.

ACKNOWLEDGEMENTS

I was astounded to read a book on the bombs that fell on Birmingham during the First World War, for although I had heard these bombs had fallen on London, Birmingham as a target had hardly been mentioned so I hurriedly researched it and found it to be true. Walsall was chosen because it was the gateway between Birmingham and the highly industrialised 'Black Country', hence its nickname, and where many of the munitions for the Great War were made. The internet is a great tool and a fount of all knowledge, but sometimes it is wise to check facts, so I have also used *Brum Undaunted* and *Birmingham at War*, both by Carl Chinn.

I feel great gratitude towards my publishers Harper Collins and in particular my agent Judith Murdoch and my editor Kate Bradley who have shown me such consideration and understanding with the problems I experienced; this has been very much appreciated.

In writing this book, thanks must go to my great family,

my terrific friends and my lovely, patient and very loyal fans who have waited a long time for this book. I hope you enjoy it and it doesn't disappoint. Write and let me know, I love hearing from you.

To all of you, I owe an immense debt of gratitude, so thank you once more.

If you liked this book, why not dip into another one of Anne Bennett's fantastic stories?

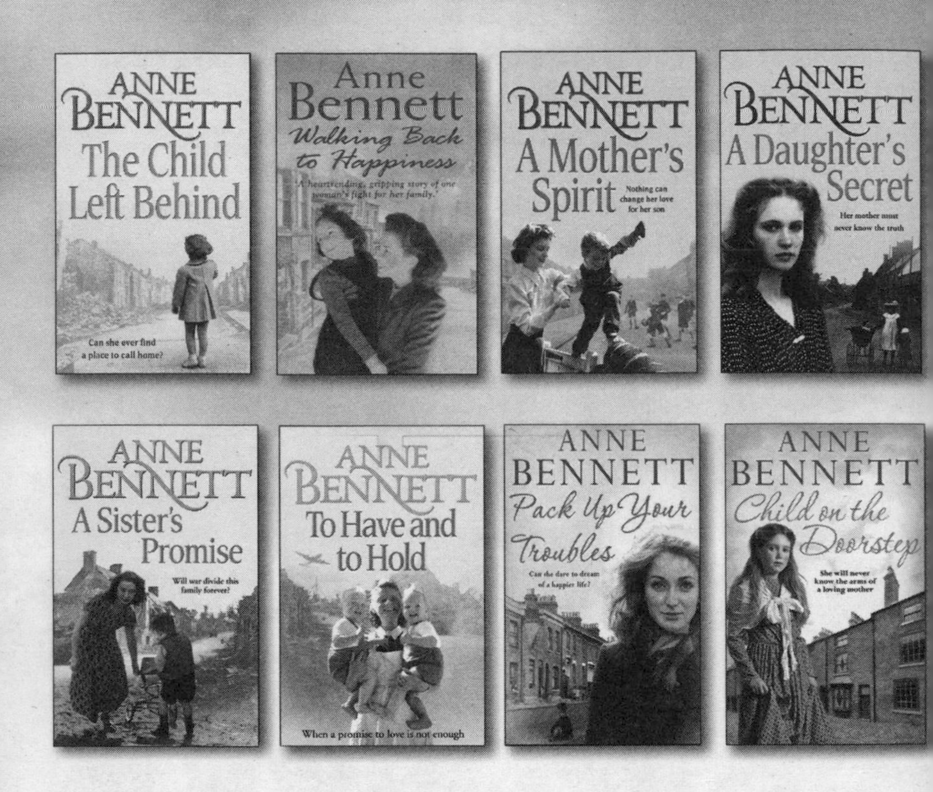

'The beauty of Anne's books is that they are about normal people and are sewn through with human emotions which affect us all'

Birmingham Post

Keep reading for a sneak peek of Anne's gripping novel, *Child on the Doorstep*. Available to purchase now.

ONE

Angela took her coat from the hook at the back of the door and stepped out into the early morning. The day was a chilly one – it was early yet but Angela was glad the bite of winter seemed to be gone at last, though it was only early March 1926. In the children's verse March was supposed to begin like a lion and end like a lamb so she knew they weren't quite out of the woods yet. But they were on the way to spring and that morning a hazy sun was trying to break through the clouds. Funny how it cheered a body to see the sun.

But then her good mood was dispelled a little when, despite the early hour, she saw Tressa Lawson on the road before her, carrying a cushion and an army-issue blanket. As the eldest in the family it was her job to lead her father, Pete, by the hand for he had been blinded by mustard gas in 1915. He wore his great coat against the chill of the day and immense pity for the man rose up in Angela.

'Why does he go out so early?' she'd asked Tressa one time.

'He says he gets the best pitch then,' Tressa had said. 'He positions himself by the tram stop in Bristol Street.'

Angela had nodded; she knew he did, for she had seen him there herself and never passed without greeting him and dropping some money in the cap on the floor before him.

'He says he gets the people waiting for the tram and those getting off, as well as those walking into the city centre by foot.' Tressa had chewed on her bottom lip before going on, 'Sometimes though, for all he sits for hours, often chilled to the bone, especially in the winter, despite his cushion and blanket, he has collected precious little. I hate the look on his face then. He hates the thought that Mammy has to take in extra washing from the big houses in Edgbaston, that he can't provide adequately for his family. He often says he feels a failure.'

Angela's intake of breath had been audible and she had hissed to Tressa, 'Your father is no failure.'

'I know that,' Tressa had said, 'but it's what Daddy thinks.'

Angela remembered him marching away to war, so proud that he had the opportunity to serve his King and country. And when it was over, four gruelling years after it had begun, they called it the 'Great War'. Personally Angela thought there was actually not anything great about that war at all. It was supposed to be the war to end all wars and all the men fighting in it had been promised a land 'fit for heroes', but in fact those who returned had nothing but the dole queue and poverty awaiting them.

Somehow, Angela could never see the decent and respectable Pete Lawson without feeling a pang to her heart. That bloody 'Great War' had also taken away Angela's beloved husband and Connie's father Barry, and at the time Angela had thought she would never get over the tremendous loss she'd felt.

The lovely letter of commendation that she had received from his commanding officer, who had said how brave and courageous a soldier he was, hadn't helped the searing ache inside her. The letter had told her that Barry had eventually lost his life saving another. While her mind screamed 'Why?' she imagined in the heat of battle there was little time for logical thought and Barry would have acted instinctively. But that act was the culmination of this very brave soldier's career; the officer had said he was recommending him for an award and in due course she received the Military Medal.

Angela still thought it cold comfort and if her husband had been a little less brave he might have been one of the ones who had marched home again. His mother, Mary McClusky, on the other hand, had been 'over the moon' that her Barry had received a medal for gallantry and Angela thought Connie might like it as she grew. It would show her what a fine father she'd had, for she was too young to remember him at all, and Angela had put the medal away carefully to show her when she was older.

In the end, despite commendations and medals, she had learnt to cope with her profound loss because she had Connie to rear and Barry's mother Mary to care for too, for they lived together. Anyway, she was by no means the only widow and when the Armistice was signed and the men who had survived were demobbed, it was only too obvious how few men there were about.

As Angela made her way to the Swan public house where she cleaned, she reflected anew on all the changes brought about because so many men had not returned from the war.

She could well remember what George Maitland, her old employer, had said on a similar subject.

He had no children and this was a great regret for him, but when the war began and the casualty figures began appearing in the paper, he had said to Angela one day when she was collecting her groceries, 'You know I've never had chick nor child belonging to me and at times that has been a cross to bear, for I would have loved a family. But now I look at my customers and see the ones who have lost sons and wonder if it is worse for them who have given birth to a boy and reared him with such a powerful love that they would willingly give their life to save him. But they are unable to save him from war and when he dies for King and country, the loss must be an overwhelming one. I have had women in the shop crying broken-heartedly about their beloved sons who will never return and at times I am almost thankful I have no sons of my own to suffer the same fate.'

Angela had often thought about George's words as the war raged on and could understand his reasoning so very well, but then she often did. In her opinion he was a very wise man. She had worked in his shop for two years before her marriage and just after it and had become very fond of him, and he had thought a lot of her too. So much so that, after he died, she found he had left her his mother's jewellery, which he had lodged in the bank with authorisation saying it was for Angela alone. It was totally separate from the will, in which everything presumably was left to his wife, Matilda.

Angela had never taken to Matilda, mainly because of the way she had been with George. She was a cold woman, who never seemed to have a high regard for him, and in Angela's hearing had never ever thrown him even a kind word, and there was no place in her life for children, or sex either, so people whispered.

By now Angela had reached the pub and would have to settle her mind to the job in hand. She went in the side door and called out to the landlord, Paddy Larkin, as she did so. She was very grateful to Paddy for offering her this job after the war, for she couldn't in all honesty say either her father-in-law, Matt, or her husband, Barry, were regular visitors there. She was more than happy to have it though, because it eased the financial pressure, and with Constance at school and Mary to see to her in the holidays, it was perfect for them all.

Angela seldom saw the landlady Breda Larkin for she was usually getting herself ready upstairs. She often wouldn't come down before ten thirty or so to open the pub at eleven and Angela would usually be on her way back home by then. However, one morning when she had been at the cleaning for three years or so, Breda got up early. She greeted Angela pleasantly enough, but when she had left she turned to her husband and said, 'She's wasted on the cleaning, that Angela McClusky.'

'What do you mean?'

'Look at her, you numbskull,' Breda said impatiently. 'Despite everything she is still a beautiful woman, blonde, busty and pleasant. She has a smile for everyone and she will bring the punters in, especially on Friday and Saturday night.'

Paddy might have bristled at being called a numbskull by his wife but he had to acknowledge what she said made sense. Angela was not only a very good-looking woman, but she had something a little special, and though she was always agreeable, she was not flirty – too flirty a woman behind the bar could cause all manner of problems. And so he put the proposition to Angela the next day. She knew it would be extra hours and so extra money and she also knew she couldn't have considered it if she hadn't Mary at home, for she would not leave Constance alone for the hours she would be behind the bar. She told Paddy she would have to ask Mary, for she would be the one looking after Connie, but it was only more for courtesy.

As she'd anticipated, her mother-in-law had no objection.

'Why would I even think about objecting?' Mary said to Angela. 'It is only two nights a week you'll not be here and I shall do what I do every night: sit before the fire and do a bit of knitting and a bit of dozing. But surely to God you won't be doing the cleaning as well?'

'No, well, I'm going to put a proposal to Paddy,' Angela said. 'He wants me Friday and Saturday night and Sunday lunchtime. So I could do the cleaning on Monday to Thursday, and if he was agreeable ask Maggie to take over the cleaning over the weekends.'

'Oh you do right to think of her,' Mary said. 'That poor girl.'

Angela knew how Mary felt for her best friend, Maggie, who was also Connie's godmother. She had married Michael Malone after the war, having been sweet on him for years, even before the war began, and had written to him when he was in the army. A few of the men from their town had been part of a pals battalion and had fought alongside each other and Angela had found out later that the shell that had killed Barry while he'd been trying to save another had blown Michael's left leg clean off.

He had thought any future with Maggie was scuppered,

that she wouldn't want to saddle herself with a one-legged man, but Angela knew her friend was a bigger person than that. And Maggie had said that it made no difference to the way she felt about him and Angela knew she spoke the truth. She also knew if Barry had lost his leg, but came home to her, she would have rejoiced. Though getting Michael to understand that took Maggie some time.

A major slump after the war meant that, with strapping able-bodied men finding any sort of employment hard to come by, no one was prepared to even consider employing a one-legged man, and he felt bad that he couldn't provide for Maggie. Maggie had said she didn't need providing for, and besides, as he had been so disabled in the war, Michael had been awarded a pension of twenty-eight shillings a week. Angela was pleased for them both, but was a little confused that as a war widow she qualified for a pension of only eighteen shillings, with an extra shilling added for Connie.

'No understanding the way governments work,' Mary had said when this had been explained to her after the war.

Angela had quite a sizeable nest egg in the post office because of her well-paid war work in munitions making and delivering shells, as well as the money Barry was sending her. But savings didn't last for ever if you had to draw on them constantly and so when Paddy Larkin had offered her a job she hadn't even had to think about it. She knew Maggie too wouldn't hesitate, because any job was better than no job, and it would do her very well for now.

'It'll be money the government won't know about because Paddy pays you in hand,' Angela pointed out. 'Will Michael mind that it's you working and not him?'

'He may well mind,' Maggie said. 'But he is above all a

realist. And so he will not show any resentment to me or give me any sort of hard time.'

'He's a good man you have there, Maggie.'

'I know it,' Maggie said. 'But the war exacted a heavy price from us one way and the other. Oh, I know Michael survived and Barry and our Syd didn't so maybe I shouldn't moan, but I would like to take the look of failure from his face. He knows in the present climate he hasn't the chance of a sniff of any form of employment and I can't even give him a child.'

She caught sight of Angela's face and went on, 'I see you think it irresponsible to bring another life in the world just now when our financial position isn't great and not likely to improve very much. But, oh, Angela, how I long to hold my own child in my arms – a wee girl like Connie, or a boy the image of his father. I don't think it will ever happen, that's the point, and that's hard to bear.'

Angela was upset to see her friend so downhearted and the worst of it was everything she said was true; none of the girls she worked in the munitions with had become pregnant. This was such a phenomenon across the country that investigations had been made and it was found that the sulphur many of them worked with had made them infertile.

Angela had wished at the time she had become infertile too and then there might have been no repercussions from the terrible attack that day she had driven to the docks for the first time. She had been one of the first and only female delivery drivers, transporting munitions around the country. It had been on one of these trips that something terrible had happened, something she had tried to push out of her mind but which had come back to haunt her and caused her to make the most heart-breaking decision of her life.

One dreadful night she had been attacked and viciously raped when making a munitions delivery at night in a strange town. Her assault had left her scarred, but worse, it had left her with child. With no other course available, with a husband away fighting at war and nowhere to turn, Angela had been forced to leave the child, a young girl with fair hair and blue eyes like her own, on the workhouse steps. The shame and the pain of it had stayed with her and Angela had had to shut off the past to keep the pain at bay.

At least she had Connie, though, who she loved with all her heart and soul, while poor Maggie had nothing. Angela had pushed all the awful memories away. Better to focus on the present and Connie's future.

Maggie was grateful for the chance of employment at the Swan and took herself off to see Mr Larkin. They got on fine and the upshot was that she was to take on the weekend cleaning, while Angela worked behind the bar.

In fact Paddy felt it was scandalous that two women, one a widow and one with a disabled husband, should have to take on jobs like the ones he was offering to keep the wolf from the door.

'Those men fought for King and country, both of them,' he said to his wife one night as they prepared for bed. 'You'd think their relatives would be taken care of if they were killed like Barry McClusky, or crippled like Maggie's husband, or Pete Lawson, blinded, and so many more.'

'You've just said it though, haven't you?' Breda said. 'So many more. Think about it, there were thousand upon thousand killed and even more injured. I should think it takes a great deal of money to fight a war and so they haven't got the money to provide adequately for all the dependants.'

'And since when have the government cared about the likes of us anyway?' Paddy said morosely. 'Cannon fodder, the common people are.'

'That's about the shape of it,' Breda said. 'And people do what they can to survive. And now Maggie doesn't have to make a decision this winter whether to order another hundredweight of coal or buy the makings for a dinner, and neither does Angela, so at least we have made two of those dependants happier.'

'And that's all we can do, I suppose.'

'It is,' Breda said decidedly. 'Now come to bed and stop fretting about things you can do nothing to change.'

As Angela worked, whether it was pulling pints behind the bar or cleaning, she was always well aware of what she owed Mary, for without her stalwart help in caring for Connie, she knew their lives would have been financially harder. But she didn't just appreciate Mary for the help she gave but she was glad she was there with them. She had been part of her life since as far back as she could remember and she hadn't a clue how she was going to manage without her. And though Mary might have years to live yet, she somehow doubted it. The news of Barry's death had hit her for six, combined with the death of two of her other sons in 1912 as they had travelled to America on the *Titanic* to seek better prospects, and the grief had done much to hasten the death of her husband. The bad times were wearing her down and Mary hadn't the resilience of youth.

It wasn't all bad. Mary still thought a great deal about

her other two sons in America who had gone ahead some years before the *Titanic* disaster, and she was glad they were so happy in their new lives. She often wished she could see them again just the once, but she had known when she kissed them goodbye it was final. They wrote regularly though, and she was grateful for that, especially when they included dollar bills folded inside the letter. They wrote about things she could barely imagine, like the flashing neon lights in a place called Times Square and the trolley buses and the trains that ran underground in the bowels of the earth and the motor cars they helped build that were now filling the wide straight roads of America.

And they wrote of their marriages – for Colm had followed his brother Finbarr and married a Roman Catholic girl – and sent pictures of their weddings. But Mary could barely recognise her sons and their wives, and the babies born later were like the photographs of strangers, names on a page, and sometimes she was heart-sore knowing that she would never hold her sons' children in her arms and take joy in them. Connie helped there, for she still had to be looked after, and Mary knew Connie loved her with a passion that eased the pain in her heart.

As Connie grew up, she became very good friends with a girl in her class called Sarah Maguire. Angela had no problem with her having Sarah as her special friend as she herself had been best friends with Maggie Malone, née Maguire, at a similar age. She was friendly with Sarah's mother Maeve and knew them to be a respectable family and was glad to see Connie making friends of her own. It wasn't as if she'd be all that far away in any case, for the Maguires lived just a wee bit down Bell Barn Road on the corner of Great Colmore Street.

The Maguire home was so different from Connie's – although cramped and noisy it was filled with a vibrancy and vitality often lacking in her own. She liked them all, even Sarah's parents. She saw little of Mr Maguire but what she saw she liked. He was called James and his eldest son, wee Jimmy, was named after him. He had big swollen muscles that often strained against the fabric of his shirts, which he usually wore folded up to the elbow so that his lower arms looked like giant hams, and led to large, red, gnarled hands. His face was equally red, with his nose sort of splashed against it and his wide, generous lips tilted upwards so it looked as if he was permanently smiling. He did smile a lot anyway and laugh, and a full-throated and very infectious laugh it was too. Added to this he had a fine head of brown hair which was sprinkled only lightly with grey.

Mrs Maguire, Maeve, had an equally dark head of hair though it was always tied away from her face in a bun of some sort. She wasn't as pretty as Connie's own mother – few people were – but Maeve Maguire's face had an almost serene look seldom seen on those with a houseful of children. Connie had never heard her raise her voice and Sarah said she almost never did. So her face had a contented look about it, with no lines pulling her mouth down, although there were creases around her eyes which were a strange grey-green colour.

'Do you mind me coming round so often?' Connie asked her once. 'My granny says I mustn't annoy you.'

Mrs Maguire gave an almost tinkling laugh. 'Child dear, you don't annoy me in the slightest,' she said. 'You are like a ray of sunshine. And anyway, when you have so many, one more makes little difference and there is more company for you here. The children's friends are always welcome and you help Sarah with the jobs she must do, so you must assure your granny you are no trouble.'

Maeve Maguire had hit the nail on the head, for Connie, though she loved her mother and grandmother dearly, was often lonely. There was something else too. Sometimes her mother seemed far away. She was there in person but when Connie spoke, she sometimes didn't answer, didn't seem to hear her and her eyes had a faraway look in them. She had asked her grandmother about it and Mary had said that her mother was still remembering her daddy, Barry.

'You said that when I asked you why she was sad at Christmas.'

'Yes. She's remembering then too.'

'But, Daddy didn't die at Christmas.'

'No, but Christmas is a time to remember loved ones, especially those you might not see again,' Mary had said and added, 'Don't you feel the same when you remember your daddy?'

Connie didn't; in fact, if she was absolutely honest, she didn't remember her daddy at all, just the things people had told her about him. But even though she was a child she had known her granny would not like her to share those thoughts and so she contented herself by saying, 'Mmm, I suppose.'

So she went for company to Sarah and the Maguire house. They sat together at school and met often on Saturdays and holiday times and on Sundays at Mass.

'Beats me how you don't run out of things to say,' Angela commented dryly as they sat down for an early meal before she went to serve behind the bar one Saturday evening.

It was funny but they never did. They often talked about

their families and one Saturday as they went along Bristol Street, fetching errands for Maeve and pushing the slumbering baby Maura in the pram, Connie suddenly said, 'Aren't your mammy's eyes an unusual colour?'

'I suppose,' Sarah said. 'Neither one thing or the other. Mine are the same. Look.'

'Oh, I never noticed,' Connie said.

'All us girls are the same,' Sarah said. 'Well, that is, Kathy and Siobhan are. Too early to tell with Maura yet and the boys both look like Daddy.'

'It must have been more noticeable with your mother because she has her hair pulled back from her face,' Connie said. 'But now I come to look closer you look very like your mother.'

'Oh, the shape of my face is the same and my mouth is and thank goodness my nose is like Mammy's too. I would hate to have a nose like my father's, which isn't really any shape at all. Looks like it's been broken and not fixed properly or something. I asked him once and he said that if it had been broken he hadn't been aware of it. Mammy said she grew up nearly beside him on the farm in Ireland and Daddy grew up with a rake of brothers, seven or eight of them with only a year between them all. There were girls too, cos there were thirteen altogether, and Mammy said near every time she saw the boys two or three of them would be scrapping on the ground like puppies. She said Daddy's nose could have been broken a number of times and their mother wouldn't have had time to blow her own nose, never mind notice that one of the tribe had theirs busted.'

The two girls burst out laughing. 'Why do boys do that, fight and things?'

Sarah shrugged. 'Who'd know the answer to that or care either? It's just what boys do.'

'Glad I'm a girl.'

'And I am,' Sarah said. 'And it's a blooming good job because there's nothing to be done about it if we were unhappy. And never mind the likenesses in my family, what about yours? You look just like your mother. I've never seen hair so blonde and your ringlets are natural, aren't they? I mean, you don't have to put rags in your hair or anything.'

Connie shook her head so the ringlets held away from her face with a band swung from side to side.

'No,' she said. 'They're natural all right, it's just that I can't ever wear my hair loose for school. Mammy insists I have it in plaits.'

'That's because of the risk of nits,' Sarah said. 'The same reason Mammy won't let me grow mine long. But still, you're luckier than me because when you're old enough you can wear your hair any way you like and you've got the most startling blue eyes.'

'I know, I seem to have taken all things from my mammy and none from my daddy at all.'

'D'you remember your daddy?'

Connie shook her head. 'Not him, the person. Sometimes I think I do because I've been told so much about him, but I know what he looks like because Mammy has a picture of him in a silver frame on the sideboard. Remember I showed you? I don't look like him at all.'

'That's how it is sometimes though, isn't it?' Sarah said.

'Oh yes,' Connie said as Sarah's words tugged at her memory. 'My mammy was born with golden locks and blue eyes like mine, my grandmother said, but she's not my mammy's real mother. My mammy's real mother died in Ireland when she was a babby, like I told you before.'

'Yes,' Sarah said, 'she lost the rest of her Irish family and that's when she went to live with the McCluskys who came to England. Their son Barry was your daddy.'

Connie nodded and added, 'And my daddy was killed in the war.'

That wasn't uncommon and Sarah said, 'Yes, I think lots of daddies were. But maybe your daddy and your other granny are in heaven this minute looking down on us all?'

'I'd like to think it.'

'Don't say you have doubts,' Sarah said with mock horror. 'If you have, keep them to yourself, for if Father Brannigan hears you he will wash your mouth out with carbolic.'

Connie grinned at her friend and said, 'When I die I shall ask God if I can pop back and tell everyone it's true.'

Sarah laughed. 'You are a fool, Connie. You'll have to come back as a ghost and that will frighten everyone to death,' she said. 'Anyway, when were you thinking of dying?'

'Oh, not for ages yet.'

'Good,' Sarah said. 'In the meantime I think we better get on with Mammy's shopping or she'll think we've got lost. And it looks like Maura is waking up so our peace is probably gone anyway.'

TWO

Early in 1924, when Connie and Sarah were almost eleven, Sarah's eldest sister, Kathy had left school and gone to work in the Grand Hotel in Colmore Row, Birmingham. Though she worked long hours, she loved the job and enthused about it so much that Sarah's other elder sister, Siobhan, applied for a job there too two years later when she also left school.

Although her sisters taking live-in jobs meant that they were no longer all squashed on the one fairly small mattress in the attic, and there was more space generally and they couldn't boss her about any more, Sarah missed them a great deal. She also knew, now that Siobhan had joined Kathy, the carefree days of her childhood were at an end, for she was the eldest girl and so she would be the one now to help her mother. She had been cushioned by the presence of two older sisters but now it was time to step up as the eldest daughter and help her mother and take a hand with her younger siblings, particularly Maura who was no longer a cute baby but a spoilt toddler. Sarah was convinced that Maura's screams when her wishes were thwarted could shatter glass and her tantrums had to be seen to be believed.

Connie too had begun to rethink her life. She was coming up to thirteen now and in the senior school, and couldn't miss the reports of the miners' General Strike.

Now that the coal exports had fallen since the Great War, the miners' wages were reduced from £6.00 to £3.90. The government also wanted them to work longer hours for that, and a phrase was coined that was printed in the papers:

Not a penny off the pay and not a minute on the day.

No buses, trams or trains ran anywhere, no newspapers were printed or goods unloaded from the docks, the drop forges and foundries grew silent, no coal was mined and, much to the delight of many children, schools were closed. The strike finished after nine days but little had changed and though the miners tried to hang on longer they were forced to capitulate in the end.

'It is so sad really,' Angela said, reading it out to her daughter from the newly printed newspaper. 'We should be thankful we are so much better off than many.'

'We could be better off still if you would let me leave school next year when I am fourteen and get a job like Sarah intends.'

'Connie, we have been through all this.'

'No, we haven't really done that at all,' Connie said. 'You've told me what you want me to do with my life, that's all.'

Angela frowned, for this wasn't the way her compliant daughter usually behaved.

'You know that going on to take your School Certificate and going on to college or university is what I've been saving for. What's got into you?'

'Nothing,' Connie said. 'It's just that . . . Look, Mammy,

if you hadn't me to look after you would have more money. You could stop worrying about money, wipe the frown from your brow.'

'If I've got a frown on my brow,' Angela said testily, 'it's because I cannot understand the ungratefulness of a girl being handed the chance of a better future on a plate, which many would give their eye teeth for, and rejecting it in that cavalier way and without a word of thanks for the sacrifices I've made for you.'

Connie felt immediately contrite.

'I'm sorry, Mammy,' she said. 'I do appreciate all you do for me and I am grateful, truly I am.'

'I sense a "but" coming.'

'It's just that if I go on to matriculate I won't fit in with the others, maybe even Sarah will think I am getting too big for my boots and . . .'

'Connie, this is what your father wanted,' Angela said and Connie knew she had lost. 'He paid the ultimate price and fought and died to make the world a safer place for you. He wanted the best for you in all things, including education. Are you going to let him down?'

How could Connie answer that? There was only one way.

'Of course not, Mammy. If it means so much to you and meant so much to my father, then I will do my level best to make you proud of me when I matriculate. Maybe Daddy will be looking down on me and be proud too.'

Angela gave Connie a kiss. 'I'm sure he is, my darling girl, and I'm glad you have seen sense and we won't have to speak of this again.'

Connie hid her sigh of exasperation and thought, as she wasn't going to be leaving school any time soon, it was about time she started making herself more useful. She decided she would take care of her grandmother, rather than the other way round, and help her mother around the house far more.

So the next morning she slipped out of the bed she shared with Mary in the attic and, while her mother set off for work, made a pan of porridge and a pot of tea and had them waiting for Mary when she had eased her creaking body from the bed, dressed with care and stumbled stiff-legged down the stairs. She also filled a bucket with water from the tap in the yard and the scuttle with coal from the cellar and told her grandmother she would do the same every morning.

And she did and Angela was pleased at her thoughtfulness. On Monday morning Connie began rising even earlier to try to be the first one to fill the copper in the brew house with water from the tap in the yard, light the gas under it and sprinkle the water with soap suds as it heated. Then she would carry all the whites down to boil up while Angela made porridge for them all before she left for work. By the time Connie had eaten breakfast and seen to her grandmother, the whites were boiling in the copper and she would ladle the washing out with the wooden tongs into one of the sinks and empty the copper for others to use. That was as much as she could manage on school days and her mother would deal with everything else after she had finished at the pub, for lateness at school was not tolerated and all latecomers were caned.

In the holidays Connie would help her mother pound the other clothes in the maiding tub with the poss stick, or rub at persistent dirt with soap and the wash board. Then whites were put in a sink with Beckit's Blue added, and sometimes another with starch, before everything was rinsed well, put through the mangle and pegged on lines lifted to the sky with long, long props to flap dry in the sooty air.

For all they were such a small household, it took most of the day to do the washing and most of Tuesday to do the ironing, unless of course it had rained on the Monday, in which case the damp washing would probably still be draped around the room on Tuesday, cutting off much of the heat from the fire and filling the air with steam. Connie never moaned about this because she knew it was far worse for many bigger families, like the Maguires for instance. She could only imagine the amount of clothes and bedding, towels and clothes they went through in a week, though Sarah said that was another thing that had become easier since her sisters had left home.

'I can't wait to do that myself either,' Sarah said.

'What?'

'Leave home,' said Sarah. 'Siobhan and Kathy are going to keep an eye out for a job at their place and as soon as I am fourteen I'm off.'

'Does your mother know that?'

'Course. Only what she expected,' Sarah said. Then she looked at Connie and said, 'Your mammy wants you to take your School Certificate exam and go to college, don't she?'

Angela nodded her head.

'Do you want to?' Sarah asked

'No,' Angela said. 'I want to get out and work. All my life Mammy has worked and provided for me and Granny and I want her to take life easy for a change. If I am earning she will be able to do that. But . . .' she gave a shrug, 'she has her heart set on it. She has been to see the teacher and she says I am one of the children that could really benefit from a secondary education and so that is what she is determined I will have.'

'How will she afford it?'

'I asked my granny that when she first said it and Granny said all through the war when Mammy was earning good money in the munitions, every spare penny was saved for that very purpose. She said there is a tidy sum in the post office now.'

'Is your granny for it too then?'

Angela shook her head. 'Granny thinks no good comes of stepping out of your class.'

'Yeah, my mother thinks that too,' Sarah said. 'I mean, we live here in a back-to-back house and when we marry it will likely be to someone from round here. And, as my mother says, where will your fine education get you then? And my father says there's little point in teaching girls any more than the basics because they only get married. He said they should spend less time at school and more with their mothers learning to keep house and cook and rear babies.'

'I can see that those things might be useful,' Connie said. 'But we sort of learn to do those things anyway, don't we? And I like school.'

'I know you do,' Sarah said. 'Everyone thinks you're crazy, especially the boys.'

'Huh, as if anyone gives a jot about what boys think or say.'

'One day we might care a great deal,' Sarah said, smiling broadly.

'Maybe we will, but we'll be older then and so will they, so it might make better sense,' Connie said. 'But for now I wouldn't give tuppence for their opinion.'

'All right but your opinion should matter,' Sarah said. 'Tell your mother how you feel.'

'I can't,' Connie said. 'She'd be so upset.'

She remembered how her grandmother told her how her mother would go to put more money in the post office.

'It was all she thought about. Granny said she was even worse when she found out about the death of Barry. Mammy said the physical loss of him was one thing but she would make sure his daughter did not suffer educationally. She said she owed it to Barry to give me the best start she could. What the teacher said cemented that feeling really.'

How then could Connie throw all the plans she had made in her face? Connie was well aware of the special place she had in her mother's heart and for that reason she couldn't bear to hurt her. She knew she had a special place in her grandmother's heart too and it pained her to see her growing frailer with every passing month.

'I really don't know what I'll do when she's not there any more,' she confided to Sarah one day as they walked home from school together.

It was mid-June and the days were becoming warmer and Sarah said, 'She is bound to rally a little now the summer is here. The winter was a long one and a bone-chilling one and, as my mother says, enough to put years on anyone.'

Connie smiled because Sarah's mother was a great one for her sayings.

'And she is oldish, isn't she?' Sarah put in.

Connie nodded. 'Sixty-five.'

'Well, that's a good age.'

'I know, but that doesn't help,' Connie lamented. 'She has

been here all my life and very near all Mammy's life too. The pair of us will be lost without her.'

'You'll have to help one another.'

'Mmm,' she said, knowing Sarah probably didn't understand the closeness between her and her granny because both her grandparents had died when she was just young. It wasn't just closeness either; she could tell her grandmother anything, more than she could share with her mother. She loved the special times they shared when her mother worked in the evening in the pub. Her granny liked nothing better than to talk about days gone by, which Connie sometimes called 'the olden days' to tease Mary, and Connie loved to hear about how life was years ago. It was the only way she got to know anything, for her mother seemed to have no interest in how things had been.

'What's past is past, Connie, and there is no point in raking it all up again,' Angela had said.

That was all very well, but now she was thirteen Connie wanted to know how it came about that Mary had brought her mother up from when she was a toddler. That bit of information she had gleaned. She knew her mother's mammy had died in Ireland, but didn't know when, or anything else really.

Mary knew why Angela didn't want to talk or even think about the past and the dreadful decision she had been forced to make. Connie didn't know that, however, and Mary thought she had a point when she said, 'Mammy thinks that what has passed isn't important because she has lived it and doesn't want to remember, but I haven't and I want to know.'

Mary thought that only natural. The child didn't need to know everything, but it was understandable that she wanted to know where she came from.

'I'll tell you, when we have some quiet time together, just

you and I,' Mary promised and she did, the following day, which was a Friday night. With Angela off to work and the dishes washed, Connie sat in front of the fire opposite her granny with her bedtime mug of cocoa and learned about the disease that killed every member of her mother's family. Angela had survived only because she had been taken to Mary McClusky before the disease had really taken hold.

'Your dear grandmother was distracted,' Mary said. 'She didn't want to leave Angela, but the first child with TB had contracted it at the school and your namesake, Connie, knew she had little chance of protecting the other children from it because they were all at school too. But Angela had a chance if she was sent away.'

'Did she know they were all going to die?'

'No, of course she didn't know, but she knew TB was a killer, still is a killer, we all knew. Angela's family, who were called Kennedy, were not the first family wiped out with the same thing.'

'And only my mammy survived,' Connie mused. 'Did you mind looking after her?'

'Lord bless you, love, of course I didn't,' Mary said. 'I would take in any child in similar circumstances, but Angela was the daughter of my dear friend and, as your grandfather, Matt, often said to me, the boot could have been on the other foot, for our children were at the same school. To tell you the truth, I was proper cut up about the death of your other grandparents and their wee weans, but looking after your mammy meant I had to take a grip on myself. I knew that by looking after Angela the best way I could I was doing what my friend would want and it was the only thing I could do to help her. It helped me cope, because I was low after

Maeve's death. She was followed by her husband who was too downhearted to fight the disease that he had seen take his wife and family one by one.'

'What part of Ireland was this?'

'It was Donegal,' Mary said. 'We came to England in 1900 when your mother was four. It wasn't really a choice because the farm had failed, the animals died and the crops took a blight, and with one thing and another we had to leave the farm.'

'So you came here?'

'Not just like that we didn't,' Mary said. 'We first had to sell the farm to get the money to come. Once here, we had nowhere to live, but luckily for us, our old neighbours in Ireland, the Dohertys, had come to England years before. You know Norah and Mick Doherty?'

'Yes, they live in Grant Street.'

'Well, they put us up till we could find this place,' Mary said. 'It was kind of them because it was a squash for all of us. In fact, there was so little space my four eldest had to sleep next door.'

'Next door?'

'Well, two doors down with a lovely man called Stan Bishop and his wife Kate who had an empty attic and the boys slept there.'

Connie wrinkled her nose and said, 'I don't know anyone called Bishop.'

'No one there of that name,' Mary said a little sadly. 'Stan's wife died and then he enlisted in the army and was killed like your daddy and many more besides,' Mary finished, deciding that Connie had no need to know about the existence of Stan's son. It would only complicate matters.